Praise for the Brack Pelton Mystery Series

"Burnsworth nails the voice of new Southern noir. This talented author will win you over with his engaging and multi-faceted hero, then keep you turning pages with his suspense."

— Hank Phillippi Ryan,
Mary Higgins Clark Award-Winning Author of *Say No More*

"Hop on board for a hard-edged debut that's fully loaded with car chases (particularly Mustangs), war veterans, old grudges, and abundant greed. A choppy start belies a well-executed plotline enhanced by the atmospheric Palmetto State setting."

— *Library Journal*

"This second case for Brack is marked by a challenging mystery, quirky characters, and nonstop action."

— *Kirkus Reviews*

"In Brack Pelton, Burnsworth introduces a jaded yet empathetic character I hope to visit again and again."

— Susan M. Boyer,
Agatha Award-Winning Author of *Lowcountry Book Club*

"Burnsworth is outstanding as he brings out the heat, the smells, the colors, and the history of Charleston during Pelton's mission to bring the killer to justice."

— John Carenen,
Author of *A Far Gone Night*

"If you have always suspected there is more to Charleston than quaint Southern charm and ghost stories, then David Burnsworth's noir series, featuring ex-soldier, tiki bar owner, and part time beach bum, Brack Pelton may just be the antidote to a surfeit of sweet tea."

— Michael Sears,
Shamus Award-Winning Author of *Black Fridays*

BIG CITY HEAT

Books by David Burnsworth

The Brack Pelton Mystery Series

SOUTHERN HEAT (#1)
BURNING HEAT (#2)
BIG CITY HEAT (#3)

The Blu Carraway Mystery Series

BLU HEAT (Prequel Novella)
IN IT FOR THE MONEY (#1)

BIG CITY HEAT

A BRACK PELTON MYSTERY

DAVID BURNSWORTH

HENERY PRESS

BIG CITY HEAT
A Brack Pelton Mystery
Part of the Henery Press Mystery Collection

First Edition | April 2017

Henery Press, LLC
www.henerypress.com

This is a work of fiction. Any references to historical events, real people, or real locales are used fictitiously. Other names, characters, places, and incidents are the product of the author's imagination, and any resemblance to actual events or locales or persons, living or dead, is entirely coincidental.

Trade Paperback ISBN-13: 978-1-63511-199-6
Digital epub ISBN-13: 978-1-63511-200-9
Kindle ISBN-13: 978-1-63511-201-6
Hardcover Paperback ISBN-13: 978-1-63511-202-3

Printed in the United States of America

To my parents, Mom and Ron, and Dad,
for their unrelenting love and support.

ACKNOWLEDGMENTS

This book almost wasn't published. The publishing industry is just like any other type of business. It has ups and downs and, like life, changes. The first person I want to thank is Kendel Lynn, the managing editor at Henery Press. It was at a meeting during Bouchercon 2016 that the subject of *Big City Heat* came up. At the time it was a mostly complete manuscript sitting on the shelf because I had moved on to a second series. She agreed it should be published and made it happen. So thank you, Kendel!

My wife Patty, if you didn't know, is responsible for all of this in that she encouraged me to pursue my dream of being a published author. She believed in me when I didn't believe in myself, and her unrelenting faith in God is a blessing.

Every writer needs a support system. If you don't think so, try to work a day job, crank out prose, plan events, manage social media, come up with promotion ideas, find a beta reader that can be trusted, and maintain a website. The only reason I can perform the first two is because I have Rowe Carenen, the Book Concierge, for the rest. Thanks, Rowe, for all your efforts over the past three years.

My agent, Jill Marr, has been the faithful, steady force behind the scenes. When the aforementioned change occurred, she moved me on to bigger and better things. Thanks to you, Jill, and everyone at the Sandra Dijkstra Literary Agency. I am in good hands.

I'm so glad my work has landed at a new home in Henery Press. They welcomed me in even before I was one of their own. Special thanks to Rachel Jackson for excellent skills in managing me, Art Molinares for giving me a bear hug as a welcoming gesture, Erin George for helping with promotion, Amber Parker for her proofreading skills, and Jesica Pena for working behind the scenes to make everything run so smoothly.

My road to Henery Press was paved by Susan Boyer. She has been the trusted friend and fellow author I've gone to for the tough publishing questions—the ones that I was embarrassed to ask but needed answers to. And she introduced me to Kendel and the gang at Henery. Susan, thank you for everything you have done to get me here.

The Brack Pelton series has, I feel, a certain nuance to it. It is this extra kick that makes it special. This kick is Chris Roerden. Like with *Southern Heat* and *Burning Heat*, Chris took my prose (garble) and polished and sharpened the words into what became *Big City Heat*. If you like what you read, it's due to her. If you find any fault herein, it's because I didn't listen to her close enough.

A special recognition to a wonderful family of friends: Stephen Black, Katie Black, Anna Kate Black, and Emma Grace Black. Thank you all so much!

And, as always, thank you, South Carolina Writers Association.

My mom and dad had the foresight to pack up and move to Atlanta back in 1982, dragging me with them. Brack Pelton resides in Charleston, South Carolina. But this book is set in Atlanta because I lived there, grew up there, and was changed there. Thank you, Atlanta, for everything you gave me. I might not be the man I am today if you hadn't helped shape me during that crucial part of my life.

And lastly, thanks to all the Brack Pelton followers! This book is for you.

Even though I walk through the valley of the shadow of death, I will fear no evil, for You are with me...

Psalm 23:4

Chapter One

Atlanta, Georgia, Wednesday night, Mid-May

Brack Pelton waited in his Porsche by a no-parking zone in a very bad part of the city and watched someone he thought he knew well climb out of an old Eldorado convertible. The man entered a ramshackle building with a neon beer mug shining through its one dirty window.

Easing away from the red-marked bus stop, Brack found a better location down the block and pulled in. Before getting out of the Porsche, he woke Shelby, his tan mixed-breed dog slumbering in the backseat, and pulled a forty-five from the glovebox. He verified a round was chambered.

Shelby licked his lips and gave a quick bark as Brack slid the pistol down the back waistband of his cargo shorts.

Patting his dog on the head, Brack asked, "Ready?"

A needless question. Another bark affirmed Shelby's stand on things.

"When we get inside, your job is to find Mutt. Okay?"

Shelby licked his face. Brack knew that as long as their target hadn't escaped out some back door, Shelby would find him. Mutt was one of his favorite people. Brack's too. That was why tracking him like this went against everything he believed in doing.

Mutt was the one who often rode shotgun with Brack as they'd right Charleston's wrongs. Now Mutt was the one in the crosshairs. Thanks to an early morning phone call from Cassie, Mutt's girlfriend, a life depended on answers his friend would give. The forty-five wouldn't come out unless trouble came up.

The barroom's rusty screen door screeched open. Shelby darted ahead, already focused on his objective. Brack entered a time warp. Uncanny how even the sour bar wash fragrance and cigarette smoke were the same. Through the old familiar haze, he imagined Mutt standing behind a peeling Formica counter pouring drinks to patrons who could barely afford their rent. Somehow, Mutt had managed to replicate his termite-infested watering hole three hundred miles west of where his original joint stood before some spoiled neighborhood brat burned it down.

"You lost?" A very large African-American man wearing a soiled wife-beater chalking a pool cue confronted the white newcomer.

Meeting his gaze, Brack said, "No. I'm looking for a loudmouth Marine named Mutt. If he's here drinking, the rounds are on me. If he owns this place, I'm going to beat the life out of him."

"Big talk coming from someone in yo' shoes," he said.

Four other men flanked him, two on each side, all with arms folded across their meaty chests. Five soiled wife-beaters in a row. A worn-out AC unit clicked and sputtered, failing to condition the polluted air in the establishment.

Shelby seemed to take longer than usual to find Mutt. Only one thing could sidetrack him. But no women had ever been present in the original Mutt's Bar in Charleston. They'd been afraid to enter the place.

Maybe Atlanta women were different.

Casually Brack removed the half-smoked cigar he'd been saving in his pocket and lit it. The only faithful friend he had left at the moment was his own adrenaline. Brack was angry at Mutt and wouldn't mind working it out of his system on these five gentlemen facing him.

Three more joined them.

Okay, these *eight* gentlemen.

Brack felt more gather behind him.

His wayward dog better have a real good excuse for not warning him.

Taking a drag on the stogie, he exhaled a cloud of smoke to add to the carcinogenic fog. "It's going to be a bad day for some of you."

Chuckles echoed around the room, undoubtedly at his expense.

Mutt pushed his way through the gathering mob. A few inches over six feet, he'd replaced his boxed Afro with a close trim since the last time Brack had seen him. His clothes were of a more recent vintage, another change, and to Brack's untrained eye, quite stylish.

"Opie, you always got to do things the hard way, don't 'cha?"

Brack couldn't decide if he wanted to punch him or shake his hand. The fact that his friend sported a bridge that replaced his missing front teeth also caught him off guard.

Shelby was not with Mutt.

From behind, Brack heard the gruff words, "You want us to take this cracker out back, Mutt?"

Mutt knew as well as Brack did that they were greatly outnumbered. But Brack figured Mutt also knew that a few of his patrons would spend the next few weeks in the hospital if things went south.

Before either of them could say anything, a husky female voice came from somewhere in the crowd.

"You got the prettiest dog."

All the men turned in the direction of the voice. Through a break in the undershirt line, Brack observed a heavyset black woman in a way-too-tight purple body suit. Clearly she'd fallen in love with his dog. Her extra-long orange day-glo fingernails scratched behind his ears.

Sitting on his haunches with closed eyes, Shelby flapped his tongue and panted in what Brack recognized as pure bliss. Two other women wearing similar attire also gave Shelby their full attention.

Brack was about to get pummeled by eight or more hulks itching to right the wrongs of their world, yet his dog had managed to pick up what looked like all the women in the establishment.

The spokesman for the wife-beater ensemble said, "We ain't finished wit you, white boy."

Brack turned back to him.

Mutt got between them.

"Easy, Charlie. He's my brother."

The men looked at each other as if Mutt and Brack could possibly be related. Of course, they weren't in the traditional sense.

"Summertime" by Billy Stewart began to play somewhere in the room. A real classic.

Circling Shelby, the women moved their ample hips to the beat. The dog, in plus-sized heaven, spun around, not sure which lady to kiss first.

A fourth woman Brack hadn't noticed until now came from behind the bar to stand beside Mutt. Almost as tall as Brack, with dark brown skin, a buzzed haircut, and toned figure bordering on muscular. Her inked-up arms momentarily distracted Brack.

The man Mutt called Charlie said, "I don't care who you think he is. He ain't got the juice to come in here talking about beatin' you up."

Mutt turned to his old friend. "You said you was gonna beat me up?"

"Something like that." Brack cocked his head. "I get a call begging me to drive here from Charleston. It's Cassie. She's scared half to death because some men threatened her, and she doesn't know what you do when you leave her house late at night. Put yourself in her shoes."

The woman bartender looked at him. "You must be Brack."

Mutt interrupted. "Opie, I'ma tell you like I tol' Cassie. What I do is my bidness. She ain't got no right to ask."

Charlie moved in like he was about to throw a punch.

Before Brack could react, the toned female bartender grabbed Charlie by the shirt collar and said, "You really don't want to do that."

Mutt said, "Easy there, Tara. We all friends here."

She didn't let go.

Charlie backed off.

Brack dropped what was left of his cigar on the floor, crushed it with his foot, and turned back to Mutt. "You better tell me what's going on, or I *will* beat the ever-living daylights out of you."

Chapter Two

Thursday morning, two a.m.

Mutt and Brack cruised along Peachtree Street in the Porsche, top down, with Shelby asleep in the backseat. It was way past Brack's bedtime, and traffic was light. Tara stayed behind to close up the bar. She could definitely handle herself.

"Cassie told me on the phone that her kid sister's missing. What do you know about it?"

Mutt pulled out an electronic cigarette contraption Brack had heard called a vaporizer. "Regan been gone 'bout a month."

"And now Cassie is in danger?"

He took two drags off the vaporizer. "I started asking around and found out Regan got in wit some bad people."

"How bad?"

"Lemme put it to you this way," he said. "All I did was ask a few peoples if they knew where she was at, and the next day these dudes on motorcycles threaten Cassie."

"Threatened like how?"

"They caught her when she was leaving the restaurant late one night. Tol' her I shouldn't ask no more questions or someone might get hurt."

He looked at Brack. "All I did was ask if anyone'd seen her sister."

Brack slowed for a light. "Who'd you ask?"

"Everyone we know."

"That doesn't help."

"This ain't Charleston, Opie. You mighta gotten away with a lot there, but the playas here mean bidness."

Brack said, "When did you start vaping?"

"Cassie seemed to think it was a good idea."

"Well, you look good, Mutt. You look good."

He lifted the collar of his new sport coat. "You like this?"

"I couldn't wear something that nice on a regular basis, but it looks good on you."

Mutt checked out Brack's faded Blue Oyster Cult t-shirt and frayed shorts. "You in the big city now, Opie. We gotta get you something else to wear."

"What we need to do is take care of the bikers and find Regan."

After another puff on his fake smoke, Mutt said, "I found out where she is."

It was Brack's turn to look at his friend. "Where?"

"There's a guy here, runs most of the illegal stuff in the city. Name's Vito. She workin' for him."

The light turned green and Brack accelerated. "I guess we know where to go next."

"We can't go bustin' up in his crib and expect him to just hand her over."

"Maybe you can't," Brack said. "Where we headed, anyway?"

"Turn right at the next light."

"That still doesn't answer my question."

"My house," he said. "You and Shelby need a place to stay, don'cha?"

Eleven a.m., Thursday

After oversleeping, Brack and Shelby drove out to Midtown to see Cassie Thibedeaux at her new restaurant. They'd slept at Mutt's house, a pretty decent rental a few blocks from his bar. Brack awoke and found Mutt already gone, which irritated him to no end. He must have walked back to get his car.

When Cassie had gotten him up with the phone call at two a.m. the Tuesday night before, Brack realized she'd taken up with Mutt. And that Mutt had so-called "retired" on his fire insurance proceeds and moved to Atlanta a year ago to be nearer to his daughter who lived with his ex. Cassie had run a great soul food restaurant in Charleston and opened a similar place in Atlanta. Mutt told Brack she'd convinced her New York City sister, Regan, to join her here. With Regan now missing, Cassie had good reason to be scared.

Brack assumed that Cassie had called him because he and Mutt were friends. That he and Mutt had already been through a lot together. And that he would do anything for his friend, even driving five hours to help him any way he could.

Mutt, for all his good qualities, didn't help matters by neglecting to tell Cassie about his latest business venture—another old beer joint. Brack considered, not for the first time, that the couple's separate residences allowed Mutt to do pretty much whatever he wanted.

Pulling into her restaurant's parking lot, Brack noticed that she'd named her business after herself as she had in Charleston—a similarity she shared with Mutt. Cassie's stood among a row of premium addresses along Peachtree Street in what was referred to by Atlantans as Midtown. Decorated to look as if it came directly from the lowcountry, its pastel blue shutters were hinged across the top of the windows and propped open at the bottom to provide shade and light at the same time. The window frames were trimmed in white. The only touch missing was a palmetto tree, yet Brack was sure he'd spot one somewhere.

Not knowing if it was okay for Shelby to come inside, they walked around the perimeter. Because Brack owned two establishments in Charleston—a run-down bar called Pirate's Cove on the Isle of Palms, and a new place his manager, Paige, was in the process of opening on Kiawah Island—he knew enough about drainage, convenient parking, and entryways and exits to realize that Cassie's new place appeared well-planned.

Once the pair made the full loop and faced the entrance again, a squat figure wearing a bright green flowing dress barreled out the door.

"Hey, handsome!" She threw her short meaty arms around Brack before he could stop her.

He tried not to squirm. "Good to see you too, Cassie."

A few inches over five feet, with thick features all around, this woman was strong enough to force the air out of his lungs.

Shelby, Brack's sometimes best friend, gave a jealous bark.

Cassie released Brack and knelt to give the four-legged lady-killer a more gentle welcome. "How you doin', baby?"

Shelby promptly rolled onto his back and let her scratch his belly.

Brack said, "Thanks for calling me."

"You mean it?" She looked up at him. "I wasn't sure it was the right thing to do."

"Of course it was. I'm sorry you were threatened."

Looking back to Shelby's tummy rub, she said, "Me too."

"Would you be able to recognize them?"

"No. It was dark and they was wearing masks."

Brack didn't buy it, but let her slide. "If you want to talk about something else, we can."

Still kneeling next to Shelby, she said, "No. You come all this way to he'p. And I appreciate it. I had no one else to turn to." Her voice broke.

"What about the police?"

"I filled out all the papers," she said. "B-but they said not to get my hopes up." Tears streamed down her worry-lined face.

Shelby got to his feet, and did his best to lick them away.

Brack said, "I'll do what I can to get Regan back."

She gave Shelby a kiss and stood, brushing sidewalk dust from her dress. After a deep breath and exhale, she said, "I know you will."

Her light skin color accentuated her round face and big brown eyes.

"Why didn't Mutt call me himself?"

Cassie didn't reply, letting him figure it out.

Then he understood. "Pride."

"He got a lot of that."

Me too, Brack thought.

Hungry from skipping breakfast, Brack looked past her to the restaurant. "You got anything left over from yesterday to eat?"

"Sure do, hon."

Inside, the restaurant was all light pine flooring and pastel blue walls trimmed in white, with framed photos of live oaks and African-American women clothed in the white cotton wraps associated with Gullah.

No one else was around.

"Cassie, I'm not trying to tell you what to do, but I suggest you not be here by yourself until this is over."

"Ain't nothin' gonna happen to me in daylight," she said, batting a hand in the air. "And I make sure someone walk me to my car at night since them men scared me."

He felt her reasoning about safety in daylight was about as good as his own, usually. In this case, dangerously wrong.

She donned a large apron, and while she fried drumsticks, smashed potatoes, and heated up collards for him, she deboned a plateful of chicken for Shelby.

With all of them in the kitchen—a health-code violation that came with a hefty fine if found—Brack swallowed a mouthful of delicious cornbread, hoped the inspector wouldn't show up, and asked about her sister.

She said, "I love her, but she is one wild child. Always has been."

"Is that why you think she's in trouble?"

Shaking her head, she said, "I don't know. I thought when she come here it would all be good. She'd work in the restaurant wit me and Mutt. We'd be family."

"Instead, she hit the town, didn't she?"

After a moment, Cassie said, "Yes."

"When was the last time you saw her?"

"About a month ago. I went over to her apartment."

"I'd like to take a look there," Brack said. "Any chance you have a key?"

Cassie did have a key. She'd been to Regan's every other day but said she didn't do more than just see if her sister was there. As far as Cassie knew, Mutt hadn't been over there at all, which seemed odd to Brack.

As Shelby and Brack walked out of Cassie's place, Mutt rang his cell phone.

"Where you at?"

"Leaving Cassie's. Where are you?"

"Back home now."

"I've got the key to Regan's apartment."

"Well, come get me."

"Sounds like Shaft is ready to roll," Brack said, kidding Mutt about his obsession with Richard Roundtree.

"Cocked and locked."

Arriving back at Mutt's place, Brack guided Shelby into the one-story rental house. His dog wasn't keen on being left alone, but experience told Brack that walking into someone else's apartment without permission was hit or miss. He didn't want Shelby in danger.

Ten minutes later, with Mutt riding shotgun, Brack plugged Regan's address into the Porsche's GPS.

As they followed the electronic female voice commands through the city, Brack asked, "So where were you this morning?"

"Had to go to Taliah's school," he said. "By the way, we gotta pick her up at three, so get a move on."

"Yessir," Brack said.

Taliah, Mutt's exceptionally bright thirteen-year-old daughter, was the reason he'd moved back to Atlanta. Expected to graduate early from high school the following summer, she was already taking college-level courses. In other words, much smarter than Mutt and Brack put together.

They pulled into a low-income apartment complex. The expensive new German convertible would win them no friends here, but it was too late to turn back now. Brack parked in front of the building with the number Cassie had given. As they exited the car, he wondered if there was anyone watching the apartment. Deciding there probably was, he gave a touch of the door handle, and the car horn beeped to let him and everyone else know the alarm now stood guard.

White placards with fading black numbers hung on the weathered brown siding of the units. In a small courtyard, four truants around ten years old stopped playing touch football and stared at the salt and pepper pair as they passed.

Apartment number 212 was up two flights of stairs narrow enough to have Brack question how anyone ever got furniture up or down. Mutt gave Regan's door two hard raps.

They waited a few seconds, but the only sound came from the football players below.

Brack produced the key from Cassie and unlocked the door. They entered and found themselves in very cramped quarters. The entry door split the small living room from an even smaller dining area. Worn gray carpeting. White walls. Popcorn ceiling. A hall ahead of them presumably led to Regan's bedroom.

Cassie's sister had made a modest home for herself, furnished with a decent couch, smallish TV, and a smartphone docking station and sound system. First impression: neat but dusty.

Brack asked, "Is the rent up to date?"

"Not sure," Mutt said. "I'll check in the back."

Not feeling the need to personally go through the woman's underwear drawers, Brack said, "Have at it. I'll check around out here."

Brack didn't have to look far. A bong sat on the carpet beside the couch. Under the coffee table a box that originally contained tennis shoes held a small pipe, but no drugs.

From down the hall, Mutt said, "Hey, Opie? Check this out."

Brack placed the box back where he found it and went to the bedroom.

In contrast to the modest living area, Regan had splurged on the bedroom décor. Pink curtains curled around the tall bedposts of a queen-sized four-poster. Mutt stood by the closet. When he pushed the door open wide, Brack saw leather straps with shiny metal buckles glinting in the closet lighting. They hung from hooks on the back of the door together with coiled whips and pairs of handcuffs.

He said, "What you think about this, Opie?"

Brack stood out of arm's reach of the bondage of Regan's life. Many thoughts traveled through his mind. No matter what Brack and Mutt looked into since they'd met a few years before, it always ended up involving sex or money. Or both. This situation wouldn't be any different.

"Well," Brack said, "it's not my thing."

"Me neither," Mutt said. "I knew the girl had problems, but I never thought she was into this stuff. It ain't new, either. It's got some miles on it."

He lifted a strap to show how worn the leather was.

Brack spotted a photo on a white dresser. Two women, one Cassie and the other a very attractive, bronze-skinned model wearing a white flower in her hair smiled at him. Regan was a thinner, prettier, younger version of Cassie with the same inquisitive eyes.

Closer to forty than thirty, Brack realized he'd already seen a lot in his life. Maybe more than most thanks to the Marine Corps and a couple of dead bodies. But probably not as much as Regan had seen in her twenty-five years. He and Mutt left the apartment with nothing but an understanding that this road they decided to follow her down would get darker.

Chapter Three

Three p.m.

Taliah ran to Mutt and gave him a big hug. Not something Brack expected from a teenager, but with her high I.Q. she was not typical in any respect. She seemed very happy that Mutt was back in her life.

Brack leaned against the door of his car and watched them walk toward him, hand in hand.

About five-six, Taliah had bright brown eyes and wore her dark hair pulled back into some kind of clip. Like the other girls leaving the private high-school building, she sported the typical uniform skirt and polo. Her broad smile showed off a mouth full of metal. "Hi, Mr. Brack." She held out a hand.

Brack shook her hand. "Nice to see you again, Taliah."

She had visited her father in Charleston a few times and Brack had met her then.

"You bring Shelby with you?" she asked.

"He's at your father's house," Brack said. "Would you be interested in watching him for me some?"

Her bright eyes got brighter. "Of course!"

"We better get goin'," Mutt said, gesturing toward the car.

"You got a Porsche?" Taliah pronounced it correctly with two syllables. Most people butchered it with one.

"He sure do," Mutt said. "You ready to go?"

"Yeah!"

She scrambled into the backseat, if you could call it that.

Brack gently put the seat back so as not to crush her. "Where to?"

"I've got karate with Tara."

"The woman from the bar?" Tara had made quite an impression on Brack, something that hadn't happened in a while.

"What bar?" Taliah asked.

Mutt eyed Brack and cleared his throat. "Uh, what he mean is, she look like someone we knew back in Charleston."

Brack didn't reply, realizing that Mutt hadn't told her about his current occupation. Instead, he let her guide them to a dojo across town. They parked in the mostly empty lot of a small strip mall and went inside the unit that had *karate* spelled out in lighted red letters over the door.

The same Tara as from Mutt's bar met them at a glass display counter and gave Taliah a hug.

Before Tara could greet the men, Mutt said, "This is Brack, a friend of mine."

Tara looked at Mutt for a beat, then turned to Brack. "Nice to meet you. I'm Tara."

Smiling, he said, "My pleasure."

She turned back to Taliah. "Go change, sweetie."

The teenager nodded and disappeared through a doorway.

When she was out of earshot, Mutt said, "She still don't know 'bout the bar, okay? He'p me out wit this."

"Whatever you say, Shaft."

Tara took over.

"Mutt tells me you were a Marine. They teach you self-defense?"

"Among other things." He tried to avoid sounding patronizing so he added, "So you're a black belt, huh? Bartender at night. Karate instructor by day."

"That ain't all, either," Mutt said. "She also work with animals."

Tara said, "And he doesn't mean only the ones in the bar."

Taliah emerged, dressed in her white karate gi complete with a yellow belt. "Ready to start?"

Mutt said, "I'll see you on Saturday, honey."

His daughter kissed him, then shook Brack's hand.

Tara said, "Let me know if you boys want some training."

They circled back to Mutt's one-story rental. He had to head to Cassie's and help get things started for the Thursday-night-dinner crowd. Because she was still building a business, she was open every evening.

Shelby deserved a treat for being such a good boy in Mutt's house, and Brack wanted to do something special for him. Mutt had suggested a small park not far away, so that's where they ate dinner, a sub sandwich from a food truck for Brack and Eukanuba from a large bag stashed in the car's trunk for Shelby. They washed their meals down with bottled water and played fetch with Shelby's favorite worn tennis ball until almost dark, when they made their way back.

Around eleven, after a nap, Brack left Shelby at the house and drove to Mutt's crumbling bar. "Let the Good Times Roll" by The Cars blasted through the Porsche's speakers. Feeling good, he turned into the parking lot behind the bar and saw a small group of people gathered there, Tara being one of them.

Three men in biker garb stood near their chrome-laden motorcycles, each wearing the standard leather and basic black t-shirt. Their skin tone ran the gamut of color. Two were about Brack's height and build, the third bigger still with some machine-gun pectorals on him. It didn't take a rocket scientist to see this was no friendly gathering.

A small man next to Tara got in the face of the biggest biker. One punch in the nose and the little man dropped to the ground. Tara pushed the biker and he tried to backhand her across the face, but she instantly blocked it and jabbed him in the ribs.

Brack took a flying leap and caught the two bikers who were his size with his extended arms across their necks in a clothesline. The three of them fell over the bikes with Brack on top of his targets. He drove his fists repeatedly into their scraggly faces.

The big one grabbed the back of Brack's shirt and threw him against a parked SUV. Brack ducked to avoid a left hook. The guy's gigantic fist smashed through the SUV's back window, not an easy feat. From behind, Tara kicked the giant in the groin. He grunted and collapsed to the ground holding his privates.

Tara and Brack caught their breath. The two Brack had clotheslined recovered and came at them, taking the fight up a notch. One pulled a switchblade, the other a baton. The blade swished through the air inches from Brack's face. He stepped in with two hard cuts to the guy's ribcage and the knife dropped to the ground.

Tara took a blow to the shoulder from the goon with the baton, but rallied and dropped the guy with a roundhouse kick to his head. Brack finished off the now knife-less assailant with an uppercut to the jaw.

Their monster friend stood, grunted again, and charged. Tara tripped him, and as he fell, Brack elbowed the goon in the face. He hit the ground again. This time he did not get up.

Mutt and several others ran out from the bar's rear door, but nothing remained for them to do. Brack stooped, hands on thighs, until he caught his breath. Tara massaged her shoulder.

"You two all right?" Mutt asked.

"You know it," Brack said, "but you better call the police." To Tara, he asked, "You okay?"

She rotated her arm, regaining flexibility. "I'll be fine." She looked down at the small man who'd been with her. "How you doing, Darnel?"

He held a bloody tissue to his nose.

"I'm okay."

Fifteen minutes later, each biker zip-tied, Brack was still talking with the police uniforms when an unmarked sedan pulled in. The clean-shaven man who got out had salt and pepper hair, wore a short-sleeved shirt, and fingered a Glock clipped to his belt. As if obvious that Brack was responsible for the disturbance, the detective came directly to him and introduced himself.

"I'm Detective Nichols. I understand these men on the ground assaulted some people. By the looks of it, the wrong people."

"That about sums it up," Brack said, not used to such directness.

"So that's your statement, Mr. Pelton?"

The uniforms must have given him Brack's name. His guess was he'd already been checked out. That must have proven an interesting database search.

"Not exactly," Brack said, "but it's close."

Nichols said, "What is it, exactly?"

Brack opened his mouth to speak, but Tara interrupted. "These three men attacked me and my brother for no reason." She indicated the small man nursing his bloody nose. "If Mr. Pelton hadn't arrived here when he did, it might have been us on the ground instead of them."

Detective Nichols nodded. "I see. Well, I didn't mean to sound like I had everything all figured out. Will you be pressing charges, ma'am?"

"Yes."

After taking Tara's statement as well as everyone else's, the officers hauled the bikers away and the looky-loos moved on. Tara tended to the fellow she referred to as her brother and Detective Nichols spoke further with Brack.

"I ran you through the system, Mr. Pelton. This is exactly your M.O."

"Why don't you tell me what you think my modus operandi is, exactly?"

He smiled. "Sure. You're like Sherman marching across Georgia. Exactly."

Brack's turn to smile.

"That's pretty accurate."

Nichols said, "It's my job to make sure Atlanta doesn't burn. So I'm going to say this as nicely as I can. I don't want to see you again in this capacity. If I do, I will have you escorted to the city limits."

"But I just got here."

"And already I have a mess to clean up."

"They started it."

The detective rubbed his chin. "Knowing these men the way I do, I'd say you're right. But going after them this way will only put yourself and your friends at risk. Let us do our jobs."

Brack wanted to point out that if they'd been doing their jobs, those men wouldn't have been on the street to put everyone at risk. But his observations wouldn't help, so he lay down by his dish, metaphorically speaking, and accepted his first warning, knowing there would be more.

After Nichols left, Brack said to Mutt, "Taking a wild guess, I'd say these guys might have something to do with threatening Cassie."

"I think you're right," said a familiar voice.

Brack turned to see his favorite Charleston Channel Nine news girl. Except she no longer worked for Channel Nine in Charleston and now lived here in Atlanta. Darcy Wells was slender, blonde, and driven. And beautiful.

He stood dumbfounded in her presence. Like just about every other time he'd had anything to do with her.

In tow behind her was a cameraman.

"Mr. Pelton," Darcy Wells said, "you've been in town all of about twenty-four hours and the police are already on the scene."

"The bikers started it," Brack said, trying not to sound like a whining kid.

"Darcy!" Mutt interrupted. "How you doin', sweetie?"

Darcy gave Mutt a hug and a peck on the cheek. "It's been a long time."

Brack turned his face to receive the same greeting.

She handed him a business card instead. "Put my number in your phone. As usual, you're going to need my help."

Staring at the card, which bore the job title of Senior

Correspondent for the local affiliate of a national TV network, Brack said, "How's the hubby?"

Darcy's ex-boss, Brack's aunt by marriage, had let him know that Darcy's wedding was coming up soon. Brack was merely needling her.

"George," Darcy said to her cameraman, "this is my old friend, Mutt. He runs the bar here."

George shook Mutt's hand. "And who's the new gun?" he asked.

Darcy winked at Mutt, then gestured to Brack. "This here's Opie. He brings trouble with him wherever he goes. And now he's in our city."

Raising the camera to his shoulder, George said, "Smile, Opie. You got a face for the camera. I have a feeling we're likely to get a lot of copy out of you."

"What George means," Darcy said, "is you're the first one to stand up to Vito's men."

"I had help," Brack said, nodding to Tara, who'd been focused on her brother, her uninjured arm around his shoulder.

George swung the camera to get her on film.

Brack stepped in between Tara and the camera. "You put her on TV or any other form of media, George, and you will find out what your equipment tastes like."

"And he doesn't mean your camera only," Darcy said. "I agree. Vito's men will describe her to him, but there's no reason we should help them out with a picture."

"This is warm and cozy and all," Tara said, "but who are you people?"

The three Charleston acquaintances turned to her.

Brack read from the business card still in his hand. "This is Darcy Wells, Channel Six News *Senior* Correspondent."

Darcy added, "We're all old friends."

"Why don't you ditch George here," Mutt said. "I'll close down for the night and we can all go to my house and talk."

George said, "She's not ditching anyone."

"Let me shoot my clip," Darcy said. "George will have to work on editing. Brack, you want in this or not?"

Brack thought about it a few seconds, then said, "Sure."

"You want 'em to know we're comin' for 'em?" Mutt asked.

Looking at his friend, Brack said, "You've been here less than a year, and you already forgot how we roll?"

Tara said, "Now what's he talking about?"

Mutt smiled. "Opie's just remindin' me that when we ride, it's full throttle the whole way."

Darcy's eyes widened and she rubbed her hands together. "Along with a trail of headlines for me to scoop up." She stopped with her exaggerated elation. "Except these bikers aren't like any bad guys you've encountered in Charleston. And before you go all Semper Fi on me, I'm saying the only cause these guys fight for is themselves. Sometimes for each other."

To Mutt, Brack said, "Just like back in the sand dunes, eh, Marine?"

"Oo-rah."

"You guys are crazy," Tara said. "Those bikers have beat up a lot of people. They're nasty. We got lucky tonight. They'll be back, and when they do, who's going to watch my brother then?"

"I can take care of myself," Darnel said.

"Not against flying bullets," Brack said.

Darnel turned a few shades lighter.

Mutt said, "Tara, I'm sorry 'bout this happenin' to you an' Darnel. And right outside my bar. Why don't cha take the night off and get your brother home? Let Darcy, Opie, and me talk about what we gotta do next."

"No," Tara said. "Whatever this is, I want in."

George began filming the scene, avoiding them for the time being.

Darcy put one hand on Mutt's shoulder and the other on Brack's as she stood between them and spoke to Tara. "These two don't look like much, but this is what they're good at. The police have to follow rules. These two have only to avoid getting arrested.

And killed. Give us your number and I'll make sure we get in touch."

Tara handed out several business cards.

Brack read his aloud. "Piedmont Wildlife Preserve?" Must be what Mutt meant by her working with animals.

To Brack, Darcy said, "That should make you feel right at home."

Chapter Four

Friday

It was after one in the morning by the time the group split and Brack led Darcy to his car. George had gotten his footage and headed back to the network for editing.

She said, "Porsche?" Two syllables. "I heard you were getting soft."

He opened the passenger door. She got in, lowered the visor, and opened the mirror. As he approached the driver's side, he watched her apply a layer of lipstick. She was as striking as ever. He got in the car, not believing she was again sitting beside him.

"What are you looking at?" she asked.

"You haven't changed a bit. Except your hair's a little shorter."

"I was serious about your getting soft. My trainer is the best. Let me give you his number."

He'd just confronted three bikers with weapons and she's telling him he's getting soft. Like old times.

His flat-six motor growled to life.

Mutt pulled up beside them in his Cadillac convertible. Brack had given him the car a year ago as a thank you for helping him stop a killer. He said, "You two look good together."

Darcy said, "Let's go before I change my mind."

Mutt sped away and Brack followed. After a few short miles, they pulled into the darkened driveway of a home in the Brookhaven area of the city. Darcy commented on the homes here going for high six-figures. She got out and stretched. Brack wondered why they hadn't gone to Mutt's house like he'd suggested.

Cassie greeted them at the solid wood door of a very nice one-story house, wrapping Brack in a hug, letting go, and then hugging him again. "I tol' Mutt to bring y'all here. I'm so glad you ain't hurt."

Cassie's awareness of what happened tonight suggested to Brack that she hadn't told him the whole story and probably knew more than she let on. He wondered if she knew that tonight's confrontation went down in front of the bar she also wasn't supposed to know about.

"Calm down now, woman," Mutt said.

She kissed him. "You hush up. They look hungry."

Darcy appeared about to object, especially considering the hour.

But Brack said, "Cassie makes the best lowcountry cooking you will ever eat."

They sat around an antique wooden kitchen table while Cassie warmed up shrimp and grits from her restaurant. She also pulled out a container of coleslaw that was both sweet and spicy.

After they ate all the leftovers, Brack expanded his belt a notch.

"There will be more of those guys, you know."

"Nothin' I can't handle," Mutt said.

"Three guys with knives and batons and who knows what else isn't 'nothin,'" Brack said. "You sound as stupid as I do half the time."

"Wow," Darcy whispered. "You *have* made some progress."

"I read a few books too," Brack added *sotto voce*.

Mutt, who hadn't heard Brack's exchange with Darcy, said, "What you talkin' about, Opie? They was three road-hog wannabes on mopeds afraid of their shadows."

Brack tossed his napkin on his plate. "And we'll have to get through them, and probably more, to get to Regan."

Cassie put her head in her hands. "I just want my sister back."

Brack stood. "Now we've got to find out why Vito is sending out his goons to discourage us."

"We'll start bright and early," Darcy said.

He had a feeling that meant he would get less sleep than he wanted.

Later that morning, Brack's phone buzzed. He fumbled for it, forgetting he was in Mutt's spare room that he shared with Shelby. He checked the time and the caller ID before picking up.

"You really haven't changed a bit, have you?" he said. "Up and at 'em early."

Darcy's voice sounded cheerful. "And you haven't changed either. Sleeping on the job."

"Just for that," Brack said, "you can buy me breakfast. That is, if your fiancé will be okay with that." He wondered if he was likely to meet the peckerwood, then he worried what he'd do when he did.

"Get your pants on," she said. "I'm standing in the driveway."

Five minutes later, Shelby ran out the front door. Darcy momentarily distracted him from relieving himself, but nature took over and he ran to the bushes.

Brack, on the other hand, felt confident he could not be so easily distracted.

Darcy's hair was pulled up to keep the Georgia heat off her neck. She wore a nice cream-colored silk blouse with a skirt that stopped a few inches above her knees.

Who was he kidding? She looked great.

She gave him a onceover. "I see we need to get you acclimated to your surroundings."

"What are you talking about?"

She pointed to his B-52's t-shirt and cargo shorts. "This is not the island, Brack. This is the big city. We should at least dress the part."

Funny, he thought. Mutt, of all people, had said the same thing.

"All I have to do is show up in my Porsche and I can get into any supercilious place I want."

"Wow. Such ostentatious vocabulary so early in the morning. I almost forgot you went to college."

Brack grinned.

She finished him off with, "In this town Porsches are a dime a dozen. Everyone's got one. You'll need more than that. And unless you have something else to wear, our first stop is to get you some decent clothes."

He was about to argue with her when he remembered insults were her way of trying to help. So he said, "Okay."

They fed Shelby breakfast together, and he enjoyed the attention.

After a walk around the block and another potty break, Brack put Shelby in Mutt's house, and he and Darcy left in her five-year-old Honda Accord. When she'd lived in Charleston, she'd driven a new Infiniti convertible.

Brack said, "I see you've got yourself an undercover car."

"How very observant of you," she said. "Now, first things first. We need to take care of your appearance."

An hour later, with twelve-hundred dollars' worth of clothes and a professional shave and haircut, they were on their way.

"Where are we headed now?" Brack asked.

Darcy swerved to slide between an Escalade and an F-150, undaunted by no wiggle room. "You guys said Regan's with Vito, right?"

"That's the info Mutt has." He grabbed the center armrest with his left hand and the grab handle above the door with the other in case traffic stopped in front of them, but it didn't.

"I've got a line on some warehouses he owns." She gunned the engine.

Brack swallowed hard. "Will we find Regan there?"

Slicing through another minuscule hole in traffic, she said, "Probably not. But I believe it's good to learn everything we can. You never know when it might come in handy."

Darcy was right, as usual. Brack had also assumed there might be trouble. His forty-five was now tucked neatly inside the waistband of his new khaki trousers in the small of his back. The untucked casual white silk shirt she'd picked out hid the evidence. He hoped he wouldn't have to run. The Italian loafers needed a bit more break-in time.

Still early according to Brack-time, he slipped on his new pair of Persol shades and eased the seat back just as his crazy chauffeur braked for a red light.

She looked him over. "I forgot how well you clean up when you want to."

"Thanks, I think." Not that he had a choice. At least the barbershop she'd dragged him to was the real deal.

The light turned green. She smiled and floored it again.

As he held on for another round of automobile dodgeball, Brack realized Darcy had done for him the same as Cassie had done for Mutt. And she did so in only one hour. The image of a lamb being led to the slaughter came to mind.

Vito's alleged warehouses were located on the south side of Atlanta, past the airport. Darcy pulled up to a guard shack and flashed her news credentials. The guard, an older gentleman apparently not used to having his nap interrupted, didn't know what to do. Darcy asked for the manager.

The old man shook his head. "There's no one else here at the moment."

"I see," she said. "Well, we really need to talk to someone. Do you have any contact information for us?"

"I'm afraid not," he said. "Unless you want to call my boss. His number's all I got."

Brack asked, "Do you get a lot of visitors?"

He chuckled. "You two are the first in the two years I been on this job."

"No deliveries or pick-ups?" Darcy added.

"Nope. All of that happens at night."

Darcy and Brack looked at each other. She turned back to the guard and gave him her made-for-TV smile. "Thank you, sir."

He replied, "I seen you on the news, haven't I?"

* * *

A mile down the road from the warehouse, Brack asked, "What's next?"

"I'm going to work," she said. "I suggest you do what you normally do and throw some rocks at the hornets' nest."

"You say that like it's a bad thing."

She laughed.

He had missed hearing her laugh.

"It usually is," she said. "But I think this time it's warranted."

"Wanna point me in the direction of the hornets?"

"Knowing you the way I do, and assuming you haven't changed since I saw you last, I suspect you won't have any trouble finding them."

Her bringing up the last time they saw each other was not what he wanted to think about, but the imagery wouldn't go away. A year ago she'd helped him find a killer. If he hadn't fallen into his own pit of booze and women, she might have stayed with him. Instead, she moved here and was set to marry the peckerwood. And it was mostly Brack's own fault. The more he thought about it, the madder he got at himself.

After a quiet ride back to Mutt's house, she dropped him off and went to her day job. Brack needed to work out his anger. With no bikers to beat up, the only thing left was exercise. Shelby was excited to see him. Brack changed into a t-shirt, running shorts, and tennis shoes. He clipped a leash on Shelby and they went for a run.

Returning forty-five minutes later, they found Mutt sitting in his Caddy convertible talking on his phone. He had on expensive-looking aviator shades and a plum silk shirt. Brack opened the passenger door and Shelby jumped into the seat and licked Mutt's face.

"Good Gawd!" he said, startled.

"Easy, boy," Brack said to his dog. "You don't want to get Mutt excited."

Mutt quickly ended his call. "Very funny."

"Who was that?"

"I think I got a lead," he said, not exactly answering the question.

"Great. Let me get water for Shelby and a quick shower and I'll be ready to roll."

"Opie, I think this is somethin' I need to check into myself."

Brack leaned down to meet him at eye level. "You don't really expect me to accept that, do you?"

Mutt looked away. "I don't 'spect you to understand. It's just somethin' I gotta do."

"You're right," Brack said. "I don't understand. In fact, I don't want to understand. All I know is I'm going inside to take my shower. If you aren't out here waiting on me when I get done, Vito and the bikers won't be all you've got to worry about." Brack walked into the house, Shelby at his heels.

Eleven minutes later, Brack dressed in new duds and let Shelby out. To his surprise, the Cadillac remained parked in the same spot. And Mutt still sat in the driver's seat. Shelby gave Mutt another quick lick, got out to water the bushes, and then went inside the house without any hassle. The dog was better than Brack deserved.

After locking the door to Mutt's house, Brack got in the passenger seat.

"Opie, you ain't never talked to me like that before."

"Yeah," Brack said, "well, you've been talking crazy since I got here and frankly you deserve it."

"Let's get one thing straight," he said. "I'm my own man."

Brack looked at his friend. "We're brothers. Nothing is going to change that. I want to help my brother any way I can. If that means I've got to be a jackass, then that's what I'll be."

"True that." Mutt started the car.

"Where we headed?"

Mutt gave him a sideways look, put the car in drive, and pulled out.

Fair enough, Brack thought. He hadn't demanded to know where they were going, merely told Mutt he wasn't going alone. Brack would have to live with whatever they were about to get into. So he pulled a fresh cigar from the pocket of his new khakis and lit up, ready for anything.

Chapter Five

Friday mid-morning

"Anything" turned out to be anything but. They rode south. Not wanting to say another wrong thing, Brack kept silent, smoked his cigar, and took in the sights. Within a few miles, the populace went from melting pot to mostly minorities to all black. Like at Mutt's bar, his was the only white face in a sea of ebony. And he got the stares one would expect. After all, Mutt's '76 Eldorado attracted attention by itself. Mutt kept it polished and shining, unlike Brack's Uncle Reggie—its first owner, who never put the top up and carried his surfboards in the backseat. Getting the bodywork fixed took quite a large sum of money. Brack knew because when he inherited all of his uncle's property following Reggie's murder, he paid for it.

They pulled into an alley, passed a row of plywood and sheet metal shelters, and parked by the loading dock of an abandoned building.

Mutt looked at him. "You wanted to come. Here we is."

"What is this?"

"You'll see." He got out of the car.

Brack followed, checking to make sure his forty-five was still jammed down the back waistband of his new trousers. The building was in worse shape than the worst of Mutt's bars, and that said something. Cracked brick, rusted steel, rotted wood. They climbed a set of crumbling steps and entered the building. Water pooled on the broken concrete surface of the emptiness inside, reflecting the rays of sun that forced their way through the holes in the roof.

Brack raised his sunglasses to the top of his head. Their footsteps echoed.

Mutt said, "Yo, Jacob. It's Mutt."

They waited for a reply. Nothing.

"Jacob!"

Again, nothing.

From the corner of his eye, Brack spotted movement. He touched Mutt on the shoulder with one hand while he reached for the forty-five with the other.

Mutt said, "Jacob, that you?"

A scrawny kid about twelve, tall and lanky, wearing a dirty Braves jersey, moved out from the shadows. "Mutt?"

"It's okay, Jacob. Just me and a friend."

Sensing the kid's paranoia, Brack kept the forty-five, now in his hand, behind his back but ready to rock and roll with a bullet already chambered.

"You bring me my baseball cards?"

Mutt pulled a pack from his pocket and tossed them to the boy.

Brack watched Jacob hold the pack up to the light and grin.

"Jacob," Mutt said, "you find out anything?"

Still looking at the wrapped cards, he nodded, "Uh-huh."

"Like what?"

"They come at night."

"Who come at night?"

"Motorcycles. A lot of 'em."

"Where do they go? Can you show us?"

The boy took his eyes off the prize and focused on them. "I guess so. No one there now." Jacob turned and walked back the way he came.

They followed. Brack thumbed at the forty-five's safety to make sure it was off.

At the other end of the open room, the three exited the building. The contrast between the darkened interior and the sunlight was enough to make Brack immediately pull his sunglasses down to shield his eyes. The kid rushed ahead, a directness in his steps. They cut between two more run-down buildings to the back paved lot used for the loading docks. Unlike the weed-strewn asphalt surrounding the first few structures, this lot was clear and in good condition. No weeds grew through these few cracks, as if the paving got frequent use. The loading dock, its concrete solid and smooth, had a pair of roll-up doors as well as a side door. The doors appeared decrepit, but when Brack tried each one they held firm.

Mutt said, "Jacob, you say the bikers come here?"

The kid said, "Uh-huh. And trucks. Big ones. They turn on bright lights and make lots of noise. I can hear 'em from two blocks away. Then the trucks leave."

Brack slipped the pistol back into his waistband, pulled out his iPhone, and took a video clip of the surroundings, making sure to not get Mutt or Jacob in any shot.

Mutt said, "You done real good, Jacob." He reached into his pocket and produced a second pack of cards, which he tossed to the boy.

Jacob caught the pack, grinned, and took off running, disappearing between two buildings.

Brack and Mutt returned to the Caddy and drove away.

After rolling down another street named Peachtree something-or-other, Brack said, "Darcy had a line on a warehouse by the airport. It had a little more security than the place Jacob showed us, but the same nighttime-only schedule. I'm thinking there's a connection."

"Mm-hmm."

"How do you know Jacob?"

"He come to the soup kitchen Cassie runs Saturday mornings. Always has on that baseball jersey. I got to talkin' wit him about the game and he kinda open up to me. When he mention the motorcycles, I got curious."

"And you didn't want me with you because I might've spooked the kid."

"Somethin' like that."

Brack put his hand on his friend's shoulder. "I'm sorry."

Mutt faced him. "Opie, I know you was only tryin' to protect me. I appreciate it. Really, I do. But you gonna have to trust me a little on this one."

"Okay then, why haven't you told Cassie about your bar?"

"'Cause it's mine."

"Don't try that jive on me."

Mutt pulled to a stop. "What did you say?"

Brack looked at him. "You're not going to shuck me like you think you're doing with Cassie who, by the way, already knows."

"Opie, I ain't gonna take this from you."

"Sure you are, because deep down, you know I'm right. And if that isn't good enough, then we can step out and settle this like men."

The two friends eyed each other for a moment, then Mutt looked away.

"Get outta my car," he said.

Brack complied and stood on the sidewalk, cigar in hand. He watched Mutt drive away, thinking something was really wrong with this picture.

Darcy picked him up an hour later after filming her news segment. Brack hadn't been idle. He found a shaded spot beside one of the abandoned buildings and managed to answer a few emails from Paige, the manager of both of his bars in Charleston. Not once did he have to pull out his gun in self-defense while waiting in expensive clothes in a dangerous part of town.

Darcy said, "You want to tell me why you're here, of all places, alone and with no transportation?"

"Not really." Brack tried to decide if he was more upset with Mutt for ditching him or with himself for pushing him to it.

"Okay," she said. "I'll assume it's related to Cassie's sister."

"There's a building near here that from the outside looks

abandoned like the rest of them. But when you get close, you see new locks and a shipping dock in very good condition."

"That's interesting," she said. "How is it related?"

"It might not be. But there's a homeless kid who says the place sees a lot of activity when the sun goes down."

"Like the one by the airport."

"Just like it. Except this one comes with the added detail of motorcycle riders. Lots of them."

After he showed her the building, they drove a mile down the road in silence.

Brack asked, "So where to now?"

Darcy said, "Let's see if you can use those powerful skills of observation to pick out what's wrong in what I'm about to show you."

Instead of replying, Brack reclined in his seat. Three years in Afghanistan had taught him that you couldn't tell from first glance who you were fighting. It occurred to him that on certain streets of this city the situation would be the same. Profiling sometimes created more problems than it solved. Darcy had probably spent the last twelve months observing her new surroundings. She would be well versed in the treachery hiding on the fringes of the capital of the South.

She turned down a side street, and Brack received a whole new perspective on gentrification. Whereas Charleston's poor areas had mostly been relocated to North Charleston by practices involving money and taxes, here in Atlanta on street after street he saw people in various stages of decay and despair. And this on a weekday when most were at work.

He said, "Vito caused all this?"

"Not all, but he's exploiting it."

"Cassie's sister didn't live here."

"True, but from what I could gather she went looking for trouble and ended up on Vito's doorstep. She could be a used-up hooker by the time she's twenty-six. If she lives that long."

Looking at the trash on the sidewalks, abandoned cars left on the streets, and clusters of unemployed men, he said, "Forget this. It's almost three. Let's get a sweet tea and figure out how we're going to get her back."

"Are you really sure you want to go up against one of the most powerful men in the city's underworld?"

"I'm here to help Mutt get Cassie's sister back. Then I'm heading home."

They rode in silence for five more minutes, the weathered Accord leapfrogging from stoplight to stoplight, until Darcy slowed, turned on her directional, and made a left.

She pulled to a stop at the curb, pointed across the street, and said, "Look."

Three young women stood together on the trash-spotted sidewalk wearing various renditions of the same overly revealing attire, each of them selling her wares. None were past thirty, but all looked unkempt and run-down. The scene resembled the clearance rack for Goodwill.

"The bottom of the barrel," Brack said.

"One step from it," she said. "The bottom is where these ladies end up when they can no longer make any money."

"And death soon follows." To focus on something else, Brack took out a cigar.

Darcy said, "I'd rather you not smoke in here."

Her ride, her rules. He complied.

They sat in her undercover mobile and observed a life neither of them really understood. Though his parents had been nowhere near as comfortable in wealth as Darcy's, Brack never wanted for things. Luck, more than anything else, kept him from ending up in the gutter.

For several minutes they remained parked, watching a steady stream of cars, not unlike the one they sat in, cruise the street. Some picked up and some dropped off one or another discount hooker.

Darcy started the car and they moved on. When her phone rang she looked at the caller ID. "It's Mutt."

"I'm not here," Brack said.

Using the car's Bluetooth, she answered. "Hey, Mutt."

"How you doin'?"

"You know me," she said. "What's up?"

He cleared his throat. "Um, you ain't happen to hear from Opie, has you?"

"Why?"

"I...um, can't find him."

She glanced over at Brack. "What do you want me to tell him if I see him?"

"It ain't that," he said. "I need to find him. He ain't in a good place."

Brack spoke up then. "You mean like the old warehouse district?"

"Opie? You there?"

"No thanks to you."

"Look, I'm sorry. I shouldn'ta left you there."

Brack didn't reply.

Darcy said, "You guys want me to stop and step out so you can kiss and make up?"

At the same time, both men replied, "No."

"Good. I want you both to listen. You guys are the oldest fifth-graders I know." She paused to spur the car around a smoking Chevy with big rims. "I suggest you spit, scratch your testicles, and shake hands. Maybe not in that order, but you get the picture." She stopped for a light. "If Regan is who we need to be helping, then get over it and let's go get her."

Brack knew she was right, as usual.

Mutt said, "Yeah, besides, I got someone I think we need to talk to."

"All right," Darcy said. "I've another story brewing and really need to get back to it. I'm dropping Boy Wonder off at your house, Mutt."

Chapter Six

Friday, mid-afternoon

Riding shotgun again in Mutt's Caddy, top down, Brack lit the cigar Darcy wouldn't let him smoke. Mutt took a hit of vapor and exhaled a cloud of mist. The day was Deep South hot, the sky a clear and cloudless blue. The sun wouldn't set for another few hours.

"So who's this person we need to talk to?" Brack asked, avoiding the slight tension between them from their last encounter.

"You'll see." At a stoplight, Mutt hung an arm out the car, tapping on the steel door to the beat of "Brick House" by the Commodores.

Brack took in a mouthful of the Dominican's finest and exhaled. He wanted to ask his friend more questions, but decided it would be better to let things play out.

A black four-door Wrangler, also with the top down, stopped next to them, cutting through any remaining tension. The doors were off, the same way Brack liked to roll in his old Jeep. Three bikini-topped and short-shorted young women in it were giggling, apparently at a joke directed at him and Mutt.

"How you ladies doing?" Brack asked.

The driver, a twentyish blonde, turned to the two other twentyish blondes and giggled some more. Then she turned back to the two men.

"What are you guys supposed to be?" she asked, her snotty attitude even more exposed than her body. "The pimp scene went out in the seventies."

"Why?" Brack said. "You girls looking for work?"

Mutt had been in the middle of taking a drag of vapor and choked up.

"Seriously?" she asked, still with attitude. "You guys look like you have to pay for it."

"And you three look like you're selling it," Brack said.

The driver's flame-red lips dropped open.

The blonde in the passenger seat leaned forward. "Listen here, perv—"

"Look," Brack interrupted her. "We've had a really bad morning. How about we all head to the closest watering hole and I buy you gals a round of whatever you want? Show you we aren't all that bad."

"Opie," Mutt said, "we ain't got time to be flirtin' with no girls."

Brack turned to Mutt. "Coming from you, that's real rich." Back in Charleston, the man had been like a deer in rut.

The light turned green and Mutt hit the gas, his face pinched together and jaw muscles bulging.

Brack and Mutt sat at a bar across town from his own establishment where they were supposed to meet Mutt's source who, according to Brack's vintage Tag watch, was late. To not arouse suspicion or frighten whoever they were meeting, both men had left their guns in the car.

Mutt looked around the room, then lowered his head. "Opie, we got some company."

Brack spotted what his friend referred to. Three men approached dressed in some version of the same biker get-up, black t-shirts with skulls, jeans, and leather boots.

With the three bikers still twenty feet away—ten feet from when Brack would get up and charge them—he heard a slightly familiar voice behind him, snotty attitude and all.

She said, "Those are the two that called us prostitutes."

Mutt said, "What the—"

Brack took his eyes off the men in black to see the three blondes from the Jeep pointing at him and Mutt. Next to the blondes stood three defensive lineman-sized clean-cut white guys.

Bikers in front of them.

Jocks behind.

Guns in the car.

Under his breath, Brack said, "How did we get ourselves into this one?"

Mutt replied, "You and yo' big mouth."

Returning his attention to the bikers, now eight feet away, Brack said, "I got the hogs. You take the bubbas."

Mutt said, "This gonna be fun."

Maybe for you, Brack thought. These bikers fought dirty.

Brack grabbed a beer bottle off the bar and smashed it across the closest Harley rider's head.

The other two did not startle. One caught Brack with a blow to the side of his face. The other tagged him with a gut punch. Brack doubled over, grabbed a stool, and swung it across the closest knee, catching it just right. The goon fell beside his fallen companion. The remaining one caught Brack with a good uppercut and slammed him backwards into the bar. Dazed and confused, Brack told himself he had one play left. As his opponent approached, Brack reached behind, steadying himself by grabbing the edge of the bar with both hands. Supported by his hands only, he kicked with both feet. His Italian loafers slammed into the biker's black leather vest. The goon flew backward into a support beam and crumpled to the floor.

Brack shook the cobwebs out of his head and turned to see what else might be happening. Two of the bubbas were down, but the third had a hold of Mutt's silk shirt and threw a solid widow-maker punch into Mutt's face. With whatever force Brack had left, he kicked the giant in the back of his knee, buckling his leg. As the jock twisted to face him, Brack slammed his elbow into the jock's face and his nose exploded. Blood spurted all over the three wannabe blonde hookers, who squealed and ran away.

The bubba let go of Mutt, who fell to the ground.

Brack coughed and spoke to the bloody nose. "You done?"

He sure hoped the jock was finished, because he had nothing left.

As if just noticing the blood gushing out of his broken nose, the giant put both hands to his face.

"Well?"

From behind him, Brack heard an authoritative voice say, "It's time to break it up."

Brack knew better than to turn his attention away from his opponent. In one of the mirrors, he could make out two uniformed officers walking toward them.

The Atlanta Police Department's building on Spring Street featured holding cells crowded with an assortment of races. America was, after all, the melting pot, and this jail attempted to prove the point. When Brack was put in the back of a cruiser and hauled away, he'd been separated from Mutt. Having lost sight of his friend, Brack now stood in the corner of an overpopulated cell. He kept to himself, glad there were no mirrors. His face felt as if it had grown two sizes from the beating he'd taken from the bikers, and he really didn't care to see how bad he looked. At least his bones were intact.

Brack's past experience in similar situations—and he'd had more than his share—told him he would be taken to a room called the "box" with a one-way mirror and asked a few "questions." He'd already been Mirandized so anything he said could and would be used against him. So far Brack hadn't asked for an attorney, but did think about calling his in Charleston.

True to form, a uniformed officer escorted Brack from the cell. Jeers and catcalls from his fellow detainees awarded him with the momentary status of a rock star, albeit one old enough to know better than to get arrested for a bar fight.

The officer opened a door and told him to take a seat at a table. The room had a mirror and one involuntary glance told him he looked as if he'd lost the brawl. He pulled out a chair, its aluminum legs scraping across the worn linoleum, and sat.

A few minutes later the door opened and Detective Nichols entered. He smiled, took a seat across from Brack, and placed a file folder on the table between them.

"I need to remind you," Nichols said, "that anything you say can be used against you."

"And I have a right to an attorney."

"Would you like an attorney?"

"Not yet. Where's Mutt?"

Nichols's forehead creased. "I think you have more pressing needs at the moment."

Brack said, "I've been in this situation before. More than a few times, unfortunately. Now, it was nice of you to be the one to come in here and talk to me. I appreciate that. Before I answer any questions, I want to know that my friend is okay."

"He is. We released him ten minutes ago. Seems the witnesses at the bar all agreed that the three men had attacked him and he had defended himself."

"Were they arrested?"

"Yes."

"Good. Now, what's in the file?"

Sitting back in his chair, Nichols opened the folder and spread out three sheets of paper. "These are the three men you fought with. They are very bad apples."

Brack looked up from the sheets to him. "Bad apples? That's the best you can do?"

"Okay," he said, "all are ex-mercenaries. Trained killers."

"I'm a Marine. Mercs are nothing but basic-training flunkies."

"You were a Marine. Now you're a civilian."

"Once a Marine, always a Marine."

"You haven't even asked me what the charges against you are."

"Because," Brack grinned for a second, "there aren't any."

Detective Nichols did not rein in the surprise in his face. "Why do you think that?"

"Just a guess. Witnesses to the ruckus will tell you I started it by taking out one of these pansies with a beer bottle, thus initiating it all. But I'll bet the pink slip to my Porsche that none of the bad apples, as you call them, are going to file any charges."

"Good guess."

"They are going to square things up on the street."

Nichols flipped through a few pages. "Their files suggest that's the way they work."

"So what are we doing here?"

Closing the file, Nichols said, "I told you if I saw you again like this, I'd have you escorted out of town."

"It's a free country," Brack said, jonesing for a cigar.

"I'd rather know you are safe back in Charleston than dead here on Peachtree Street."

"Me too. But I haven't finished what I came to do."

"Which begs the question," he said. "Why are you here?"

Brack told him about Regan.

Nichols said, "If she's with Kelvin Vito, you're better off simply heading home."

"But aren't you the police?"

"Yes," the detective said. "And I don't have time to be babysitting some soda cracker from out of town with a death wish. Going after this Regan, or Vito, is precisely that."

The next morning, Saturday, Mutt and Brack sipped hot French-pressed coffee from mugs at Cassie's house while she served free food to Atlanta's homeless. Brack was quiet and deep in thought. At least he pretended to be. The one thing on his mind at present was who had set them up the afternoon before. A knock at the door followed by someone letting themselves in had them both look up.

Darcy walked into the kitchen where they sat. "Detained again, I see. The more things change..." She didn't bother to finish the cliché that was growing older by the second. Instead, she said, "You guys look like you got beat up."

Brack said, "It was six against two."

"Yeah? It looks like you lost."

"Whatever," Brack said. "We walked away. They didn't."

"You wanna cup of coffee?" Mutt asked.

She sat her purse on a chair. "Of course."

Mutt worked Cassie's French press like a real barista. Considering the sludge he used to pour, his technique now was nothing short of a miracle. He served it to Darcy in a mug along with a chilled miniature stainless-steel cream pitcher. "You take sugar?"

"Why thank you, Mutt." An astonished look crossed her pretty face.

Brack realized that Cassie had done quite a number on his old buddy, and he had to give her credit. She didn't have much to work with, but she managed to domesticate the big wild pooch.

"What happened to you?" Brack asked him.

Mutt said, "Huh?"

"French-pressed coffee? Cream in little pitchers? What happened?"

Darcy said, "Shut up, Brack. It's obvious Cassie's had a positive influence on him."

"Whatever," he said. "We got bigger things to worry about than my Marine buddy being neutered."

Mutt said, "That's cold-blooded, man."

Brack smiled at him. "I'm just trying to give you some balance."

Darcy looked irritated. "Oh yeah? Where are you getting yours from?"

That one cut deep on a lot of levels. Ignoring her question, Brack said, "At this point I'm ready to bust in there and drag Regan out."

"Opie," Mutt said, "it was six to two and we barely got out of the bar. Vito's got an army. We ain't gonna bust in nowhere. That's all he needs to barbeque us alive."

"Mutt's right," she said.

"Well, of course you'd agree with him, since he served you gourmet coffee in a pink apron. I'd like another opinion."

"And I'd like to be rich," she said. "Oh, wait a minute. I already am."

"Yeah, yeah," Brack said. "The rest of us have to work for a living."

Her grin vanished in a flash. "I work harder in one day than you have since the day I met you."

Deciding she was probably right, Brack switched gears. "So, Mutt, you want to tell us about this traitor that was supposed to meet us yesterday at that bar?"

"I got fooled," Mutt admitted. "It was one of them anonymous tips. Someone called me and said to meet them there. I'm sorry 'bout all that, Opie."

Brack said, "That's okay, my friend. Regan is forcing us to grasp at straws."

"If it weren't for Cassie," Mutt said, "I wouldn't be doin' any of this."

Chapter Seven

Saturday

Even a senior correspondent couldn't relax on a weekend, so at nine Darcy had to leave for work. With some free time, Brack left Shelby with Taliah and Mutt at his rental house and drove forty minutes north of the city to the Piedmont Preserve. Tara had invited him to visit her at her day job. He remembered that she worked with elephants.

She met him by the main entrance wearing a Panama hat, white t-shirt that covered most of her tattoos, and khaki shorts and boots. A security hut nearby gave shade and a fan to the elderly attendant who staffed the desk. The temperature was already eighty-five degrees, though it was technically still spring.

"I never did thank you for saving my brother the other night," Tara said.

"How's the shoulder?"

"Sore, but loosening up."

Brack looked around. A large fence surrounding the Preserve stretched almost forever in both directions. "I've never been to a place like this."

She took his arm. "Then let me give you the nickel tour."

The firmness of her touch felt good to him.

She played guide for a twenty-minute walking tour of only part of the five-thousand-acre facility, consisting mostly of pasture, woods, and a few buildings. Thanks to this location away from the city, the air was fresh and clean.

Tara said, "And now you can help me feed Mr. Grumpy."

"You feed Mutt in here?"

She laughed. "No. Should we?"

"Who's Mr. Grumpy?"

Tara led him around a building that looked like a super-sized barn to an area in the back. Twenty feet from them stood the largest animal Brack had ever been this close to without bars between them. The elephant was over ten feet tall and weighed at least ten thousand pounds. Large tusks protruding from the sides of its trunk looked even more intimidating. The mammal was taking hay off a bale of the stuff and flapping his ears as he chewed.

"This is Mr. Grumpy," she announced.

Brack had faced men with guns and cheated death many times. But this imposing life standing two car lengths in front of him was something else entirely.

Mr. Grumpy greeted them with a loud trumpet blast from his prodigious proboscis.

Tara approached him slowly and Brack followed, realizing he walked behind her instead of beside.

"How's Mr. Grumpy doing?" she asked him in a sweet but firm voice.

The elephant gurgled a reply and continued eating.

She picked up a handful of hay from the pile and held it out to him. The elephant snaked his trunk around the bunch and inserted it in his mouth.

As Mr. Grumpy munched, Brack tentatively picked up a handful like Tara had and held it out to him. The elephant took it from him, put it in his mouth, then wrapped Brack in a long gentle hug with his trunk.

Tara put a hand to her mouth in surprise. Brack hoped he wasn't about to become the beast's next mouthful.

"He really likes you," she said, patting Mr. Grumpy and saying, "Good boy."

Then he released his captive.

"He's never done that before, Brack. He doesn't usually like anybody."

"Birds of a feather," Brack said, hoping not to reveal how intimidated he felt.

They spent some time with Mr. Grumpy, Brack getting more comfortable with the beautiful beast, as well as with a few other elephants roaming freely, then Tara walked him to his car.

He said, "I need some exercise. You want to work out with me when you get done here?" He always kept a gym bag in the car with fresh clothes and tennis shoes.

She smiled. "Are you sure you can handle my routine?"

Brack thought of his trainer back in Charleston, an ex-University of South Carolina linebacker who still benched four hundred pounds. Although his routine balanced both cardio and weight training, it was no picnic.

"I guess I'll find out."

Brack leaned against his Porsche and smoked a cigar while waiting for Tara in the Preserve's parking lot. A voice in the back of his mind told him he should be hunting for Regan, but his gut was telling him a connection existed here that he ought to pursue. Sometimes the right thing to do seemed the least logical. At least that's what he told himself. His hunches had blown up in his face before.

Tara came out of the back gate and walked toward Brack. He clipped the burning end off the cigar, crushed the ash with his loafer, and put the remainder of the cigar in his pocket.

"Tsk, tsk," she said. "You know those things are not good for you."

He popped a mint in his mouth and smiled. "I gave up booze. Cubans and Oreos are all I have left." He'd also given up chasing women with questionable morals, but he wasn't about to announce that little tidbit to her—at least not today.

"Wow," she said. "*Two* things we have to work out of your diet."

"Where are we headed?"

Showing off a mouth full of gleaming white teeth, she said, "Follow me." She got in an older Toyota 4Runner.

The Porsche followed her back to the northeast Atlanta suburbs. They parked at an upscale shopping center. Taking up half the center's footprint stood a modern gym. Big glass windows exposed a multitude of people working out on various cardio machines.

The cigar was probably not the best warm-up activity he could have done. The only thing going for him was his two-hour session every other day with his personal trainer. Thanks to that USC linebacker, Brack was in the best shape of his life, tobacco and junk food notwithstanding.

The gym session was as tough as Tara had promised. She matched him set for set on the machines and with the free weights, even after he stepped up his reps. Though Brack worked out more frequently than most men, Tara was a machine when it came to personal fitness. They finished with strength building in what could be called a dead heat if they had been competing, and Brack expected they'd hit the treadmill to close out the session with a nice run. Where Shelby and he lived on the Isle of Palms, Brack enjoyed regular five-mile jogs around the island, so he wasn't concerned.

But Tara guided him to the stair machine for what she called a casual climb. Except that she set the speed on a seventy-steps-per-minute interval with no time limit. Brack's body was used to a decent clip on flat island roads. This was more like a sprint up the stairs to the top of the Empire State Building.

He managed to keep up with her for seventeen and a half minutes before he jumped off, ran to the closest trash can, and threw up. After everything he'd eaten for breakfast had exited, Tara handed him a towel. "Ready to give up those cigars now?"

His first instinct was to tell her where she could go, but lucky for him he had to toss more of his innards first. Another trainer came by to say that none of Tara's challengers ever made it to the stairs before they dropped out, so Brack could consider himself in pretty good shape.

With his head in the trash can, his mind managed to form two words: just great.

After his stomach settled and a warm shower in the gym's locker room relaxed him, Brack walked out famished and a little ashamed. As if to add insult to embarrassment, Tara said she had a bachelorette party to go to and took a rain check on Brack's offer of dinner.

While Brack drove back to Mutt's house to spend time with Shelby, Darcy called with a tip from one of her sources. So at nine o'clock that evening, he and Mutt sat in the Porsche watching the address of the exclusive club they'd been tipped about. Atlanta's classic rock station played through the high-end speaker system.

They'd been parked maybe five minutes when the vehicle Darcy told Brack to watch for arrived.

The black Mercedes G63 SUV pulled to the curb, the rear door opened, and Kelvin Vito stepped out. Mutt recognized him from all the press coverage he'd received, both from his links to the underworld and from the charitable events he hosted to counter the former. Vito turned to extend a hand inside the open door. An African-American woman took his hand and exited the large SUV. Holding her head high, as a queen would, she resembled the photo Brack had seen in Regan's bedroom. Thin, really too thin, Cassie's sister wore a beautiful black dress with gold highlights. Arm in arm, the couple strolled into the private club followed by two very large, very muscular beefcakes. Rambo wannabes. And by the cut of their sports jackets, Brack could tell they covered more than muscle tissue.

"Well, I'll be," Mutt said. "Darcy was right. And there's Regan."

"So that's her," Brack said. This was all a lot of trouble for one very small woman.

Mutt reached for the door handle to get out.

Brack put a hand on his shoulder. "Easy there, cowboy."

"Let's get her so we can go on home," he said.

"What about those two meatheads?" Brack asked. "They got heaters in shoulder rigs."

"What you worried about, Opie? We handled worse than them before."

"Yeah. But I don't feel like being in a shootout today."

Mutt shrugged and took out his vaporizer, which brought to mind Brack's exercise routine with Tara. Somehow he didn't feel like joining Mutt in lighting up a smoke. Instead, he remarked, "Shaft and Mike Hammer ride again."

"Mike Hammer?" Mutt said. "I thought you wanted to be James Bond."

"Hammer is more my style."

"Yeah," Mutt said. "Rough around the edges."

The station commercial break ended and the wail of Prince's guitar in the intro to "When Doves Cry" wafted through the speakers. RIP, Prince, Brack thought.

Mutt said, "We got to get in there."

"They aren't going anywhere."

When the song ended Brack drove up to the entrance of the club. Slipping the valet a twenty to park the Porsche, he and Mutt bypassed the line and walked directly to the bouncer who manned the roped section designed for celebrities and those with enough cash to avoid waiting. Mutt slid the big man a bill and he unclasped the velvet rope to let them by. Their next stop was the window to pay the cover charge.

The young lady behind the glass might have been all of twenty-one. Mutt handed her two more bills identical to the one he'd slipped the bouncer. She nodded once with a tilt of her pretty little head, motioning the newcomers to move on.

As Mutt and Brack opened the double doors and entered the darkened nightclub, Brack marveled that this time it was his friend shelling out for cover charges. So far Mutt was in for one-fifty. And the evening was just getting started.

Like camera flash bulbs, spotlights and strobes bounced over the walls and the crowd at the speed of machine-gun fire. Mutt and

Brack strolled casually to the bar, first, because Brack was thirsty, and second, so they'd have a place from which to observe and locate their target.

Brack ordered a club soda and lime and Mutt got a draft beer. He pulled out his vaporizer and took a few more puffs.

"The best thing about this," he said, showing off the contraption, "is I can smoke anywhere I want."

Not quite, but he had a point.

Taking in the crowd of millennials, Brack spotted their target and his entourage in an elevated far-corner booth.

Mutt saw them at the same time. "How you want to play this?"

"We'll never get past the meatheads without some form of violence," Brack said. "Not that I have too serious an issue with that. But let's hold back. Sooner or later, Vito has to take a whiz."

After another hit from his vaporizer, Mutt said, "I ain't got nothin' better to do, anyway."

Across the room, Brack spotted a familiar face among a group of women, one of whom wore a tiara on her head.

Tara must have sensed his gaze and looked his way. She smiled, left the tiara wearer and the rest of her party, and made her way over.

Mutt noticed and turned his head toward Brack's ear. "You better watch yourself with this one."

Tara came up to Mutt and gave him a peck on the cheek and a hug, then did the same with Brack.

"What are you guys doing here?"

Brack mimicked the girl in the cover charge booth and merely gave a head nod in the direction of Vito and his crew.

"I figured as much," she said. "He's a real piece of work, you know."

"I've been described that way myself," Brack said.

"Yeah? Well, whatever you are or have done, I'm sure it pales in comparison to Kelvin Vito. He may look like a hip club owner who makes things happen. But he's into a whole lot of very bad things from the skin trade to exotic animal poaching. It makes me so mad that we spend all this time and money to help people and to preserve endangered species, and he profits from the destruction of both."

Mutt said, "We're here for Regan."

"This is the first time I've seen her out with him," Tara said.

"You come here often?" Brack asked, instantly regretting the pick-up line phrasing.

She took it in stride. "My brother likes these places. So do some of my friends. If it wasn't for them," she said, motioning to the group, "I wouldn't be here."

"Opie and me was tryin' to figure how to play this. Straight up or wit a slant."

She said, "With Vito, better play the slant. In fact, the greater the angle, the better your chances. Like I said, he's a real piece of work."

Her advice resonated with Brack, although probably not how she thought it would.

Mutt looked at him. "What you thinkin'?"

Brack reached into his wallet, took out the valet ticket for the Porsche, and handed it to Mutt. "I'll be right back. Get the car if something goes wrong."

Mutt started to say something, but Brack stepped away too quickly to hear it and strode toward the target. He reasoned that if Vito was so sharp it took a pretty wild slant to fake him out, he must have prided himself on the angles. Playing this one like a head-on collision might be the only way to succeed. And since Brack didn't live here or have to stay and suffer the consequences, what he was about to do was better done alone.

He got within a couple of feet of the elevated platform before the two meatheads came to their senses and rose to block him from stepping up to their level. They crossed their arms over their massive chests and stood with their feet apart.

Brack calculated he was half a foot shorter than each of them and about half as strong as either one. But the Marines had taught him to improvise, adapt, and overcome. These two seemingly immovable objects were about to get a lesson on what happened when they underestimated their opponent.

Another movie scene came to Brack's mind. One from Clint Eastwood's *Heartbreak Ridge*.

The beefcake standing above Brack's right arm put his hand on Brack's shoulder and opened his mouth to say something. Brack jerked both his arms out in front of him, grabbed each man by his crotch, and squeezed hard. So hard that the surprise in their faces turned to horror, then agony, all within two seconds. Both tried swinging at Brack's arms, but succeeded only in losing their balance. They fell off the platform and landed with loud thumps.

The music might have stopped, but Brack hardly noticed. With both of them now out of the way, he had unrestricted access to Kelvin. And the arrogant jackass had the audacity to merely sit there and watch, as if he weren't in any danger. He wasn't, of course. Brack was already way out on a limb. If he harmed Vito but failed to kill him, there would be no place on earth where he'd be safe from the gangster's unlimited resources.

"They were two of my best," he said. "Take a seat."

"No thanks," Brack said.

Vito pursed his lips as if to consider. After a beat, he said, "Okay. So what can I do for you?"

Staring into Vito's eyes without blinking, Brack said, "The young lady with you, Regan. Her sister is worried about her. A quick phone call letting her know everything is okay would go a long way to easing her burden."

With amusement in his smile, Vito said, "You went through this whole exercise and all you want is for Regan to call her sister?"

"I do whatever it takes."

Regan said, "I don't have a sister."

Neither Vito nor Brack made as if they heard her protest. Instead, Vito said, "For someone who beat up six of my guys already, Mr. Pelton, you sure are playing this fast and loose."

So he did know who Brack was. "Yeah, well, I'd keep my head down if I was you." Brack slowly reached into his pants pocket and took out a fat roll of hundreds he'd withdrawn from his own safe before he left Charleston. Cash always came in handy, like right now. He peeled ten bills off the roll and laid them on the table. "For any inconvenience I might have caused."

Brack turned around to leave. One of the giants had gotten to his feet but was still hunched over. The other lay in the fetal position on the floor. Strolling past them, it occurred to Brack that most of his moves had come from all the movies he'd baked his brain watching when he should have been doing something his mother called "more constructive."

Because he didn't see Mutt or Tara, he headed for the front door. His Porsche was already waiting at the curb with Mutt in the driver's seat. Tara sat in the back. As soon as Brack got in, Mutt revved the motor and got them out of there in a hurry.

Chapter Eight

Saturday night

A block down the road, Mutt said, "Da-amn Opie! I knew you had stones, but I didn't think you'd do anything like that."

"Me either," Brack answered.

"You realize," Tara said, "that he's onto you now."

"He already was."

"And that you are in danger."

"Nothing new."

She asked, "And that thought didn't occur to you while you were jeopardizing those two idiots' ability to procreate?"

"I was simply doing the world a favor."

"The monks who set themselves on fire in protest get better results than what you just did," she said.

"Don't be so quick to judge," Brack said.

"Whatever," she said. "My car is at the club. I'm going to have to get it eventually."

"You want us to go back and drop you off now?" Brack asked.

"Of course not," she said.

As he drove, Mutt said, "They gonna be lookin' for us. We can't go to my bar or Cassie's restaurant."

In the end, they went to a Waffle House not too far away and got three coffees and three pieces of pie. They sat there waiting out the danger and talking junk for two hours before heading back to the club and Tara's parked SUV.

She hugged them both, lingering her embrace with Brack a tad longer, in his opinion, before heading away.

With her now safely away, Brack and Mutt proceeded back to the rental where Taliah and Shelby were.

On the way, Darcy called.

Brack answered. "Hey there."

"Hey there, yourself," she said almost gleefully. "I just heard two of Vito's henchmen will have trouble fathering children. You are my hero."

Realizing her definition of hero was in the "I will have enough news to report to keep me busy for the next month" sense, Brack said, "You're welcome."

Regan knew she was in trouble. The ride back to Vito's apartment in the backseat of the Mercedes SUV was a quiet one. Up to this point, she'd thought she could keep the fact that her sister was looking for her away from him. Using his name, she'd sent a few of his minions to try to stop her sister and Mutt from asking questions and getting too close.

But this new player was the real business. Taking out Lonnie and Mike like *that*. No fear. Bringing it to Vito in a straight line. No one, but *no one* had spit in her man's face before. Especially in public. Thinking about him aroused something inside her, the same feeling she'd felt when she first met Vito. That Vito already knew about this man was not good news for her. Even knew his name.

Vito spoke, breaking her train of thought.

"So," he said, "when were you going to tell me your sister was looking for you?"

"I told you. I don't have a sister."

"Apparently this man Brack thinks you do."

"He ain't nothing."

Vito said, "He took out Lonnie and Mike. Maybe they weren't my best after all. But he isn't 'nothing,' like you say. He can jeopardize everything."

She touched his leg. "I'm sorry. I should have talked to you about it before. I didn't want to worry you."

He took her hand in his. "Don't you understand? If you are in danger, I want to protect you."

Sunday morning, Brack had a long talk with Cassie. He felt she should know that Regan didn't appear to be either missing or kidnapped.

"She gotta be hypnotized or something, Mr. Brack," Cassie said. "My sister shouldn't be with a man like that."

As painful as he knew it would be to hear what Regan said about not having a sister, Brack nevertheless told her.

Cassie's eyes watered. She wiped them and blew her nose.

He let her get it out.

She said, "There's someone I want you to talk with, if you don't mind."

He didn't mind. If she still wanted to pursue this, Brack wasn't going to let Mutt try to handle it on his own. Not after he'd just kicked over the hornets' nest.

Brack left Cassie and drove down Peachtree Street toward Buckhead, taking in the city he'd called home a very long time ago. The significant increase in population had brought a sprawling metropolis and everything that came with it.

Traffic wasn't that horrible, especially for a Sunday. The real problem, as he saw it, was that any place he wanted to go was located across town from wherever he happened to be. That and Atlanta drivers behaved much more aggressively than the drivers on the South Carolina island he now lived. Here cars weaved in and out, drivers vying for any advantage by constantly changing lanes. Since he was seldom in a hurry, Brack rolled along just fast enough to keep a minimum distance between his front bumper and the rear of the car in front of him.

Mutt had to go to the restaurant to handle some restocking. Cassie had suggested Brack visit a women's shelter she supported to talk with the director. Regan had not called her, of course. So after breakfast and a long walk with Shelby, Brack left him alone in

Mutt's house and arrived at the shelter in Buckhead five minutes early for his appointment.

The building was a large nondescript brick home a little north of the big money district. Brack pulled into visitor's parking and approached the lobby, expecting to find a receptionist behind a desk. Instead, he entered a small room with white walls and cheap gray tile. Between two hospital-type waiting room chairs, a small table held a phone. Opposite the entrance stood one very substantial door. A small tinted dome was mounted in a corner ceiling and probably housed a camera. After verifying his assumption that the door was locked, Brack picked up the receiver. He saw no card anywhere with printed instructions about calling anyone.

In place of a dial tone, a friendly female voice said, "May I help you?"

"I have an appointment to see Mrs. Royce."

"Your name please?"

He gave it to her.

After a long moment, the voice said, "Please have a seat and someone will be with you shortly."

The phone then went dead.

Another glance around the room revealed no magazines or wall-mounted flatscreen TV to hold a visitor's attention. Brack sat in one of the chairs and waited.

Ten minutes later the fortified door opened. A stout woman a few inches shorter than him came into the room. Big glasses accentuated big eyes. Gray-streaked hair and a weathered face put her a decade or two older than him.

She smiled and held out a hand. "I'm Susanna Royce. It's nice to meet you, Mr. Pelton."

Taking her offered hand, Brack said, "Please call me Brack."

Finished with the formality, she said, "My office is on the second floor. I believe we should talk there."

"Lead the way."

She held the door for Brack, then guided him through the

ground floor. They passed empty rooms that looked like hospital exam rooms, along with a lot of closed doors. Everyone Brack saw—and he counted about twenty between the entry door and the stairwell—was female.

They took the stairs. Cream-painted concrete block and steel walls surrounded them. The second floor's cubicle inhabitants greeted them, and Mrs. Royce meandered through a maze to the end of a hall and an actual office. Hers, Brack presumed.

Motioning him in, she closed the door behind them. Her decently sized office held a large black desk and two visitor chairs. Against the wall by the door sat a couch. She settled heavily into one end of it. Brack took the other end and they faced each other.

She said, "Cassie spoke highly of you and asked me to talk to you about her sister."

"Yes, ma'am."

"Can I ask what experience you have with abused women?"

Thinking about her question, Brack said, "I've dealt with a few situations in which women were kidnapped and harmed."

"What kind of credentials do you carry?"

"Usually I don't carry any. But I fought as a Marine in Afghanistan and have a licensed Colt forty-five locked in the glovebox of my car."

She sat back a bit, as if trying to add more distance between them. Judging by her reaction, his answer must not have been a good one. Or at least not one she wanted to hear.

Brack tried to give her a friendly smile, but it didn't seem to work.

"Mr. Pelton," she said, "we don't condone violence here. Most of the women who come to us have seen enough of it."

"Yes, ma'am."

"Cassie gave me the impression that you were a man who believed in justice."

Brack's form of justice sometimes flew in the face of the legal system. He said, "I believe we should protect the innocent. There's a difference."

"How so?"

"If someone uses a gun to rob a store, there's a chance an innocent bystander could get killed. I believe in taking out the robber before that happens, even if it means the robber dies. Justice would say the criminal should get five to ten years or whatever *if* they're caught after the fact. Some would call me a bit extreme."

Clasping her hands together on her lap, she said, "What happens if someone innocent gets hurt *because* you are trying to stop the robber?"

What Susanna Royce didn't know was that something similar had happened only last year. He and Mutt had tracked a killer to an apartment complex. Riding with them at the time was a Charleston Police detective who received a partial shotgun spray and lost an eye. One could say it was due to Brack's negligence. He was often reminded of the moment because since then, the detective had married Brack's business manager, Paige. The man didn't seem to hold a grudge, but who knows.

Brack said, "There's always a risk."

"Yes, there is." She sighed. "Well, I suppose I have to trust Cassie. Although when she talks about you, she gets a dreamy look on her face. I think her judgment might be compromised. But I'm going to give her the benefit of the doubt."

"She is a very nice person."

Mrs. Royce said, "She's concerned about her sister."

"Yes."

"Her sister has been on the wrong side of things since as far back as I can remember, and I've known Cassie's family a long time." She removed her glasses and wiped her eyes with a tissue.

He waited for her to continue.

"I've been doing this work for twenty years and it still gets to me."

"As soon as it stops getting to you, that's the time to hang it up," he said.

Her eyes met Brack's. "You're giving *me* advice?"

While she might have not meant those words as a compliment, he wasn't offended. He believed what he said, and he thought she did too. He said, "I've seen a lot of death. In Afghanistan and elsewhere. More than most people will ever see."

Sniffling, she asked, "What's supposed to be my takeaway from that?"

"Eventually it stopped getting to me. That's one reason I didn't re-up. I came back with depression and a drinking problem. It's taken me a few years to get a handle on both."

"You're not kidding, are you?"

"No."

"And you say you've got a handle on your problems?"

"Not all of them. Most days I don't drink or sit around feeling sorry for myself. But a few other days are not worth repeating."

"Amen to that," she said.

"Tell me about Regan."

"Very pretty. Think of a taller, more slender version of Cassie. Mostly her eyes. Looks wise, the girl has it all."

"I've seen her," Brack said, not really wanting to go into details of the night before.

"From what I hear she's Kelvin Vito's woman."

"And that's a bad thing?"

She straightened up as if taken aback. "Of course it's a bad thing."

"I mean, isn't it better than being in the trade?"

"I'm not sure."

"Okay. So what does being Vito's woman mean?"

"She is at his beck and call, I guess."

Thinking out loud, he said, "I wonder if she gets to run some of the business now."

Mrs. Royce lowered her head, moving it from side to side. "I hope not. Bad enough she enlisted for this lifestyle. If she becomes someone who perpetuates it, I don't know how Cassie will be able to handle it."

"Tell me about Vito."

"Born with a silver spoon up his butt, pardon my French. Handsome. Cruel."

"I met him as well. How come he isn't in jail?"

"In addition to most of the brothels in town, he has a line of what I've heard called top-shelf girls for his select clientele."

"By 'select clientele' you mean powerful men?"

She nodded.

"I see."

"I'm glad you do, because no one else seems to," she said. "There's something else too."

"What's that?"

"Thanks to his connections, Vito's got some type of diplomatic immunity."

That wasn't good news. "How's that?"

"All I know is that it has something to do with his family. He's not a natural born citizen."

Brack spread his hands open. "Okay. Where should I look first?"

She straightened her skirt and stood. "If you've got time, I'd like you to talk with a few young women we have with us."

"How do you feel about someone from the press being present?"

"You mean Darcy Wells? Cassie told me of your relationship with her."

Mrs. Royce could go either way in her decision to allow Darcy to join him, he realized. He wasn't sure why he'd thought of including her, besides the obvious reason, of course. Maybe that was the only reason.

Susanna Royce said, "From what I've heard, Darcy is one of the best reporters in the city. She's already broken several crime rings wide open. As long as identities are protected, I don't have a problem. In fact, it might be a good idea to have a woman with you when you do talk to our clients."

She raised her bulk from the couch and led him outdoors to make his call. Cell reception in the building was not very good.

Darcy answered on the second ring. "What's up?"
He told her where he was and what he was about to do.
She said, "I'll be there in thirty minutes."
"Thirty minutes?"
"If traffic isn't too bad."

Chapter Nine

Sunday, mid-afternoon

The wait gave Brack time to think about how to handle these fragile women. Normally he would smoke a cigar while he thought, but after the workout session with Tara he really wasn't in the mood. Susanna Royce was right that having Darcy with him would be a good idea. So he sat in the front waiting area for Darcy to enter. There were no windows to look out of, probably for confidentiality reasons.

Twenty-five minutes almost to the second, his favorite reporter entered the lobby. She looked as beautiful as ever.

"Thanks for coming."

"Are you kidding?" she said. "I've been trying to get an interview here since I moved to town."

"So it's worth something to you?"

Stopping in her tracks, she asked, "What do you want?"

He had a whole lot of answers to that question. Actually, only one real answer existed, but he wouldn't be offering it at this time. So he said, "My contact here says we have to protect the anonymity of the women we interview."

Darcy said, "I figured that."

"Good. And afterward you can buy lunch."

She gave him one of her trademark smiles, the fake one that she reserved for people she had to tolerate to get what she needed. It was okay. At this point Brack would take whatever he could get.

They entered the reception room and he picked up the phone, again asking for Mrs. Royce.

Within five minutes, she opened the locked door.

Brack introduced the women to each other.

Darcy said, "Thank you so much for this opportunity. Brack has explained to me the need to protect the identities of the women we talk with. I give you my word I won't print names or describe their appearances in a manner that would divulge who they are."

"Good," Mrs. Royce said. "I want you to know that the reason you are here is because of Mr. Pelton. And the reason he is here is because of my relationship with Cassie Thibedeaux."

Darcy nodded. "I understand, and you won't regret it."

Holding the door open for them to enter, Mrs. Royce further informed them, "You are the only reporter I have ever allowed in here. I'm familiar with your work. If I didn't feel you would handle this properly, I wouldn't have agreed."

Another way of saying Darcy's reputation was on the line. That shouldn't bother her, because Brack knew it was on the line with every story she reported.

Mrs. Royce led them to a generic room on the ground floor, with a table, four chairs, and a window that faced a fenced back lot. She said she'd return in a moment with the first woman they would get to talk with.

To keep his eyes and thoughts off Darcy, Brack stared out the window.

She said, "Like old times, huh?"

"Almost," he said. "Thanks again for joining me. I don't think I'd have gotten this far without you." It was a true statement that applied to most of the past few years.

When she didn't reply, Brack looked at her. She'd been watching him, then turned away.

She said, "I heard you and Paige are opening up a second location."

"When did you talk to her?"

Darcy said, "All the time."

Great. Paige neglected to tell him she kept in touch with Darcy. If that hadn't struck a nerve, he would have focused instead on the second thought he had, which was to wonder what else she wasn't telling him.

He said, "I see."

Darcy gave him her trademark made-for-TV grin. "I'm guessing you're out of the loop."

"Apparently for a lot of things."

"You said it," she said. "So, what about the bar?"

"It's on Kiawah. Beachfront costs a fortune. We got a deal on a second-row property that needed a lot of TLC. Paige hired someone to run the Cove and has been working full time ever since to get the new place in shape."

"What are you going to call it?"

"Reggie's Shipwreck." He didn't have to explain the meaning behind the name. She knew his late Uncle Reggie had owned the Pirate's Cove until a few years ago when Brack got it as part of his will. She'd helped Brack catch Reggie's murderer.

"Good choice," she said. "And smart move giving it to Paige to run. You guys are set to create an empire."

He wasn't sure he wanted to grow larger than operating two bars. Even one was a lot of work. More than he'd anticipated. Though the money was great, some days he wanted to pack his things and move to Hawaii with Shelby. He still might.

The door opened and Mrs. Royce entered with a young woman about twenty. Attractive but tired-looking, the client had natural olive skin, big brown eyes, and hair to match pulled back in a ponytail.

Darcy introduced herself, looking the woman in her eyes and making sure to take her hand in both of hers. She said, "We don't need to know your name. Give us something to call you."

The young woman visibly relaxed. "How about Sonia?"

Her accent was from somewhere south of the border.

Brack said, "Hi, Sonia. My name's Brack Pelton."

The four of them took seats around the table.

Mrs. Royce began, "Um, Sonia, why don't we start with your describing how you happened to come here?"

Sonia looked down at her hands and fidgeted with a tissue. "I come to the city to find work. A man find me in bus station and tell me he can help. Two years later I am here."

"Who is the man who found you in the bus station?" Darcy asked.

"His name is Levin, but I not sure if it is real name."

"Does he work directly for Vito?" Brack asked.

"I not sure."

"When was the last time you saw Levin?"

The fidgeting stopped. "About six month ago. He was one of my non-paying customers."

"Non-paying?" Mrs. Royce asked, as if that was a detail she hadn't heard before.

"Sí. We had paying ones and non-paying ones who worked for Vito."

Darcy said, "And you couldn't refuse to work." It wasn't a question.

Sonia looked at her, at first with a hint of anger in squinted eyes and clenched teeth, but then her face softened as she realized Darcy's intention.

"No. We would be punished."

"Like how?" Brack asked, almost immediately regretting his hasty question.

"They would beat us, not give us food, lock us in a small box. Things like that."

Darcy asked, "If we showed you a picture, could you identify this Levin?"

"Sí. I never forget him."

"What else can you tell us?" Brack asked. "Anything will help."

"I can tell you I am glad I got away. If they find me here, they kill me."

The need for anonymity became crystal clear.

"We won't tell anyone," Darcy said. "We only want information that will help us take down Vito."

Sonia asked, "And Levin?"

A smile tugged at Brack's mouth, but he suppressed it. "If I find him, I'll deal with him personally."

Sonia made no attempt to hide the hint of satisfaction that tugged at the corner of her own mouth. Brack had a feeling that her knowing of the dirtbag's suffering would ease hers.

The next young woman Mrs. Royce had them talk with came from Costa Rica. Her story was similar—except that her dirtbag was someone other than Levin.

Outside, in the Deep South oven, Darcy and Brack stood talking by her car.

"What do you think?" he asked.

"Sounds like a story we've heard before."

"Yep. So what do we do now?"

"Not sure about you, but I'm ready to burn Vito's house down, editorially speaking."

"You take care of the paperwork. I'll bring the gasoline and matches."

"We can't just blow up his enterprise," she said. "People might begin to feel sorry for him. And the women he 'owns' might be hurt. We don't want that."

"I never gave much truck to what others thought," Brack said.

"The police have got to come down on our side for whatever we do. Otherwise, well, you know how it could go."

He certainly did. They'd slap on the cuffs and throw them both in jail before they could finish what they started.

Later that afternoon at Mutt's house, while Darcy worked on her story, Brack explained to Mutt and Cassie what they'd discovered. Shelby lay by his side on a rug Mutt had given him.

Mutt said, "I already knew most of that, Opie."

Cassie said, "No, you didn't. Not about Levin."

"You right about that. I say we go find us this guy."

"I got the impression Levin was pretty high in the food chain," Brack said. "Might be hard to get to from the bottom."

"Then we gotta get 'im from the top."

Cassie stood. "I can't stand to listen to any more of this macho talk. One or both of you is gonna get killed."

Mutt's eyes met his. Brack knew what he was thinking and shook his head no. They would not remind Cassie that it was her sister they were trying to rescue.

Brack reached down to give his dog a pat. "Let's see what Darcy digs up. You know she's the best investigative reporter around."

Cassie got them back on track. "Susanna was helpful?"

"Yes." As dangerous as all the other times were when Brack and Mutt had "looked into something," they paled in comparison to what Vito and his band of bikers promised. Brack felt it as strongly as he felt the ground beneath his feet. Getting Regan back to Cassie would get bloody.

Yet part of him looked forward to it—the part that he kept locked in a cage and released only for desperate situations like this one.

"You guys aren't thinking about going after Vito, are you?"

That was exactly what Brack was thinking. However, something told him Cassie would not want to hear that at this particular time. He said, "What I want is to bring your sister to you."

Mutt said, "Yeah, baby. We ain't gonna do anything stupid."

Not something Brack would have promised, but he was making a conscious effort to not lie. Mutt must be working toward a different set of goals.

"Don't you be shinin' me on, Clarence Alexander," Cassie said. "I will toss your black behind out the front door so fast you'll wonder if time stopped."

Chapter Ten

Sunday, afternoon

Johnny Cash—Mutt's choice—belted "Ring of Fire" through the Porsche's stereo as they rolled through the steady traffic of the city.

"You know this man got some brother in him," Mutt said. "Ain't no full-blooded Wonder Bread got that kind of anger. Same with you, Opie."

"Thanks, I think." What Brack really thought was how little time he'd spent with his dog since he'd arrived in Atlanta. Not that Shelby seemed to mind. He'd adopted Taliah as his new favorite female admirer and barely noticed how often Brack walked out one door or another.

"You're welcome," Mutt said. "Turn right at the next light."

"We've actually got a destination?"

"I always got a destination. You, on the other hand, follow where the wind blows."

Brack couldn't argue. Sometimes his life felt like a tumbleweed. The thought in Brack's head was, isn't it time for someone to die? Usually by now, as in the last few escapades they'd had, someone would kick the bucket because of something he and Mutt did or because the bad guys targeted a victim. Either way, the grim reaper was late. And Brack balanced his itchy trigger finger with a guilty conscience about his friends being in danger.

Mutt guided him into one of the not-so-nice parts of town. Because Atlanta stretched out in all directions with no end in sight, there were more of these not-so-nice parts than Brack cared to count. Such was life in the big city. He now understood why Darcy drove a beat-up Honda. He and Mutt stood out in his shiny new sports car, especially in parts of town where everyone lived below the poverty line.

"Who are we going to see?" Brack asked.

"A friend of mine I shoulda been talkin' to already."

"Who's that?"

"Name's Delray. After he did ten for running girls, he switched to robbery. He's pretty much retired now, but he still knows what goes on."

Mutt had him turn down a side street, pull into a cracked driveway, and park behind an eighties Seville on blocks. The neighborhood was probably mostly crack houses and meth labs. Delray's house, a one-story faded-gray mill house, was as run-down as the immobile Cadillac in the drive. The yard looked as if it hadn't been mowed in this decade. The sidewalk could not be seen through the weeds. And the hole in the front porch could swallow a medium-sized dog.

They got out of the car, forced their way through the undergrowth to the porch, and carefully avoided falling in the hole. Mutt gave the front door two solid raps.

After a half-minute, the peephole darkened. "Who there?" came a scraggly voice.

Mutt made himself visible by standing in front of the door. "It's Mutt. I brought a friend with me."

The door opened and a heavyset man about Brack's height stood in the doorway. "Well, come on in if you're comin'."

"Thanks, Delray. This here Brack. He's in town from Charleston."

"Any friend of Mutt's be welcome here."

"Thanks." Brack held out a hand and Delray took it.

A television blared somewhere in the small row house. They stepped inside, smelling old sweat.

Mutt said, "You got anything to drink, Delray?"

"Yeah. Sure do. Go get us a couple quarts outta the fridge." Delray walked ten paces and eased himself into a worn recliner that faced a nice flatscreen showing a basketball game.

Mutt left and returned with two quart bottles of beer plus a can of store-brand cola, which he handed to Brack. "My man Brack here off the bottle."

Delray gave Brack a sideways glance but said nothing. They popped the tops off the quarts and Brack opened his can. The three clinked drinks and took long swigs.

Mutt said, "Cassie's sister left home and we want her to come back."

Delray said, "Well, she ain't here. Ain't no woman been here in way too longa time."

"Who you kiddin'?" Mutt asked. "You got more women tendin' to you than we got Miss America contestants."

The big man said nothing. Brack simply listened.

Mutt added, "She wit Vito."

"What you want from me? I ain't in the business no more. Can't you tell?"

Setting his bottle on a cigarette-burnt end table, Mutt said, "We go back a long time, Delray. I know you. You know me. You think I just show up here asking questions like I don't know what I'm doin'?"

It was a profound statement for Mutt. Or maybe Brack hadn't been giving his friend enough credit. Either way, Delray must have known he wouldn't be able to give Mutt a snow job.

"I mighta heard something."

Mutt said, "I'm listenin'."

"Her name's Regan, right?"

"Yeah."

Delray turned his head from side to side as if stretching his neck. "And she with Vito."

Mutt said, "I just tol' you that."

"No," Delray said. "She *with* him. Like, not working *for* him no more."

Susanna Royce had said the same thing to Brack, but it was good to get a second source. Regan looked cozy enough with Vito that Brack had no doubt.

Mutt said, "Really?"

"She was supposed to be for the top customers." Delray rubbed his hands together. "We called girls like her Bank Rolls. They always makin' money."

"And within a month she hooked up with Vito." Brack's first contribution to the conversation.

Delray added, "I hear she's even running some of the houses now."

When Brack had mentioned that to Mrs. Royce, he was merely speculating. He didn't really expect it to be true.

He asked, "How after only a month can she have gotten so far?"

Delray said, "You askin' me? Shoot, man. Why do any man fall on his sword for a woman?"

Mutt said, "He must be in love with her."

Brack thought Mutt might just be right. He asked Delray, "Any idea why she won't call her sister?"

The fat old man examined his bottle, then took another swig. After another moment of silence, he said, "I had this girl one time. Country girl. Didn't know squat. At least I thought so at the time."

Mutt nodded.

Delray continued. "I fell in love wit her, just like you said, Mutt. Big mistake. Next ting I know, she running a few girls for me. Her father come lookin' for her. I didn't want no trouble wit him so I tol' him where she was." He shook his head. "She shot him."

"What for?" Mutt asked.

"'Cause she crossed over and waren't goin' back."

There wasn't much to say after that. They finished their drinks and left Delray to what was left of his life.

Outside, a police cruiser sat behind the Porsche, blocking them in.

Two uniformed officers got out of their car as Brack and Mutt approached.

On the one hand, Brack was grateful their presence had prevented anything from happening to his ride. On the other, prevention wasn't their job today, so they obviously were here for another purpose.

The first officer was a medium-build white guy approaching retirement age. "You want to tell us what you're doing here?"

Brack said, "Visiting a friend."

The other officer, a tall black man about twenty-five, said, "I didn't know Delray had friends."

Mutt grinned and Brack knew this was about to get interesting.

Brack said, "Everyone's got friends."

The older cop said, "Delray's got a lot of things. A record for running girls. An arrest for aggravated assault."

"And he got us friends," Mutt said.

"And who are you?" the young officer asked Brack.

"Call Detective Nichols. He'll tell you."

The uniforms glanced at each other. The one with less seniority went to the cruiser and used the radio. Mutt and Brack stood waiting, hands in pockets, while the older cop eyed them. One of his hands rested at his side, the other stayed close to his Glock.

After a minute the younger man came back, whispered something to his partner, then faced them. "Detective Nichols said he wants you to go home. He said you were trouble and if you're here, you need to tell us why."

Brack said, "I think you made up that last part. If he wants to know why, he has my phone number."

The four of them looked at each other. Then the officers got in their cruiser and left. It was obvious to Brack that Detective Nichols had at least vouched for them.

Then the phone in his pocket vibrated.

Brack answered.

"What are you still doing here in my city? I thought I told you to leave town."

Brack said, "You weren't that specific so I didn't listen. I seem to have a problem with authority."

"The officers said you are in drug central."

Looking around, Brack realized they should probably get in the Porsche and find a more neutral locale. "Not for long."

"Why are you at Delray's house?"

"Visiting an old friend."

"Don't play games here, Pelton," Nichols said.

"Well, since you know where I am, pick a place and I'll buy you an R.C. Cola."

"This is Atlanta," he said. "We drink Coke."

"Okay, pick a place and I'll buy you a Coke."

After a moment, he rattled off some place in Virginia Highlands and hung up.

Brack told Mutt the name.

"I know where that is. Let's git outta here."

"You got it."

Ten minutes and several seven-thousand-rpm shifts later—so Brack could enjoy hearing the Porsche's engine rev—they entered an old but high-dollar suburb of the city known as Virginia Highlands.

Mutt pointed to a bar and grill. "There it is. But I still don't understand why we gotta meet with the po-lice."

"Because every time I don't," Brack said, "I end up regretting it. I like to cover all the bases."

"This ain't baseball, Opie."

"I know. This is more fun."

Mutt sighed. "You ain't right."

Brack couldn't argue with that. He wasn't right. He hadn't been right in a long time. That's why he needed good friends to keep him in line, provided he occasionally listen to them.

He parked in a lot among other expensive German cars, almost as if he sought to return to some form of deluded white reality after immersion in the poorest of the Atlanta poor he'd just experienced.

The place Detective Nichols chose to meet resembled the fifties diner in the movie *Pulp Fiction*. Sort of a modern, more sterile interpretation of the original.

Their police host sat at a booth facing the door.

Brack smiled and sat, scooting in to make room for Mutt.

Detective Nichols said, "Why is it I think I'm going to regret this?"

Mutt said, "I say the same thing every time Opie come up with one of his crazy ideas."

Brack said, "Thanks for meeting us."

"So what were you doing at Delray's?"

Before he could answer the detective, their waitress came to take their order, a young woman with platinum blonde hair and an hourglass figure. An over-the-heart tattoo of the Godfather of Soul peeked through a very low-cut dress. Decidedly not fifties fashion, but not out of place.

Mutt seemed to lose focus.

Brack ordered a strawberry milkshake for himself and a vanilla one for his tongue-tied friend.

The detective ordered coffee.

Peek-a-boo Tattoo departed and Mutt turned to Brack. "You getta load of her James Brown?"

"Is that why you couldn't form a complete sentence until now?" Brack asked.

Mutt shook his head to clear away the distraction. "All I got to say about that is 'How!'"

Nichols said, "And you two actually think you're going to get close to Vito?"

"We ain't done too bad so far, have we, Opie?"

"We usually finish what we start," Brack said. "One way or another."

"One way or another," Mutt repeated.

"Why don't we start with what you found out from Delray. And then you can finish up with why you confronted Vito last night. You gave a new meaning to grabbing a bull by the horns."

Mutt chuckled. "My man here crazy."

Before Brack could reply, the waitress returned and placed their drinks on the table.

Mutt said to her, "I love James Brown."

To their surprise she spun around, and with a growl in her voice like James, sang the chorus to "I Got the Feelin'." She followed that routine with a few gyrations that would go over well in a gentlemen's club, and continued gyrating all the way back to the kitchen. Her impromptu performance guaranteed that Mutt would empty his pockets of any and all cash for her gratuity.

The things they ran into never ceased to amaze Brack.

Given that Mutt would now be useless for another fifteen minutes, Brack focused on the detective and offered, "Quid pro quo?"

After a long moment, Detective Nichols nodded.

Brack went first. "The woman we're looking for, Regan? According to Delray and another source, she's Vito's woman now."

"What does that mean?"

Brack related the story of how she'd been one of the special girls saved for the exclusive clientele, but apparently had moved up to run some of his houses.

"You think Vito's going to just let you take her back?" the detective asked.

"No." Brack took a sip of his milkshake. "The question you should be asking is how much he's willing to risk to keep her."

Nichols said, "These guys don't like people messing in their affairs."

"The nice thing is that Vito isn't respectable enough for too many police officers to care when we go after him. Your turn, detective."

"Word is Vito told his crew he wants you dead."

"I figured he and I would never be barbeque buddies. What else?"

The detective's eyes widened. "I just told you that one of the biggest hoods in the city wants you dead and you brush it off? You *are* crazy."

Coming out of his waitress-induced trance, Mutt said, "It took you this long to come up with that?"

"Not really," Nichols said. "But it's nice to have my assumption confirmed."

"Again," Brack urged. "What else?"

Nichols sat back in his seat, tapped a finger on the table, and sighed, his eyes focused on the ceiling. After five seconds, he said, "Don't make me regret this." He took an envelope from his pocket and slid it across the table to Brack.

"I hope that's the winning Powerball ticket."

"Almost. Vito's having a fundraiser tonight for some kind of human rights charity."

Brack laughed.

Nichols said, "I know, right? He's the biggest offender in the city. Anyway, that's a pair of tickets to the ball."

"I thought you wanted me to leave the city."

With a slight grin, Nichols said, "Maybe I changed my mind, unofficially speaking, of course. You didn't get the tickets from me, and you're on your own from here."

Mutt said, "I ain't gonna be your backup on this one, Opie."

"You wouldn't look very good in a dress anyway, my friend."

Detective Nichols finished his coffee and got up. "Remember, Pelton. Don't make me regret it. I'll catch you guys later."

"See you on the other side," Brack said.

Nichols tapped the table and walked out.

"You think we can trust him?" Mutt asked.

Brack held the tickets up. "We don't have much choice." Something told him this was a nice break in the case, or whatever they were working on could be called.

Chapter Eleven

Before she moved to Atlanta, Darcy had been Brack's date to some of Charleston society's fundraising events. Now that her socializing time belonged to her peckerwood fiancé, he needed a stand-in. Tara agreed to join him—with two conditions. First: she continue as his personal trainer during his stay in the city, which worked out great for him—he couldn't afford to let his conditioning slip. Her second condition wasn't so easy: no cigars tonight.

Brack's only other choices for a companion were Cassie or Mutt, so he acquiesced. Besides, since their training session he hadn't wanted a smoke anyway. Did the training alone achieve that, or his humiliating failure to keep his breakfast down?

Tara greeted him at the door of her apartment wearing nothing but a towel wrapped around her taut, muscular body. Before he could close his gaping mouth, she said, "I'm running late. Mr. Grumpy was ornery and wouldn't take his meds until we bribed him with watermelon. Make yourself at home while I finish dressing."

Brack stepped in. She closed the door behind him and ran off down the hall. The apartment smelled refreshingly of coconut oil. Polished hardwood floors creaked under his feet. The framed photos on her white walls of people and of animals mixed in tasteful groupings. A beige couch and loveseat along with a mahogany coffee table comprised most of the living room. Everything looked as if it came from Pottery Barn or Pier One. The only thing missing was a television. Or not—if she didn't watch it.

From down the hall, she called, "Help yourself to a drink in the kitchen if you want."

Brack turned away from the living room and spotted the kitchen area behind a large opening in the wall between the two rooms, making the space seem a lot bigger than it was. In the fridge he found bottles of beer, cans of soda, and one of those pitchers that filtered water. He selected a glass and poured himself some cold water.

A few moments later, Tara appeared. He had wondered whether she owned attire suitable for a black tie event, but she did not disappoint. The spaghetti-strapped number she had on accentuated her figure and her brown skin. Even with her inked-up arms, the first word that came to his mind was elegant.

"Do I look okay?"

Brack nodded. "That is a very nice dress."

She gave him a big smile and brushed a piece of lint off his jacket. "Thanks. And you look very handsome."

His tuxedo was a real Armani, and only a few years old. He'd learned to never travel without it, or risk having to buy another or rent one.

He finished his water and they left the apartment. Walking to the car, Brack saw the sun beginning to set, but the air was still hot.

As he opened the passenger door for her, he asked, "Do you want me to put the top up?"

"Are you kidding?" She slid onto the hot leather seat. "I'd kill for a convertible."

His kind of woman.

They drove to a large mansion located in a part of Atlanta he hadn't seen before. The valet handed him a ticket and drove his cherished car away. Brack was relieved to see how skillfully he backed the Porsche into a spot out front between a Ferrari and a Range Rover.

Tara took Brack's arm. He escorted her inside and couldn't help but notice all the men stealing glances at her.

The ballroom floor had black tile alternating with squares of white. A very high ceiling with globe lighting made the women's jewelry sparkle. Tara chose a flute of champagne from a tray presented by a uniformed server. Brack scanned the room and found Atlanta's elite to be a little younger and a little more ethnic than Charleston's. The vibe he got added at least one zero to the net worth of the average donor here compared with his home base. Though Uncle Reggie's will had made him extremely comfortable, in this sea of money here he was but a small fish.

The orchestra played a slow waltz and several couples moved gracefully across the tiled dance floor.

Brack asked, "So how did you end up working at Mutt's Bar?"

His date grinned. "How do you think?"

A thought came to mind. "Cassie."

"We're friends."

Of course they were. That confirmed Cassie hadn't quite told him the whole truth. If Cassie knew Tara, then she definitely knew about the bar, and everything else Mutt had been hiding. Brack didn't hold it against her. She was only trying to protect Mutt and get her sister back.

Tara finished her champagne and gave the glass to a passing server. Then she asked, "Would you like to dance?"

"That was supposed to be my line," he said.

"Convention was never my strong suit."

He wasn't about to comment on that. Instead, he took her hand and led her to the dance floor. Thanks to lessons he had taken a decade ago with Jo, his deceased wife, he knew what to do, and slid his free hand behind her back. Tara rested hers on his shoulder. They moved around well together, Brack thought. She smiled, showing off her very nice teeth. He forgot for a moment why they were here and simply enjoyed her company.

The music changed to a mild salsa number. He led Tara through a few spins. She backed into him, their arms crossed in front of her and they swayed to the beat.

And then as the song ended, Brack caught sight of Darcy in the arms of another man and his stomach tightened.

* * *

He and Tara exited the dance floor and she excused herself to head for the restroom. Brack watched Darcy dance with her fiancé to another song. When they turned and her date's back was toward Brack, she spotted him and lifted her hand in a slight wave.

Brack nodded.

Then her eyes grew wide as she looked past his shoulder.

Brack heard from behind him Kelvin Vito's voice. "I could have you thrown out."

"You'd have to," he said, turning to face Vito. "You certainly couldn't do it by yourself."

Vito smirked. "You know, it's a shame they let anyone in here."

"Present company included," Brack said.

Vito turned to watch the couples dancing and his slicked-back hair reflected the overhead lights. "Mr. Pelton, if I were you I'd watch my step while I was in town. Accidents happen all the time here." He walked off.

Tara returned and they started toward an empty table in a corner. It would give him a good vantage point, since he'd been advised to watch his step.

En route to their destination, Darcy stepped into their path.

With her came the man Brack assumed was her fiancé. She turned to Tara and said, "It's good to see you again. That's a lovely dress."

Tara smiled. "Thanks. Yours is gorgeous. Versace?"

Nodding, Darcy said, "Good guess."

Brack held out his hand to the peckerwood, whose name he'd learned through some internet sleuthing: Justin Welcott the third. "I'm Brack Pelton."

First impression: a few inches shorter, brown hair going thin at the temples, thick-framed stylish glasses hiding brown eyes, small mouth, weak smile. A real peckerwood.

Welcott took the outstretched hand. "So you're the one who got my fiancée shot."

His hand felt soft. No calluses, unlike Brack's own. Before he let go, Justin turned to Darcy. "We really must be going, dear."

She gave her fiancé a quick smile, then turned to Tara. "It was a pleasure seeing you again."

Brack watched the soon-to-be newlyweds retreat and thought that the peckerwood really needed something bad to happen to him.

Tara interrupted his thoughts. "I wouldn't mind another drink."

His focus returned to her. "I'm sorry. A lot of water under the bridge there."

"I could tell." She gave him a friendly smile. "We all carry things with us. They make us who we are."

Looking toward the floor-to-ceiling window, he said, "And sometimes who we turn into isn't all that pleasant."

Touching his cheek, she said, "You helped me and my brother. As far as I'm concerned, you're Sir Galahad."

"I've been called worse," he said.

A male voice behind them said, "Excuse me."

Brack's gut told him trouble, but he'd already known there would be at some point. Precisely why Detective Nichols gave him the tickets—and why he'd shown up.

Tara and Brack turned to face a very tall and very stout Aryan. Even before Brack took in his blond flat-topped hair, he noticed the man's height—a few inches taller than himself. He filled out a tuxedo jacket that obviously had been custom-tailored to show off his large shoulders and biceps and rather trim waist. Brack ordinarily didn't cower from anyone, but his instincts told him not to mess with this guy. *Professional* was practically stamped across his forehead. Green Beret or Ranger or, worse, SEAL. Probably a high-paid mercenary now. Very lethal.

Brack decided all this in a split second.

"Yes?" he responded.

The giant's blue crystalline eyes bore into Brack, and from his thin lips he heard, "Mr. Vito would like you to leave."

Tara seemed to size up the situation pretty quickly. She squeezed Brack's hand.

His better judgment slipped away from him. "Yeah, well, we're busy right now."

"Ignoring his request would be a mistake."

"For whom?"

"It doesn't have to go down this way," he said. "You won't get the drop on me."

"I figured as much," Brack said. "But you won't do anything in front of all these witnesses."

"There's always another time."

"While you're basking in your apperception, I should probably tell you there won't be any rules."

The giant nodded. "Understood."

"And one of us will not walk away."

The giant's mouth formed a slight grin, and his upper lip showed a minute tremor, which Brack took to mean the hulk couldn't wait to throw down right here and now.

Brack put his arm around Tara's waist and eased them both back a few steps. The giant did not take his eyes off Brack's. A safe distance away, he and Tara turned and walked onto the dance floor, where they danced until midnight.

The valet retrieved the Porsche in mint condition and Brack drove Tara back to her apartment, U2's "The Unforgettable Fire" streaming through the sound system. The low-key tunes and Tara's seemingly peaceful visage helped him keep his speed in check, although the muted growl of the boxer engine taunted his right foot for anything but restraint.

He managed to make it all the way back to her apartment complex without so much as one moving violation.

Brack walked his date up the stairs to her place, his thoughts focused more on the angles of getting at Vito than on the curves revealed by Tara's dress.

At her door, she turned to him. "Thank you so much for a wonderful evening."

He said, "I'm glad you enjoyed yourself. I did too."

Closing the distance between them, she gently placed her hands on his chest and kissed him. "That's for saving me and my brother."

Startled, he put his arms around her.

She kissed him again. "And that's for treating me so nice."

"What do you mean?"

Resting her head on his shoulder, she said, "No one has ever invited me to a ball before. I felt like Cinderella."

"Yeah," he said. "Too bad the clock struck midnight."

Giggling, she pulled away and looked at him. "You're not going to turn into a pumpkin, are you?"

"I think I already did."

She said, "I like you, Brack."

He had nothing to say to that.

"But," she said, "your heart belongs to someone else."

As Brack returned to his car in the parking lot of Tara's apartment complex, he thought about what she'd said. She was right. His heart did belong to someone else, and he couldn't shake that, even if the object of his love was about to marry someone else.

Still five hundred feet from his car, his cell vibrated in his tuxedo pants pocket. He answered.

A disguised voice said, "Get out of town or the next time you won't only be a witness."

Brack stopped walking. "What?"

His Porsche exploded in front of his eyes.

Chapter Twelve

Monday, one a.m.

Kelvin Vito watched the carnage from the passenger seat of his Mercedes at the far end of the parking lot. The very nice Porsche convertible lit off like one big firecracker. The explosion shook the SUV. The whole thing made Vito smile.

Levin, his second in command, who'd been with Vito from almost the beginning of his empire, watched from the driver's seat. "I still don't understand why we don't just kill him."

Vito kept watching the fireball achieve maximum magnitude and then begin to taper off. "A guy like that can do a lot of damage. We just need to point him in the direction we want him to go."

"You're saying we're going to use him?" Levin asked. "Personally, I think he's a big dumb hero wannabe who's bound to be killed sooner or later."

"Exactly," Vito said. "So why not take advantage of the opportunity?"

"But all this will do is rile him up and get him to come after us harder."

Vito said, "Who is our biggest enemy right now?"

"Kualas, of course," Levin said. "But you know that."

"What would happen if my good friend Xavier Kualas got word there was a new gun in town aiming at us?"

"He might try to join forces."

Vito smiled again. "And when Xavier comes out of his hole, we're going to make sure he doesn't crawl back in."

Levin said, "We need to make sure Pelton doesn't survive

either. And then I think we need to deal with Regan. She caused this whole mess."

Vito looked at Levin, "When I want your opinion, I'll tell you what it is. Just so we're clear, Regan is off limits to you or anyone else. Now, get us out of here."

Levin started the SUV and slowly drove away.

Chapter Thirteen

In Brack's engineering courses, he learned Newton's second law: Force equals mass times acceleration. He was two hundred and ten pounds of force projected through the air by a tremendous amount of energy. The speed at which his body hit whatever it was that stopped its flight must have been pretty significant itself, because the world went black.

"Brack..."

Whoever called his name sounded far away.

"Brack."

But getting closer.

"Brack!"

He coughed and opened his eyes.

The prettiest set of green eyes stared at him. He said, "Jo?"

"It's Darcy."

Using the back of his hand, he wiped his eyes. "Darcy?" The light surrounding him was blinding. He wanted it to stop. As more details came into focus, he realized he was in a white room. Fluorescent lighting above caused the brightness. "Where am I?"

"Atlanta Regional."

Something soft held his hand. He blinked and realized it was Darcy's hand.

"What's going on?"

She gave his hand a squeeze and let go. "The doctors say you have a concussion, but otherwise you're fine. Lucky, in fact."

Brack coughed again to clear his throat.

"Someone blew up your car. Good thing you and Tara weren't in it."

The words of the phone call he'd received in her parking lot came to mind. "They planned it that way."

His favorite reporter stared at him.

He said, "Whoever it was called me and gave me the good news seconds before they set it off."

Tara came into view. "The explosion shook my apartment."

Darcy said, "She dragged you to safety and called 911."

Another voice in the room, a familiar one, said, "You one lucky soda cracker."

"Not really," Brack said to Mutt. "My insurance company wouldn't let me have anything but liability."

Darcy and Mutt laughed. Brack didn't think it was all that funny. The sticker price on the Porsche was a cool one hundred and twenty-five thousand. And he didn't think his agent was likely to call the explosion an accident.

Detective Nichols took Brack's bedside statement and said explosions tended to pique the interest of the anti-terrorist factions of the government. But almost in the same breath he added that what they'd found so far was not much to go on.

Not wanting Mutt's house to blow up next, as soon as the hospital released him Brack checked in to one of the only major hotels that accepted dogs. Then he did what he should have done about Shelby from the start and placed a phone call to Charleston. It was answered on the third ring.

"Hi, Trish," he said.

"Hello, Brack," she said. "How's Shelby?"

"He's fine. In fact..." He paused, gritted his teeth for a second, then said, "As usual, he's the reason I'm calling."

This was risky territory. Trish's love affair with his dog went back two years. More than once, Brack had the feeling she would be pleased if he disappeared so she could adopt him herself. But she was the only person besides himself Shelby would eat for. If anyone else set a bowl of food in front of Shelby, he merely looked at it and walked away. So Trish, the wife of Brack's attorney, Chauncey Connors, was his only option—until he resolved his situation.

She said, "You guys are in Atlanta, aren't you?"

"Yes."

"Is he all right?"

"He is. I was, um, wondering—"

"You want me to come there and get him?" she interrupted.

"Do you think Chauncey would let you come for a few days?"

She said, "I'll pack as soon as we hang up."

That afternoon, Brack sat on a bench in front of the hotel with Shelby sleeping at his feet. A Volvo pulled to the curb, Brack's favorite pastor and friend Brother Thomas at the wheel. Trish, defying her sixty-plus years, leapt from the car and ran to Shelby. Brack's dog, who seconds earlier was snoring away every care he'd ever had, jumped to full wakefulness and danced around the ever-ready dog sitter as if Trish were his favorite person in the whole world. Which couldn't be, because Brack held that title. At least that's the lie he kept telling himself as he stood to greet his Charleston rescuers.

"Thanks for coming, Trish. And for bringing Brother Thomas."

Trish had already gotten down on the ground, ignoring the dust and grime and whatever a city sidewalk could do to her nice, no doubt expensive travel wear of linen walking shorts and matching polo shirt. She wrapped Shelby in a hug and spoke in a voice usually heard around babies. "Of course I'm going to come for my favorite sweetheart, yes I am."

Brack left his four-legged Benedict Arnold in the arms of his new best friend and held out a hand to Brother Thomas. About the same height as Mutt at six three, Brother Thomas was three hundred and fifty pounds of presence. He wore his usual attire, a black suit and minister's collar.

The preacher took Brack's offered hand in both of his. "I sure am glad you called me to come and he'p you out, mm-hmm."

"You're welcome," Brack said, knowing full well that he had not called him because he didn't want another good friend anywhere near here. "Except you shouldn't be here. This place is a ticking time bomb."

"All the more reason, mm-hmm. How's Mutt and Cassie?"

"Holding it together," Brack said.

"Yeah. Well, I did hear you got your car blown up already. How many does this make?"

Ignoring the question, "Needless to say, Brother Thomas, things have gotten a little out of hand."

Brack felt his shoulder grasped by a warm hand.

"Obviously, Brother Brack. Otherwise you would not have called Ms. Trish to guard your companion, mm-hmm."

"Trish has a reservation here," Brack said. "I can arrange for you to have a room as well, or if you prefer you can stay with Mutt, who has plenty of room."

"Where you gonna be?" he asked.

"I'm not sure, yet. I need to get another set of wheels."

Trish asked, "Then what will you do?"

Brother Thomas said, "He goin' to try to right all the wrongs of the world with fists and guns, mm-hmm. And if he don't get hisself killed, which he think will never happen, he'll wait for the next time he can go to war."

Brack stared at his friend, then blinked. Brother Thomas had always given him the straight answer, but he'd never been this brutally direct. His words would have upset him if Brack weren't so surprised by his brevity and intuitiveness. He recovered and asked, "What's wrong with that plan?"

"One of these days, you are gonna die," he said, "and leave behind a lot of people who love you, whether you think so or not."

Brack's confusion of feelings was saved by the bell. Darcy called, her timing impeccable as usual. He suggested they meet at Cassie's house, not telling her who'd come to town.

* * *

Brother Thomas, Trish, Shelby, and Brack arrived at Cassie's twenty minutes later and piled out of the Volvo. Cassie had said over the phone that she would let her staff open the restaurant and wait for them to arrive. Shelby spotted Darcy and ran to her. If Trish was the dog's first love, Darcy came a close second, followed by any other female in the vicinity.

Cassie let out a shriek and ran to Brother Thomas to wrap him in a hug. She hit him with such force that she knocked him back two steps.

He hugged her as well, petting the top of her head like the father figure he was.

Mutt stood in the doorway watching everything.

Brack said, "Let's all go inside where it's nice and cool and formulate our plan for taking Vito down."

Trish asked, "Who's Vito?"

"Kelvin Vito," Darcy volunteered. "In addition to being a respectable businessman, he pretty much runs the sex trade in the city, among other illegal enterprises."

In her kitchen, Cassie poured glasses of iced tea loaded with sugar and lemon for everyone. Perfectly refreshing. She had the kitchen radio tuned to the station Mutt liked, the one that specialized in Motown from the sixties to the eighties. Dionne Warwick, while not technically on the Motown label, sang "Walk on By."

To Brack, Darcy's having left Charleston and any chance for a relationship with him made the lyrics seem sadly appropriate.

Mutt, quiet until the song ended, said, "Opie and I got this Vito thing, Brother. Why'd you come?"

Brother Thomas tilted his head back and let out a laugh. "You two? Please."

"This ain't funny now, hear?" Mutt's dark face became even darker.

Brack's friend and pastor was one of the few people not

intimidated by Mutt. It could be because they were the same height, but it wasn't. The three of them—Brack, Brother Thomas, and Mutt—had been through a lot together. Nothing intimidated any one of them. They shared the understanding that only the truth as each knew it would be spoken.

Brother Thomas said, "As soon as I heard Cassie callin' for Brother Brack, I know'd there was trouble. Only a matter of time before somethin' happened, mm-hmm. I just didn't think he'd lose *another* automobile."

A wise man once said that if someone suspected you a fool, don't open your mouth and prove them right. So Brack offered no comment.

All six friends sat around Cassie's large dining table. Shelby lay at Trish's feet. To Cassie, Trish said, "This Kelvin Vito is the one you believe has your sister?"

Brack answered for her. "Mutt and I saw her with him. This isn't a kidnapping. She's *with* the man. There's no doubt."

Brother Thomas asked, "So why don't we just go over there and get her?"

"Because," Darcy said, "our resident Romeo here already tipped our hand. Vito knows we'll be coming. That's why a certain brand-new Porsche with less than two thousand miles on it got blown up."

Later that night, Brother Thomas took Trish and Shelby back to the hotel, saying he wanted to meet with a pastor friend of his. Because Darcy's informants had tracked several of Vito's henchmen to a biker bar on the south side of the city, Brack sat next to her in her old Accord undercover mobile and scoped out the scene.

It wasn't his ride, so the radio was set to some modern pop station. A Taylor Swift song serenaded them, but their focus was on the saloon's front door and the five shiny motorcycles parked at the curb.

"My source says they hang out until either they pick up women or the clock strikes eleven. If any of them are still on the hunt, they head to Limey's."

"Let me guess," he said. "Limey's is one of Vito's businesses."

"Not sure," she said. "We'll have to do some digging on that. It's a few steps lower than the mainstream gentlemen's clubs. But I hear it makes a ton of money."

"There's always a market for flesh."

"Men will be men."

"Present company included," he said.

A smirk lined the corner of her mouth. "Present company included."

They both knew that with Brack's past he lacked the standing to criticize. After Darcy moved away he tried to become a better man, concentrating on his dog and on running the Pirate's Cove. He'd lived like a priest. But if he thought about it longer than five seconds, he would realize he had done it because of Darcy. He'd read somewhere that to find someone of quality, he had to *be* someone of quality. And Jo's quality was very hard to replace. His late wife still crept into his thoughts. She'd been his everything until a tumor took her away.

Darcy interrupted his internal monologue. "Earth to Brack."

"Yes?"

"Deep in thought over there?"

He angled the rearview mirror to make sure no one was sneaking up on them. "Sorry, only reminiscing."

As if by instinct, her hand went to her shoulder, where two years ago a round from a Sig nine millimeter had torn through. It happened on a stakeout a lot like this one. "Don't remind me."

"How about if you watch the front and I'll keep an eye on our six?" he asked.

"That's military speak for behind us, right?"

"You got it."

"And you aren't antsy to head inside the bar?"

"The old Brack would have stormed in there and gotten his head taken off. You're dealing with two-point-oh."

"Wow," she said. "Color me surprised."

"I'm trying."

Brack took his eyes off the rearview mirror to look at her. She was so beautiful sitting close to him with a broad smile on her face. It pained him to know he'd not been able to win her heart, not that he'd been in any shape mentally to try.

"Keep your eyes on our six, Romeo."

"Yes ma'am."

When the dashboard clock displayed eleven p.m. Darcy's informants proved themselves spot on. Their targets exited the building, sans female companionship. Firing up their Harleys, they roared away in a staccato of unmuffled straight-piped American glory.

Darcy gave them a city block's lead before starting the Honda and easing out of the metered spot on the street. Knowing where their targets were headed kept them from behaving in a hurry.

As an afterthought, Brack said, "Does Justin know where you are?"

"He knows I'm working."

He turned to her. "I'm not trying to be smart or get your goat, but it might be a good idea, given our objective, to let him know what's going on. Maybe even give him a way to track you."

Letting another smirk cross her face, she said, "I almost believe you're being genuine."

"I'd want to know, if for no other reason than a little peace of mind. Just thinking out loud here."

They rode in silence through two intersections before she spoke again.

"That has got to be the most unselfish thing you've said to me since you've been in town. Or ever."

"I have my moments." Brack's smile hid gritted teeth. On the one hand, he was trying to be accepting of the situation with her and the peckerwood. On the other hand, he really wanted to be anything but.

Chapter Fourteen

Monday, eleven fifteen p.m.

As predicted, they found the motorcycles in question leaning on their kickstands in front of Limey's. Business at the strip-club-slash-brothel was booming, given the steady stream of men of all ages and ethnicities entering and exiting the run-down establishment.

"Popular place," Brack said.

"The question is, what do we do once they leave? It's not as if we can run them down."

"I have an idea."

He opened his wallet and took out Detective Nichols's business card. Dialing with his thumb, he hit the call button and held the iPhone to his ear.

On the second ring he heard, "Nichols."

"Detective, this is Brack Pelton. I thought you might like to know that Vito's henchmen are at Limey's right now. If you were looking for something to add to your file on them, this could be it."

Nichols didn't reply right away.

Brack waited.

Eventually, the detective said, "We've actually got two units in the area. This might work. Did you happen to see if they were carrying concealed weapons?"

"Didn't get that close, but if you'd like I can scope out the situation."

"I don't want you to put yourself in harm's way—again—but

any intel you can give us would be appreciated. I'll call you back in five minutes." Nichols hung up.

Darcy asked, "What did he say?"

"He wants to know if they're carrying."

Her eyes opened wide. "He's coming to get them, isn't he?"

"Maybe," Brack said. "In the meantime, I'm going in."

"You're what?"

He didn't answer. Instead, he stepped out of the car. The front doors to the house of ill repute stood wedged open. Several men exited past Brack as he made his way into the cheap brothel. He knew Charleston had its own share of these places. But thanks to his actions a few years ago in tracking down the man who killed his uncle, Charleston now had at least one fewer. That loss hadn't exactly won him friends in certain circles.

Some hip-hop recording played on the sound system as he entered the building. Inside and to the right, a very large round black woman wearing a red brassiere and some sort of sheer flowing cape over her shoulders stood behind a raised desk. She gave Brack a huge smile to match her proportions. "How you doin', sugar?"

Other women, large and small, paraded around wearing not much of anything. Some of them were actually attractive, but probably had been judged not good enough for the classier places.

It had been his experience that places like this were always protected by men with guns. Sometimes they watched everything from behind the bar. Other times they kept out of sight or attempted to blend in.

Because most of Limey's clientele here was on the rough side, Brack had to scan the room twice until he found the pair he thought were the guards. In a back corner sat two black guys sipping drinks from glass tumblers. Their attention on the entryway and lengthy sideways glances at him gave them away.

Brack showed the lady in red a big smile. "I'm a little lonely this evening."

She leaned over the desk, any pretense of modesty vanishing.

"Pretty boy like you shouldn't be that way. What can *I* do for you?" She placed a lot of emphasis on "I."

Standing close to so much flesh, as well as surrounded by the semi-nude women in the room, he felt his face redden. "I'm not sure."

"Well," she said, batting her eyes, "why don't you make yourself at home. Maybe something will come to you."

Brack strolled to the bar, took a seat three chairs away from the guards, and gave them a nod, figuring he had less than a minute left before Detective Nichols called and his men stormed the fort. Pretending to check out the merchandise, he watched for the bikers. Apparently they'd wasted no time in choosing their partners because he didn't see them.

A hand touched his thigh, breaking his concentration. It belonged to a small white woman who could have been forty, or a very rough twenty. Her pleasant smile accentuated the age lines on her face. She wore a full-length dress that separated across her legs when she took the seat next to him.

Brack said, "Hi."

She said, "Hi back at you." Her hand stayed put.

Not sure what to do, especially with the two guards a mere two seats away from her, he said, "Buy you a drink?"

"If that's what you want to do." She signaled the bartender, an Asian woman, who sauntered over, displaying an even smaller version of the attire barely clinging to the hostess. When the barkeep got close enough to hear, Brack's "date" said, "I'll take a gin rickey. Mr. Gorgeous here needs something to loosen him up."

Miss Asia nodded and got to work on their libations.

"That obvious, huh?" he asked.

"It's my job."

Before he could reply, one of the bikers walked by with a chubby Latina.

To the guards, Brack said, "Was that a gun I saw on him?"

They sized up his target and one of them said, "They know they can't come in here with gats."

The other one said, "In fact, the only one I'd question here is you."

The woman beside Brack slid her hand farther up his thigh. At the moment she touched the iPhone in his pocket, it vibrated.

She jerked her hand back.

He stood and took the phone out of his pocket. "It's the wife," he said, looking at the display, and walked toward the front door.

Nichols said, "Storm Troopers in about twenty minutes."

"The five stooges are empty handed, but there are two near the bar who probably aren't." Brack ended the call, walked down the two steps to the sidewalk, and made it across the street before he encountered two men he hadn't seen before. They nodded to him as they passed. He guessed they were the reconnaissance team.

Darcy had the passenger door open and waved Brack to hurry up. When he got in, she took off down the road.

"Is there a fire somewhere?" he asked.

"Detective Nichols said it would be best if we weren't around when they raided the place."

"And you're following his orders?"

She never followed orders.

"He offered me an exclusive on the bust. I have a cameraman on the way. They're going to give him an all-access pass, thanks to your intel."

"I'm glad I was good for something," he said.

At an all-night diner, Darcy and Brack took a booth by a window. Hungry from the night's activities, Brack ordered a large breakfast and juice and Darcy got a BLT. They picked up where they'd left off a year ago, and although he tried not to read too much into it, he did enjoy their comfortable familiarity.

When the waitress delivered the check, a guy about thirty approached their booth. Tall, lanky, with wire-rimmed glasses, he had a backpack draped over his left shoulder.

Darcy said, "Did you get some good shots?"

The walking stick-figure grinned.

Brack held out his hand, "Brack Pelton."

The stick figure took it. "Jack Roman. Detective Nichols sends his regards."

"How'd they do?" Darcy asked.

"Thirty-five arrests."

"No gunfire?" Brack asked.

Roman slid next to Darcy. "Nada."

"Nichols told me earlier they had two units in the area. That's only four officers."

"Actually," Roman said, "they had ten. Thanks to you they got the two near the bar first. Vito's bikers were otherwise preoccupied and couldn't put up much of a fight."

"Vito's men will be out by morning," Brack said.

The waitress came by and Roman ordered coffee.

Darcy asked him, "You send me the pics?"

"They're already in your inbox."

She pulled a tablet from her purse, slid her fingers across the glass, and began to type.

"You're writing the story now?" Brack asked.

Without looking up from the screen, she said, "Yes."

Roman glanced at his watch. "If we get it posted before four a.m., we'll make the headline."

Brack stood and dropped a twenty on the table. "I wonder if their bikes are still there."

"Who cares?" Roman asked.

"They may contain something interesting."

"That's tampering with evidence."

The way he said it made Brack curious about his intentions. So he said, "Wanna come?"

"Of course."

"You boys go ahead," Darcy said. "I need to finish this. Call me later."

The men exited the diner. Roman's car, a dark-colored Altima, sat in a spot a block away.

"All you news people drive incognito?"

Roman frowned. "Most of us can't afford Porsches."

"I probably can't anymore either."

Roman unlocked the doors, they got in, and he started the car. "I'm not sure whether I'd rather never know what it's like to drive one and therefore not miss it, or have had one and lost it."

"Just shut up and drive," Brack said.

"Yessir." The old Nissan sputtered and coughed, but got them on their way.

Shortly after, they parked at a meter and walked to the house of ill repute. The police were gone, as were all the patrons and staffers. So were the bikes. Someone must have worked really fast to get them collected in the narrow window of time between the cops' departure and the arrival of Brack and Roman.

Out of curiosity, Brack tried the front door to the brothel. Locked.

He stuck a piece of gum in his mouth.

Chapter Fifteen

In the living room of his penthouse suite, Vito seethed. Levin relayed the information he'd just received about five of their men getting busted in a stupid raid. Vito did not appreciate the word on the street that his men were being arrested.

Levin said, "And our friend Mr. Pelton was seen in the establishment just before the raid."

"What?" Vito's mind calculated the odds and came up craps. "He's working with the police."

"It appears that way."

Vito walked to the bar and poured himself an inch of Makers. He took a sip and an idea formed. "That is how we are going to get Kualas."

Chapter Sixteen

Tuesday morning

Brack's phone vibrated on the hotel nightstand. He sat up in bed, daylight filtering through gaps in the drapes, and the first thing he realized other than the iPhone's spasm was Shelby's absence. Before full-blown panic could set in, he remembered his dog was with Trish, the two of them probably plotting their getaway.

He snatched the phone and growled, "Yes?"

"Brother Brack? Sorry to wake you. The Lord has provided us with a lead."

Brother Thomas explained himself, requiring a lot of sleep-deprived concentration for Brack to keep up. After the call, Brack rubbed his eyes and climbed out of bed. It was almost ten a.m.

Brother Thomas, dressed in his usual black suit and minister's collar, picked him up forty-five minutes later in his Volvo and they took a thirty-minute drive across town.

The church, Three Crosses, was similar to the Brother's own in Charleston, its tall white steeple towering over a forty-year-old white and brown structure. A shorter version of Brother Thomas stood in front of the church wearing similar attire, except the smaller man had chosen a shade of deep blue instead of the black garb worn by the man behind the wheel.

They got out of the car and Brother Thomas said, "Brother Brack. I'd like to introduce you to one of my colleagues, Reverend Cleophus."

"Nice to meet you," Brack said to the Reverend, shaking his hand.

"My pleasure," he said. "Brother Thomas said you have a lot of light around you."

"I wouldn't know about that."

"Brother Brack also pretty modest, mm-hmm."

Reverend Cleophus appeared to assess his new acquaintance. "Yes, well, any friend of Brother Thomas is a friend of Three Crosses."

"So," Brack said, "what have you gentlemen got?"

Reverend Cleophus said, "The Lord gave me a powerful word for the congregation. I felt the Holy Spirit flowing through me." He closed his eyes and moved his head from side to side as if reliving the experience. "Afterward, I asked if anyone could he'p us stop the abuse of our young chil'ren. Several members came forward. Two of them are inside the church right now waitin' to talk to you."

It occurred to Brack that these men of the cloth were not telling him everything. Otherwise, why stand outside? Brack said, "What else?"

Brother Thomas asked, "What do you mean?"

"Don't give me that. I know you too well. You and the good Reverend here are holding something back. My mother raised ugly kids, not dumb ones."

Brother Thomas wiped the sweat off his brow with a handkerchief. Brack could tell he was thinking, probably measuring his words before he spoke. Either that or he was hot. It was almost noon and on its way to ninety.

"Well, it ain't what you gonna expect."

"Not much seems to be," Brack said, silencing his added thought, when you're involved. He needed as much help as he could get, and the two church members waiting inside to talk were no doubt deeply entrenched at the grassroots level. The intel they came up with would most likely prove invaluable. "Are you going to say anything else, or will I have to find out on my own?"

The blue-clad Reverend said, "Why don't we step inside and get on with it."

"A man after my own heart," Brack said.

The pastors led him inside the church. Its weathered hardwood floors meant it was older than Brack assumed. The windows were not stained glass and they opened via hand cranks. The walls were painted white. Wooden pews worn smooth held bibles and hymnals.

Reverend Cleophus guided them through the building to a hall. The aroma of percolating coffee filled the air.

"Care for a cup?" he asked.

"It smells too good to pass up," Brack said.

"Starbucks. My weakness."

"Mine's good cookin'," Brother Thomas said.

Is that all, Brack wondered, whereas he was haunted by obsessive memories of his late wife, a short-lived tendency to pacify his emptiness in the arms of many women, a desire to drink at the wrong moments, a taste for expensive cigars, and a continuing infatuation with a woman who was marrying someone else. And a not insignificant addiction to violence.

Instead, what came out was, "I'd really hate to have to carry around those burdens you two have."

Reverend Cleophus smiled and nodded. Brother Thomas did not.

They stopped at a table set up with a fairly new coffee pot, Styrofoam cups, and an assortment of sweeteners and creamers.

The reverend poured three cups. "Help yo'self to the fixins."

Brack watched as he dumped in two Coffeemate packets, exactly how Jo liked hers. Brother Thomas and Brack drank theirs straight.

"Where is this source?" Brack asked.

"They in my office around the corner." Reverend Cleophus waved a hand. "This way."

The three men entered the room and Reverend Cleophus said, "Sorry to keep you waiting, ladies. Brother Brack here been puttin' in some long hours and looked like he needed a jolt of Joe."

Two plump Asian women sat on a couch, also holding cups of the good Reverend's prized Seattle brew.

Brack wasn't sure why he was made the cause of the Reverend's own delay and weakness for Starbucks, but he let it slide. After all, who was he to judge?

The ladies nodded their acceptance of his explanation.

"Brother Brack, may I introduce Mrs. Chu and her sister, Mrs. Lee."

Brack set his cup down on the Reverend's desk and shook their offered hands. "Pleasure to meet you both."

Mrs. Chu said, "Reverend Cleophus say you wanna know about girls selling themselves."

Not exactly. But he asked, "What can you tell me about them?"

Mrs. Lee wiped tears from her eyes. "They are our daughters."

"I'm sorry to hear that." Brack pulled up a chair so he could face the sisters.

Mrs. Lee spoke again. "Brother Thomas said you could do something to get them back?"

It took all Brack had not to glare outright at Brother Thomas, who gave him a sheepish look in return.

To Mrs. Lee Brack said, "Why don't you tell me what you know?"

She took a sip of her coffee, probably cold by now. "Well, I don't know where to begin. Our daughters had everything growing up."

Mrs. Chu admitted, "We spoiled them."

Mrs. Lee nodded. "And it did no good. They were always close growing up. Last year they turned eighteen and left."

Her sister said, "We thought they would go to college together. Instead they ended up...ended up..." She wiped her eyes.

"We want them back," Mrs. Lee said. "Our husbands are no help."

"Too ashamed," said her sister. "They wanted sons anyway."

"Any idea where I can find them?"

Mrs. Lee nodded again. She set her purse on her lap, rummaged through it, and pulled out a business card. "I found this with Mindy's things."

Brack looked at the card. It appeared to be for a night club. "You think she may be here?"

"It's all I have." At that point Mrs. Lee broke down and cried.

Mrs. Chu handed her sister a tissue and put her arm around her shoulders.

Brack asked Mrs. Chu, "What's your daughter's name?"

"Kai."

"Okay." Brack stood. "Mindy and Kai. Do you have pictures of them?"

Each sister handed over a photo of a very pretty girl.

"Do you think you can find them?" Mrs. Chu gave the tissue a workout.

Before Brack could reply, Brother Thomas said, "If they in the city, Brother Brack will find them, mm-hmm."

This time, Brack did glare at his friend, then turned and walked out of the room, agitated he'd come to Atlanta to find one woman. Now he had three runaways, plus a crime boss ready to take him out.

Settling into Brother Thomas's Volvo, Brack said, "I thought we had this discussion last year. I'm not in the missing persons business."

"Brother Brack," he said, "don't you think this is connected to Regan?"

"With the only bit of intel being the business card of a club and two pictures of pretty Asian girls, I'm not sure. In the meantime, I need another set of wheels, since mine got blown to smithereens trying to convince the first missing girl to simply call her sister."

"Reverend Cleophus got a brother who sell cars."

They drove a few blocks and ended up at Elmer's Used Cars, an establishment that appeared to specialize in ten- to twenty-year-old premium German and Japanese vehicles. Most had big shiny rims. Brack did not get his hopes up.

A man who looked a lot like Reverend Cleophus met them in the lot.

"Good to see you again, Brother Thomas," the man said.

They shook hands.

Then "Brother Brack" was introduced to Elmer and they shook hands.

Elmer said, "What exactly you lookin' for?"

"Something that blends in, but with some punch."

"See anything out here you like?"

Brack took a second look around the front lot. "Too flashy." Especially with those rims, though he didn't say it.

Elmer scratched his chin. "I just got somethin' in from auction. Come on."

He led them to the back lot. Brack hoped it would be another Audi S4 like the two he'd owned before. It wasn't, of course. Instead, Elmer showed him a five-year-old black hatchback.

"This got a turbo," he said. "It scared me."

Brack raced cars in a previous life and lately had begun to wonder about getting back into it. As long as nothing was mechanically wrong with this car, he could handle it. It was almost the right color, and aside from a hood scoop appeared nondescript, which made it a good undercover car. The badge on the back said Mazdaspeed3.

Elmer continued. "New tires and not too many miles either. You can drive a standard shift, right?"

"Of course."

After Elmer put it on the rack for Brack to examine the undercarriage and look for any leaks or damage, they went for a very fast test drive. Knowing Brack's penchant for racing, Brother Thomas wisely elected to wait at the shop. When they got back, the used car dealer might have been shade or two lighter. They settled on a price and Brack's bank wired the money to the dealer's account.

Elmer said, "Lemme get you a temporary tag." He went inside his makeshift office.

Brack turned to Brother Thomas. "Thanks for the ride over. I'll see you later."

Brother Thomas held his eyes for a minute and Brack felt like a child trying to pull a fast one on a parent. But the pastor nodded, got in his car, and drove off.

Elmer returned with the temporary license plate.

Brack said, "Any chance you've got any old ones laying around that won't link the car to you or your shop?"

The car salesman looked at Brack for a long beat.

Brack said, "If you watch the news, you already know I've been on it. I have a habit of being in the wrong place at the wrong time. I'd hate to have your business linked to anything."

"Me too," Elmer said. "But if you end up toasting the car and they run the VIN, it will show that I sold it."

"I figured that much. I'm simply looking for anonymity against an initial inquiry, whether it's the police or a citizen reporting something."

The salesman nodded, then smiled. "Okay, I think I can accommodate what you lookin' for."

And with that, Brack had his own set of wheels again.

Gecko Row, named on the business card given to Brack by Mrs. Lee, turned out to be owned by Kelvin Vito. No surprise there. He clearly owned a great many enterprises throughout the city. Darcy had dug up the background for Brack but declined to join him while he scoped the place out, citing work.

At nine p.m. Brack approached the club's front doors, surprisingly open and unattended. A synthesizer beat bounced off the walls. As he walked down the hall, black lighting illuminated his white shirt, tinting it purple. A second set of double doors were all that separated him from what would happen next.

Nevertheless, he was here, so he opened the right door and slipped inside, careful not to call attention to himself. Taking in the open space as he followed the wall to his right, he realized his caution was futile. Only the staff and the strobe lights populated the room. Apparently the boss arrived after the real activities were underway. Brack's own experience in running a business was that if something wasn't important to him, the owner, it wasn't important to his employees either. He'd bet Vito was losing money on this place.

That thought led him to an interesting idea. A shoddily run club might be the perfect spot to hide ill-gotten gains.

One of three waitresses, a tall slender twenty-something, asked if he needed anything.

"What time does your boss get here?" Brack asked.

Pursing her lips, she took a moment before asking, "Our manager?" Her bright red lipstick sliced through the staccato lighting.

"The one who pays you. What's his name?"

"Kelvin Vito?"

"Yeah," Brack said. "Him."

"He doesn't come here very often," she said. "Maybe once or twice a month?"

"Part-time boss, huh?"

She smiled.

"Lucky for you guys."

She moved in a little closer. "My name's Shana. Can I get you something? Anything?"

His personal space officially violated, Brack returned her smile. "I can think of a few things, but I'm here for a business matter."

"You want to speak to my manager?" Shana asked.

"Not really." He pulled out the photos of Mindy and Kai. "You ever seen these two here?"

She looked at the photos, then back at him. "Oh, you want to meet *them*."

That was an odd way to answer his question. "I'm looking into a missing persons case and their names came up."

Her face brightened. "I'm sorry. I thought it was for something else. They work the rooms a few hours a night. Sometimes here, sometimes not."

"I see." He slipped out a business card and a fifty and handed them to her. "If they show up tonight, can you give me a call?"

She looked at the card. "You're from Charleston?"

"Yes."

"This says you own a bar. I thought you were some private eye."

"I seem to be a lot of things lately."

She said, "If they show, I'll call. And maybe if they don't show."

"How late do you work?"

"I get off about one. Normally end up at Jacko's. Why don't you check me out then?" Another warm smile.

As focused as he was on killing Vito, her offer wasn't lost on him. "I just might."

She winked and returned to her work.

Outside, Brack decided to screw up a perfectly fine evening and called Darcy.

She actually answered, and after he told her Gecko Row was a bust, she said, "I've got a line on Vito. Want to do a little stakeout?"

Chapter Seventeen

Tuesday, eleven p.m.

A vast ocean extended the horizon. Jo held his hand, the two of them walking barefoot along the edge of the surf, the water tickling their feet.

She looked at him, sadness in her eyes. "You have to let me go now."

Brack opened his eyes.

Darcy said, "Can I have my hand back?"

At once, he realized he'd fallen asleep, and that he'd somehow reached for Darcy's hand. He let go. "Sorry. Um—"

She cut him off with the words, "Vito's on the move."

Rubbing his eyes, he sat up in his seat. She started the Accord and put it in gear.

Brack glanced down and spotted a lipstick smudge on his white shirt, the same shade that Darcy wore, along with a few strands of blonde hair. She too must have fallen asleep—but with her head on his shoulder.

They sped down the street after Vito's black Mercedes SUV. Brack really wished his gun hadn't gotten blown up with his car. He needed another one.

Both falling asleep on this stakeout was a careless mistake. A different careless mistake on their stakeout—not watching their six—had gotten her shot. Neither of them could afford any more careless mistakes.

Fumbling in his pocket, he found his gum and popped a piece in his mouth.

"What flavor is that?" she asked.

"Grape. Want one?"

She gave him a sideways glance. "Grape? What are we, ten?"

"Would you rather I lit up a cigar?"

"Point taken," she said. "Chew away, Calvin."

Their target had expanded his lead by a block.

"You better speed up," Brack said.

"Yessir."

He switched on the radio and found a classic rock station, catching the intro to the Outfield's "Your Love."

She said, "We're still living in the eighties, I see."

"When I find something I like, I tend to stick with it."

No snarky retort was forthcoming.

Vito turned down a street and Brack knew where he was heading, because he'd been there earlier. "He's going to Gecko Row."

His phone vibrated. He noticed the call came from an Atlanta area code. He answered it.

A female voice asked, "Is this Brack Pelton?"

"Who's asking?" Brack said, suspicious because the last time he got a call like this his Porsche blew up.

"This is Shana, from Gecko Row. We spoke earlier."

"Yes?" he said, not knowing what else to say.

"Those two girls, the ones you were looking for? They're here."

"I'm headed your way," he said, even though this could be a trap.

"Um," she said, "one thing though."

"What's that?" he asked.

"They aren't alone."

"No problem."

"You don't understand," she said. "They're with some really connected guys with bodyguards."

"This just gets better and better," he said. "Thanks for the information."

"You owe me," she said with a coy tone in her voice.

"Maybe this will buy me some credit," he said. "Vito is about five minutes from walking in the door there in case you and your co-workers aren't exactly, you know, working."

"That's a start." She ended the call.

Darcy said, "Don't tell me you, too, have sources in this town."

He took the moment to bask in her envy. "Of course I do."

"Well," she said, "what did your source tell you?"

"Two eighteen-year-old Asian girls are at Vito's Gecko Row place together with some connected men and their bodyguards. Of course, this could be a trap."

She tapped her steering wheel. "If it isn't, I'm guessing those girls have fake ID saying they are old enough to be there."

"What are you thinking?" Brack hoped she wanted to confront the situation.

"If we go in there, Vito will have you taken out."

She was right, of course. If she hadn't been here with him, he would have stormed the fort. Instead, he made a call and they took a detour.

Around midnight at Three Crosses Church, they sat opposite Brother Thomas and Reverend Cleophus at a folding table in a makeshift office.

Darcy and Brack explained what they'd learned about the two missing daughters.

Reverend Cleophus said, "This situation has gotten out of hand."

"When Brother Brack is involved," Brother Thomas said, "things always get out of hand, mm-hmm."

Darcy added, "And I get great ratings."

"And I end up having to remind everyone of the reason we're all doing what we're doing here," Brack said. "Like getting Regan. And Mindy and Kai."

"Just a little comic relief, Brother Brack, mm-hmm."

"Yeah, well, I'm not laughing."

*   *   *

Early the next morning, Mutt and Brack sat across from Detective Nichols in a booth at the Majestic Diner.

Brack asked, "So why haven't you arrested Vito yet?"

The man with the badge chewed his hash browns, then wiped his mouth with a napkin. He took a swig of coffee to wash it down. "You ask like you already know why."

"Diplomatic immunity," Mutt said.

"The man runs the largest illegal sex-trade operation in the city," Brack said, "and all you guys do is stand around with your guns in your holsters and let him do it."

"It's not that simple," he said, pushing his plate away.

Ignoring the BLT he'd ordered, Brack said, "Yes, it is that simple."

Nichols said, "Why are you here busting my chops if you've got all this figured out?"

"Because the men who work for Vito don't have diplomatic immunity," Brack said.

"Yeah," Mutt said, "and you ain't roustin' them neither."

The detective leaned forward to stare at Brack. "Look, our hands are tied."

"You're sitting on a public relations time bomb and you're telling me your hands are tied?"

"Yes."

Mutt blew out a long breath. "Man, if I didn't know any better, Opie, I'd think this cracker here was trying to get us to do his job for him."

"Or someone higher up is being paid off," Brack said.

"Like I said, my hands are tied."

Thinking as he spoke, Brack said, "But ours aren't."

Nichols stood and took out his wallet. "You guys are smarter than you look."

"Yeah," Brack said, "well, breakfast is on us. What do you think about that?"

Nichols smiled. "Suckers."

Brack watched him walk away. "You believe that guy?"

"Opie," Mutt said, "we just got the green light to blow up this town."

"My Porsche hasn't even been dead a week and you're already cracking bomb jokes?"

"Sorry," Mutt said. "I didn't realize you two was so close."

"We didn't have enough time to get fully acquainted." A lot like the Mustang Brack owned two years before. In a high-speed chase with some bad guys, it had been squashed between a speeding SUV and a beer delivery truck.

"You gonna eat your food or what?"

Brack looked down at his plate. "Yes."

"Good, 'cause we're gonna need all the energy we can get."

Taking a bite of his sandwich, Brack chewed absentmindedly while thinking that Vito didn't have any idea who he'd picked a fight with. Diplomatic immunity worked only as far as any official channel went. Its antonym could be named in a thesaurus as "Mutt and Brack," they were so unofficial. Brack hoped Mutt knew exactly what was at risk. As for himself, he was unattached. All he stood to lose other than his life was some money in the bank and a couple of restaurants already going to Paige if anything happened to him. But Mutt had a daughter. The more Brack thought about that, the more he had to make sure his friend didn't do anything as stupid as he himself could be.

Before Mutt left to escort Cassie to her restaurant for the Wednesday night crowd, he handed Brack one of his own thirty-eights, a loaner until the 1911 Colt that blew up with the Porsche could be replaced. After a session with Tara in the gym, Brack stood across from the Westin Peachtree Plaza, the setting sun still hot in the clear sky, watching the hotel entrance. Two lovely young ladies, Mindy and Kai, strolled out of the hotel, arm in arm with a much older gentleman wearing an expensive well-tailored suit.

Accompanying them was clearly the man's bodyguard—all muscle and sunglasses. Each man bore the dark complexion of a Middle-Easterner. Brack guessed the businessman's expense report might show a few additional entertainment charges or consulting fees. If Vito's organization was as crafty as it needed to be to operate so covertly, it included pseudonymous businesses that wouldn't raise any red flags.

He tracked the foursome to a long wheelbase Cadillac Escalade. A second burly man wearing a black suit and sunglasses held the back door for the partiers. After the trio was seated, the first bodyguard got in the front passenger seat.

In the small notebook Brack carried for just such occasions, he recorded the plate number. It would probably come back as a rental, but with the right palms greased they'd have the name of whoever signed the contract for it.

How Brack came up with the intel on the Arab and his entourage was another story. Shana from Gecko Row had called again. She'd noticed the businessman writing a note on a piece of Hotel Westin's stationery he had in his pocket. With that and the name on his credit card—also nicely provided by Shana for a promise from him of some sort of repayment—Brack was able to have Darcy track him down. Her sources tagged the man as a big spender and philanderer. She got his itinerary, and Brack volunteered to sit on him. Because this could also be a trap, Brack didn't want anyone else he cared for shot on his watch.

He flagged a taxi and said something he'd wanted to say for a long time. "Follow that car."

The driver of the well-used livery Camry did as he was asked and kept the Escalade in sight. Brack wanted to know where the girls would be dropped off. After an hour's drive through traffic around the city, it seemed as if the businessman would never be done with them.

Brack should have anticipated that things were just getting started. Apparently the john had rented the girls beyond Tuesday evening. Their first stop was what a quick internet search on

Brack's iPhone said was a five-star bistro. From a metered spot across the street, Brack and the cab driver watched the women slip back into their dresses as they exited the SUV. Too surprised by the audacity of this trio to speak about what they watched, Brack felt very far away from his South Carolina lowcountry home with its relaxing beaches and low-key lifestyle.

His cab driver, a Jamaican-accented man with dreadlocks, said, "Your's de best fare I got all week, mon."

"I'm glad," Brack said, "because I'm going to need your services for a few more hours."

"If it's gonna be like dis, you got it."

Brack called Darcy and asked if she could use her pull to have the Escalade's plate number run.

"Where are you now?" she asked.

He told her where and what he'd just witnessed.

"I'm sure you really hate that," she said. "Call me again when they leave."

They ended the call.

The driver, whose identification card showed his name was Darius Jenkins, asked if Brack minded his smoking.

That wouldn't allay Brack's jones for a cigar, but it might help him enjoy a false fix.

"Your ride."

Darius reached for a pack of Camel Blues pinned to the roof by the sun visor and offered one to Brack.

"No thanks."

"You musta quit, eh, mon?"

"Why do you say that?"

He lit a cigarette with a Bic lighter and exhaled smoke out his open window. "The way you lookin' at 'em. You want one, ain't no one gonna judge you here."

Brack wondered if Darius was referring to the cigarettes, to their intermittent voyeurism, or to his own likely other vices.

He stuck a piece of gum in his mouth. "I did quit." He knew he was talking about more than smoking.

An hour later, the threesome exited the restaurant. Darius started his cab and followed. While he was no Mutt when it came to companionship, this guy was all right.

The next stop was another bar Darius said was popular in the city. He and Brack watched the three go inside. Brack thought about his next move and decided some closer observation was in order. If Mutt had been here, he might have tried to talk Brack out of it, but he wasn't.

Brack paid the fare, gave Darius a fifty-dollar tip, and asked him to wait another fifteen minutes. The driver said this was the most excitement he'd had all year and readily agreed to hang tight. Brack got out of the cab and entered the establishment. A room that was more deep than wide welcomed its patrons with a long marble bar to the right and tables to the left, set off by a waist-high divider.

A male bartender wearing a black button-down shirt greeted Brack with a smile as he laid a napkin in front of him. "What can I get you?"

"A sweet tea, two lemon wedges," Brack said.

The barkeep nodded and got the drink.

Turning his back to the bar, Brack took in the room and all the patrons. He spotted Mindy and Kai first, then the gleaming bald head of his target. They sat at a corner table in the back. What Brack didn't figure on were three more goons sitting at the table with them. Actually, his thinking of them as goons was a kindness. Short dark hair chemically spiked upward, big shoulders stretching silk shirts, tattoos peeking out below short sleeves. Experience told Brack they were hired muscle, ex-military by the look of them.

Why did this guy need extra protection in addition to the two he already had driving his ménage à trois-athon?

Squeezing both lemon wedges into his tea, Brack contemplated his next move and called Darcy.

"Currently the target and his two companions are having drinks with three questionable characters."

"Don't be so dramatic," she said. "Can you get a picture of them?"

"I'll try, but I'm flying solo and selfies are so last week."

She acknowledged his attempt at humor by ending the call.

A thought occurred to him and he signaled the bartender.

He came right over. "What can I get you?"

"Is the owner here?"

"Some corporation owns us. I can get my manager if you want."

"No thanks."

Just then, Mindy and Kai excused themselves, got up from the table, and headed to the rear of the establishment, undoubtedly to use the restrooms. Taking advantage of the opportunity, Brack tracked them behind the divider that separated the dining area from the bar, which gave him cover most of the way. Lucky for him the restrooms required a ninety-degree turn around a corner that put them out of view of the eating area.

He caught up with them around the corner. "Mindy? Kai?"

The girls froze in their tracks and said nothing.

"My name's Brack," he said, getting down to business. "Your mothers asked me to find you."

They turned to face him but still didn't speak.

"You both are eighteen, so you can make your own decisions. What I want to do is get in touch with Regan. Do you know her?"

At that moment they screamed.

In a hundredth of a second, Brack's mind calculated the time before the three armed hoods would rush around the corner and put more holes in him than a donut shop. Instantly he pushed past the girls and crashed through an "Emergency Only" exit. The alarm sounded, but he kept running across the back lot. He heard the door bang shut, then slam open again. He rounded a dumpster in time for the bullets to merely ricochet off its steel side. Around another corner and he found himself back on the sidewalk of the main drag and immediately ducked into the vestibule of a clothing store. The goons ran right past him. Good thing he paid Darius to wait. He flagged him over, jumped in, and told him to get them out of there real fast.

Chapter Eighteen

Wednesday afternoon

Mutt called and asked to meet Brack at Piedmont Park. Brack could tell that Trish did not like giving up his dog even for a little while, especially since she'd initially decided to stay in town to spend a mini vacation with Shelby. But, he wanted to spend some time with him while he could.

However, Brack's easy access to his own dog might change Trish's mind about vacationing in Atlanta. This move was like skating on thin ice.

He clipped a leash on Shelby, who didn't seem to mind. Shelby looked happy simply being outside. Bringing him on this escapade wasn't the smartest thing Brack had ever done, though he'd done so for a selfish reason—he needed the companionship. Last fall, he'd asked Trish to watch Shelby only to take him from her in a bad case of misjudgment that almost got him and his dog killed. But leaving him in Charleston for this didn't seem like the right thing to do. It didn't help that Brack then had to ask Trish again to care for him, having to come all the way to Atlanta. Good thing she minded doing that about as much as Brack minded smoking a good cigar. At least he used to enjoy them.

Piedmont Park, established in 1895, consisted of a hundred and eighty-nine acres a mile from the heart of the city. Brack liked that some of the water fountains accommodated canines. Also, as he discovered, it contained two fenced-in dog parks. He and Shelby played fetch while they waited for Mutt and Taliah to show up.

Though it wasn't the same as the semi-private stretch of beach on Sullivan's Island they were used to, Shelby adapted quickly. He placed the tennis ball in Brack's hand for each fetch and took off running again at each throw. Brack cocked his arm back and let 'er fly. It always amazed him to watch Shelby spot the fluorescent green ball in the air, estimate its landing, and run it down.

From behind him, Brack heard Mutt say, "You call that a throw?"

Brack turned. "I never said I was good at this." To Mutt's daughter, he said, "It's nice to see you again, Taliah."

Her chin-length hair was held back from her face with bar barrettes, and she wore a pink polo shirt and khaki shorts. With a big smile she gave Brack a hug. "It's nice to see you again too."

Shelby ran up and got between them. When he succeeded in separating Taliah from Brack, he dropped the ball at her feet and gave her a friendly bark.

"Taliah," Brack said, "can you throw the ball for Shelby?"

She knelt and kissed Shelby on the head. "Of course I can."

What could Brack say? Shelby was the four-legged version of a Prada purse, or whatever was popular with young females these days.

Mutt and Brack walked over to a fountain. Brack stooped to take a drink.

"Taliah did some digging around."

"Oh yeah?" Brack wiped his mouth.

Mutt inhaled a major lungful from his vaporizer and exhaled. "She so smart."

"I already knew that."

"Sometimes she too smart for her own good. She just wanna help, but I made her promise me she wouldn't go any further."

Brack raised himself up to his six-foot height. "I agree with that. So what did she find out?"

"You ain't gonna like this. I don't like it."

Brack zeroed in on one thought. "Darcy."

"Yep."

"How's she connected?"

"You remember the time she got inside that Chinese brothel in Charleston that was blackmailing all them big-money businessmen?"

The Chinese hoods had shot her.

Brack rubbed his chin. "Uh-huh."

"She's at it again," he said.

"The question is, why didn't she tell us?"

"You think I know women?"

Taliah and Shelby had abandoned fetch the ball and played tag, a game Brack was surprised Shelby knew how to play. He watched as she chased Shelby around the area, touched his back, and reversed direction. Shelby gave chase, caught up to her, nudged her with his snout, then slid to a stop like a car without anti-lock brakes, his head and chest lowered and his hind end raised. He spun around and ran in the other direction, Taliah fast on his heels, his ears back and tongue hanging out in absolute bliss.

Their joy gave Brack a moment of peace. Here, in sight of the tall buildings of this grand yet brutal city, these two were having a blast.

Mutt said, "Would you look at them."

"Your daughter has taught my dog a new game."

What Brack saw in Mutt's eyes was what he imagined parental pride was. In Taliah, he had a lot to be proud of. Mutt was smarter than the average bear, but Taliah was off the charts.

The men didn't say anything further until Taliah and Shelby, their "kids," took a break by the water fountain.

Brack wiped the sweat off his forehead. "I think we need to talk to Darcy."

When Brack was young, his family moved to Atlanta to be closer to his mother's sister. Her daughter, his older cousin, took Brack to Little Five Points. During the mid-to-late eighties, Little Five Points was considered Atlanta's version of San Francisco's Haight-

Ashbury district. Dead Heads commingled with the punk scene. As an eight-year-old boy seeing what he later learned were Clockwork Orange skinheads—teenaged boys dressed up like characters from the movie of the same name—he had nightmares for weeks afterward. Today, with Mutt's loaded thirty-eight, Brack secretly wanted to spot one of those posers.

With the gun stuck down the waistband of his khakis, Brack sat in a coffee shop, a large cup of steaming black decaf on the table in front of him. His car was parked at a meter that needed three swipes of a credit card to register the transaction, then charged him twice.

Darcy walked in and Brack stood, hoping his face didn't betray the butterflies in his stomach.

She came over and sat across from him. "How's it going?"

"Can I get you a coffee?"

"Wow," she said, a smile creeping across her face. "Um, sure. A half-caf soy latte."

Brack ordered her drink and brought it to her.

"Thanks. This must be important if you're buying."

"Actually, and you'll appreciate this, your name came up when we were digging into Vito's businesses."

Her cup hovered in space, as if she couldn't decide whether to set it down or take a sip.

"The funny thing," he continued, "at least for me, is you were found out by a thirteen-year-old."

"Huh?"

This opportunity to have a little fun was just too good to pass up. "Granted, she is a registered genius."

"Taliah found something that links me to Vito?"

"Yep. She is one smart cookie."

Her cup made it back to the saucer. "I'm not sure I follow."

"The way it was explained to me—and we both know that requires breaking it down to a fifth-grade level—is a link exists to some outstanding parking tickets that were issued near several of Vito's businesses. If she can find your car, how long do you think it will take before someone else does? The kid is sharp, but it really proves there's a traceable trail."

Darcy looked out the window of the shop. "One that leads to me."

Brack nodded and finished off his coffee. "You want something to eat? I'm going to get a cookie."

"No thanks."

Darcy sat at the table and Brack sensed a feeling of vulnerability over her. It was obvious to him, if to no one else, that what he'd said troubled her.

"Outstanding parking tickets," she repeated.

"Funny how those things catch up with you."

"I totally forgot about them." She tapped a finger on the table. "But this doesn't make sense. My car isn't registered to me anyway."

Brack opened his mouth to toss her another smart remark and stopped. What she said *really* didn't make sense. He asked, "Who's it registered to?"

"A fake business I created."

"Hold on a minute." Brack took out his phone and called Mutt. He answered, "Yo."

"Mutt, I'm with Darcy. We need to speak with Taliah, find out exactly how she found the link to Darcy."

"She's at her mother's," he said. "I just dropped her off."

"Does she have a cell?"

"Who, her mother?"

"No, Taliah."

A pause told him Mutt didn't want his daughter any more involved than she already was.

Brack said, "Darcy's car isn't registered to her. How Taliah found her name is important."

"Look, Opie. You know I'll go all the way to the grave wit you. But Taliah is different."

That wasn't what Brack wanted to hear. What he wanted to hear was cooperation. Instead he got another roadblock. Only this time it was from Mutt. Having learned the hard way, Brack actually took time to think before he spoke. While he wanted to say anything but, he said, "Okay. You're right. We'll find it another way."

"Thanks for understanding."

"Well," Brack said to him, "we do tend to collect collateral damage."

Darcy said, "That's an understatement."

They exited the coffee shop, the sun bright and hot.

Brack said, "Why didn't you tell me you were already on Vito?"

"All I had on him so far was background and a list of his businesses." She frowned. "It wasn't anything. I mean, I was simply doing my job. He's a big player and I smelled dirt."

"What do you think now?"

Darcy checked her phone for messages. "I think something doesn't add up."

"There's a lot about this that doesn't add up," Brack said.

They walked to her car.

He asked, "What company did you register this under?"

"A fake one," she said. "I already told you that."

"Yeah, but what did you call it?"

"Doesn't matter."

"Under the circumstances," he said, "it couldn't hurt."

"Well, I'd rather not say."

That wasn't like her. "I don't think we can find out—and protect you—any other way."

She got in her car and started it.

Brack opened the passenger door and ducked in, waiting.

After a few seconds of listening to the four-cylinder engine idle, the AC laboring to work up to its role, she said, "PC Industries."

He got in the car and closed the door. "PC Industries? Computers? How'd you come up with that?"

"The question is, how did Taliah link it to me?" She put the car into drive, pulled away from the curb, and headed down the street.

Four stoplights later, she glided into a parking garage under a very tall building.

"This must be the office," Brack said.

"A little different from Charleston," she said.

Brack wasn't sure if she considered the difference a good thing or not.

She parked in a spot identified as for *Darcy Wells, Sr. Corresp.* They took the elevator up to the thirtieth floor and he realized that this place, unlike the *Palmetto Pulse*, his aunt's local news conglomerate in Charleston, probably didn't allow dogs. And then he realized how much he missed Shelby.

The elevator doors opened to plush carpeting, bright lights, and colorful signage denoting Darcy's current employer. A large number of people bustled around and held phones to their ears. While Darcy would always be a star in his book, here she had to fight with many eager young go-getters to distinguish herself.

With cube walls out of vogue, her space consisted of a desk and a few chairs set in the middle of a bull pen of other desks, chairs, and employees. To someone who spent his afternoons staring at the Atlantic lapping the shore of his island, the sound of this commotion was deafening. As soon as Regan came home, Brack was getting out of this town.

Darcy sat in her swivel chair and logged onto the system, while he took a seat in front of her desk and unwillingly absorbed the energy of the place.

A tall, skinny kid about twenty stopped beside her desk. "Staff meeting in five. Nancy says to try and grace us with your presence, pretty please." His tie sported a purple argyle design that contrasted with his white shirt, his hair already thinning at the corners of his forehead.

Darcy looked at him. "Tell Nancy I'll think about it."

"She's not going to like that." He swished to the next desk.

"I don't think he liked your answer," Brack said.

She stood. "Yeah, well, since I've blown off the last few meetings, I probably need to make an appearance."

Slouching in the seat as if ready to take a nap, Brack said, "I suppose you don't need backup."

"You're right. You better stay here."

Twenty minutes later, he was startled out of a deep slumber by the slamming of a desk drawer.

"Those idiots think we're full of smoke," Darcy said, "That *I'm* full of smoke."

Shaking off the sleep and remnants of a dream about his beach home, Brack asked, "Trouble in paradise?"

"Every story I've written has paid off. Every news segment I've filmed has had off-the-charts viewer feedback. Yet I'm still the new girl from the small town."

"They're wannabe suits," he said, rubbing his eyes. "Don't worry about them."

"Yeah? Well, we have to worry about them when they tell me to work on something else."

Brack lowered his hands.

"That's right. I was mocked and told to find some other story."

"Take a leave of absence. It's not as if you need the money."

Her family owned one of the largest importing firms in Charleston. The way she used her funds to grease the wheels of information suggested that she already had some access to that wealth, whether in the form of a trust fund or straight-up allowance. He didn't know or care which.

"I can't," she said.

"Meaning you won't," Brack countered.

"No," she said. "I promised Justin I'd give this place an honest try. I can't renege on that."

It was hard for Brack to ignore the reference to the peckerwood, but he really tried. "You know what all this means, don't you?"

A glimmer of a smile crept across Darcy's face. "It means we're onto something."

Vito's tentacles may reach all the way up to the thirtieth floor of her employer's building.

Chapter Nineteen

Wednesday, three p.m.

Regan traced a finger up Vito's bare stomach. He lay with his eyes closed in what she hoped was post-coital bliss, his head propped on a pillow. "I was thinking something."

He opened his eyes, looked at her, and smiled.

At that she knew he was hers to do with as she pleased. Making her voice low and husky, she said, "You heard what happened with Mindy and Kai, right?"

He nodded.

"If it's my sister causing all this trouble, why doesn't something happen to her?"

"You want me to take out your sister?"

"Don't you see?" she purred. "It's the only way we can live happily ever after."

Vito waited a beat as if thinking about it. He said, "If she gets killed, you will be the prime suspect."

"Okay," she said. "Why not just get her out of the way so we can get back to business as usual?"

"It's this Brack Pelton," he said. "He has a bad habit of turning up where he doesn't belong."

"So take him out." She slid her hands around Vito's waist and kissed him. "You can do it, baby. Do it for me."

"I already have a plan for him," he said. "Soon enough he'll get his due."

Chapter Twenty

With Mutt at work and he and Darcy with no new leads, Brack took it easy in his room after a late lunch in the hotel coffee shop. Alone. Trish had taken her baby-sitting role a little too far, almost approaching dognapping. He'd expected her to keep the room he'd reserved for her at the pet-friendly hotel. Instead, she'd elected to escort Shelby fifty miles outside the city for a vacation in the mountains. Taking his dog with him to entertain Taliah yesterday must have prompted Trish to make Shelby less available, as if Brack had absconded with his own dog. He kept telling himself that at least Shelby was safe.

As he was about to fall asleep on his hotel bed, he got a call from Paige.

"When we decided to open the second location," she reminded, "you agreed to free me up to handle it. We didn't talk about my having to manage the construction of the new place and still pick up your slack at the Pirate's Cove."

"What happened and why am I just now getting a call?"

"Our new manager apparently got mad about something and walked off the job."

"She what?"

"You heard me."

Paige rarely presented a problem she didn't already have a solution to. She was that good. Therefore, he was sure she was toying with him. At least he hoped so.

He said, "What would you like to do?"

"I'd like to put Maura in charge."

Maura was their assistant manager.

"Isn't she already in charge?" Brack asked.

"Let's make it official."

He said, "Do it."

"Thanks, boss," she said. "How're things going in Atlanta?"

"Not very well."

"Remember that I'm in your will. If something happens, I get just about everything."

"How could I forget?"

"Good," she said. "I'd rather have you alive so I can bust your chops. But if you get stupid and die, I'll gladly take the business we've built." She hung up.

Paige had become a little tougher over the few years he'd known her, probably because he'd gotten into some very dangerous situations that he almost didn't make it out of. She was right about the business, which ran a very handsome surplus these days— hence, the new Porsche he used to have. The rest of his assets— what Paige was not slated to inherit—would go to Brother Thomas's Church of Redemption in Charleston as well as a few animal protection charities.

Instead of dwelling on the aftermath of his demise, he turned his attention to the task at hand. He really wasn't in Atlanta for Cassie. Or Regan. He'd like to say he was here to help Mutt, who'd always been there to help him. But if he was being honest with himself, which he sometimes neglected to be, Brack would admit he was here for Darcy.

His phone rang again. It was Darcy, as if she could read his mind.

"Howdy," he said.

"Howdy? This isn't Texas, pardner."

Not wanting to admit how much he'd missed hearing her voice the past year, sarcastic or not, he affected a slightly annoyed attitude. "What can I do for you now?"

"You can check out a few things for me."

"You want *moi* to check out a few things *pour vous*?"

"Easy there, Pepe Le Pew," she said. "It's three thirty already, and I'm filming in about five minutes so I've got to be quick. I'm emailing a list of addresses for you and Mutt to run down."

"Vito owns them, doesn't he?"

"Yes. I'll call you when I'm done here." She hung up.

At least she was calling. Brack wondered what her peckerwood fiancé thought about him being here, working with her again. Not that it mattered. Too soon she would become his wife and Brack would be back in Charleston.

He got in his Mazda turbo and drove to get Mutt, hoping Cassie wouldn't object to their new assignment. And that Mutt wouldn't say anything stupid, like "I don't gotta tell you where I'm goin', woman." That would be bad.

Brack pulled into the parking lot at Cassie's restaurant, Barry White's "Can't Get Enough of Your Love" blaring through the hatchback's speakers. Because it was early, the front lot was almost empty—except for a black Ford Expedition with darkened windows. As he passed by, its driver started the engine, and when Brack parked at the far end, the SUV drove away. The small voice in the back of his head said to follow. Ordinarily he listened when that voice spoke. As for listening when common sense and logic whispered, not so much.

The Expedition turned onto the main thoroughfare and Brack gave chase, partly to test the incognito tailing ability of his Mazda. If the Ford's presence turned out to be nothing, the driver wouldn't be looking for a tail. If the person or persons in the SUV were up to no good, this was about to get interesting, especially since no one driving that SUV could outrun the Mazda.

Brack stayed five cars back in the center lane, ready to follow no matter which way it turned. The first mile or two was smooth sailing. The driver made lazy turns, using his indicator well in advance.

But Brack's luck ran out when, on a backed-up left turn, everyone in between them kept going straight and he ended up directly behind the Expedition. When the green arrow flashed the first cars in front of the SUV moved ahead, the Expedition easing from a full stop a few feet ahead of him, then making a wild U-turn at the last moment. It passed him on his left heading in the opposite direction.

Brack revved the Mazda's engine, dropped the clutch, and spun the front tires, whipping around in a tight hundred-and-eighty-degree spin. Knowing the Expedition could not outrun him, his only concern was being outgunned.

The black SUV weaved through the congested Atlanta traffic as if carting a pregnant woman to the hospital. Although it could not outrun him, Brack realized it might be able to out-maneuver him. And given the self-absorbed driving style of the locals, out-maneuvering was a given. Brack did his best to read the plate number of his target before it ran a red light directly in front of him, cut across five lanes to make a very shaky right turn, and disappeared down a side street.

Brack was stuck.

With the plate number fresh in his memory, he called Detective Nichols.

Back at Cassie's restaurant, Brack parked in his original spot and walked inside. The bartender, a medium-skin-toned African-American woman about thirty with flowing black hair, bright eyes, and a small nose, gave him a cautious smile and said they would not be serving for another hour.

Mutt came through the kitchen doors and said, "Nina, this here's Opie. He's welcome anytime. Opie, this is Nina."

"Nice to meet you." Brack offered a hand, which she shook. He said, "My name's Brack."

Nina went back to stocking the bar.

He said, "Darcy gave me a few addresses to run down. Can you get away? If not, I can always see if Nina wants to come."

The woman smiled but showed no interest.

Mutt said, "Don't be botherin' the staff, Opie. Especially when they're my relations."

"By marriage," Nina said. "And you aren't married anymore."

Brack laughed.

Mutt didn't seem to know how to reply.

Cassie came into the room, rescuing them all. "Hey, Brack."

He said, "Can Mutt come out and play?"

"If you don't let him go," Nina said, "this one will try to get me to come with him." She gave Brack a wink. "It might be better not to find out how that would end."

Brack was speechless. He'd never before been rejected and accepted at the same time, or with such panache.

Cassie rubbed her chin. "What do you have to do an hour before we open?"

Before either man could respond, Nina told Cassie, "Opie, or Brack, whichever it is, said he's got some addresses that someone named Darcy gave him."

Cassie put a chubby hand on a thick hip. "Sounds like a lot of trouble."

It probably was.

"It ain't gonna be no trouble now, baby."

From the sound of Mutt's words, Brack wasn't sure if his friend was kidding Cassie or himself.

Brack said, "I'm not making any promises."

Cassie nodded. "I figured. That's why I already added two extra staff each night until this gets settled."

"Then why ask me to work tonight, sweet pea?"

"Maybe," Cassie said, "I wanted to spend time with my man."

For Mutt's sake, Brack hoped he kept his mouth shut.

Nina walked around the bar, stood between the men, and put her arms across their shoulders. "You boys better go before my 'relative' here gets himself in more trouble."

Mutt turned and gave her a peck on the cheek. "Thanks, honey. I owe you."

"Yes, you do," Nina said. "Take Hugh and the boys to a ball game some time."

"You got it."

Mutt and Brack walked out.

Brack asked, "Hugh's her husband?"

"Yeah. And my ex-brother-in-law. Sorry, Opie."

"Story of my life," Brack said.

They got in the Mazda. Brack finished telling Mutt about the Expedition moments before Detective Nichols called back with its plate number. Its registration was in the name of a Jack Townsend. The name didn't mean much to Mutt. But the interesting thing Brack discovered was that Townsend's address matched one of the addresses Darcy asked them to check out. They went there first.

After an hour spent in busy traffic, they'd almost reached Townsend's house when Mutt answered a phone call.

Things went south fast.

He yelled, "What?"

Brack, alarmed, pulled to a stop at an empty meter.

Eyes wide, Mutt said, "Cassie's headin' to the hospital." Into the cell phone he asked, "Which one?"

When Mutt named the hospital, Brack wasn't sure where he needed to go, so he punched its name into the Mazda's navigation system.

Mutt hung up. Brack wanted to ask what happened but figured his friend needed to sort out what he'd learned before he spoke.

The GPS found the location and mapped the route.

Brack waited for a break in traffic, then sped away, redlining the engine through three shifts.

When they reached speed, Mutt sighed deeply and said, "They got her."

"Who?" Brack asked, although he knew who. The same ones they'd been tracking.

"I don't know."

"Where? At the restaurant?"

He sighed. "Yeah. She in critical condition. They beat her up good. The Fire Department is there now. Someone tried to torch it."

Blue lights flickered in the rearview mirror. Brack looked at the dash and saw he was doing seventy. The last speed-limit sign he remembered said thirty-five.

"Hold on," he said. "We gotta make a detour." Or else have to do a lot of explaining. Especially if the cops decided to search the car. And, Brack thought, given the appearance of himself and Mutt, they'd want to search the car—where they'd find Mutt's two unregistered pistols.

Mutt looked back.

With a flick of the wrist, Brack slid the Mazda onto an empty side street and gunned it.

The cruiser, an older Crown Victoria, barely made the turn.

Two more high-speed corners and they lost the tail. Five minutes later, they stormed into the hospital drive. Brack slowed in time to ease over several speed bumps. He dropped Mutt off at the emergency entrance and found a corner spot hidden by a tree on one side and a large van on the other.

The plate on the hatchback was a fake, a temporary tag that Elmer had provided. Not only could it not be traced back to Brack, but Elmer's name would not come up in the system either. A legit tag sat in the glovebox that Elmer registered the car under so he wouldn't get in any trouble. If stopped, Brack would look like he'd swapped the fake one on himself. Elmer apparently had some experience dealing with folks a shade or two outside of normal convention. Brack figured Elmer's brother, Reverend Cleophus, didn't know about the fake plates since he'd asked Brack to not say anything about them to anyone.

At the reception area, Brack asked about Cassie and realized he'd forgotten her last name. It took a few minutes for the young woman behind the desk to find the latest emergency admission and explain where he needed to go.

Brack found Mutt leaning against a wall, his face downcast.

"How is she?" he asked.

Mutt looked up at him. "Not good." His eyes teared up. "They tortured her."

Mutt did not need Brack to overreact at this point so he emptied his mind of thoughts.

"And," Mutt said, "they killed Nina."

Chapter Twenty-One

Wednesday, six p.m.

They sat in the hospital waiting room, a wait measured by never-ceasing clicks of the old-fashioned clock on the wall. Long enough for Darcy to have finished her segment. She walked in still wearing her work clothes, a snazzy skirt and blouse ensemble that might have been silk and surely was expensive.

Brack barely noticed that she ignored his presence and went directly to Mutt, giving him a hug. He needed her comfort more than Brack craved her attention. They spoke softly, then she came over and sat next to Brack.

He said, "It was good of you to come."

"I know what these places are like."

And she did, having spent time in one after her own gunshot wound. Also his fault. He said, "Townsend, one of the names on your list, was at the restaurant before this happened. At least his SUV was. What do we know about him?"

"He runs Trinity Security and has one client. Guess who that is."

"Vito."

She nodded and pulled up a photo on her phone. "And apparently Townsend's a hands-on type."

"This is the big guy who attempted to intimidate Tara and me at the charity event." The blond-haired blue-eyed monster was unmistakable. "Who are the bikers he's with?"

"Local toughs. Vito's street thugs."

Shifting in his molded plastic seat, Brack said, "Any word as to which of them did this?"

"No, but I'd put money on the wannabe road hogs."

It made sense that they would be in on it. If Townsend had any kind of sense as a businessman, he'd do his best to keep his hands clean. He'd probably been scouting out the restaurant when Brack chased him earlier. What didn't make sense was why Cassie was the target. To Brack, it should be himself or Mutt. He said, "Any thoughts as to what's next?"

Her response was to stare at him.

"What?"

"Well," she replied, "ordinarily you'd be running out the door, armed and dangerous and ready to destroy everything in your path. Which is exactly what you'd end up doing. Right or wrong."

"True. I want to get them. All of them. But I think we need to be smart about it."

"We?"

"You can walk away any time you want," he said. "I'm going all the way with this one."

After a moment, Darcy nodded. "I figured you'd say that."

Brack stood and leaned against the wall—which Mutt had been doing every few minutes—and put his hands in his pockets. He asked Darcy, "So, you in or out?"

"What do you think?"

"I'm not sure. You might want to run this by your better half."

She watched him as if to see whether he was serious or joking. He wasn't joking. She got up to leave. "You're right. I'll let you know."

Realizing his stupid emotions had gotten in the way, he said to her retreating back, "In the meantime, I'll sit on Townsend."

As she exited the room, he heard her say, "You do that, sport."

Brack walked out to his car alone. Mutt had chosen to stay by Cassie's side. Darcy was gone. And probably irritated by his jealous comment. The tall buildings of the Atlanta skyline stood over him like impersonal giants observing a mouse in a maze.

Leaning against the Mazda, he pulled out a cigar and his Uncle Reggie's Zippo. He stared at both for a moment, but decided not to indulge. Within a few minutes his jumbled thoughts dissipated. If he was honest with himself at this moment, he'd say he didn't want to be alone.

A bizarre notion came to mind. He needed to be like the deaf, dumb, and blind kid in The Who's "Pinball Wizard:" no distractions. And at this moment, solitude—him with himself for company—was distracting.

To free up his hands, he put the cigar and lighter back in his pocket, got out his iPhone, and unlocked the screen. Scrolling through recent calls, he found the one he wanted and tapped it.

After a moment, Tara answered.

"This is Brack."

"I heard about Cassie and Nina."

"I just left Mutt at the hospital. I'm still in the parking lot."

"How's Cassie?"

"I think she'll pull through, but she's in a bad spot right now."

"That's terrible."

"I'm going after the ones who did this. Remember the big blond guy from the ball? He's tonight's target."

No response.

He continued. "Care to join me in a little surveillance?" He pushed the thought of involving another innocent in this mess out of his mind because at this moment he was being a selfish jackass.

More silence.

He added, "It'll be dangerous...maybe even life-threatening."

She said, "I'm in."

"You sure?"

Letting out a long breath, she said, "Yes. I'm doing this for Cassie and Nina."

"Good reason," Brack said. "I'll pick you up in thirty minutes."

As usual, he was on the opposite side of town from where he wanted to go. Thirty minutes turned into forty-five, thanks to the late rush-hour traffic. Tara was ready when he finally arrived. She opened the door on his first knock, a medium-sized purse hanging from her shoulder. She turned off the light.

They walked down the one flight of stairs to his car.

"How's Mr. Grumpy?" he asked.

"Fine. I think he liked meeting you. The next day he looked around as if to see if I'd brought anyone with me for him to play with."

"I really like my dog and everything about him, but Grumpy is, like, on a whole other level. His personality is magnified by his size."

"He's my baby."

"If anything that weighs five tons could be considered a baby."

Brack held the door of the Mazda open for her and she got in. He noticed she wore flat shoes, Capris, and a tank top to battle the night heat.

When he slid into the driver's seat, she asked, "So what do we know?"

He told her about the list of addresses Darcy had given him. As he narrated the link to Vito and the Expedition he'd tried to follow earlier, he realized how easily he'd been allowed to tail that SUV. Those gangsters had intentionally waited for him to arrive at Cassie's to then lure him away from the restaurant.

But why wouldn't they simply get rid of him after they'd warned him with the Porsche? Now they knew what his latest ride looked like.

As he started the car, Tara said, "I've never done this before."

"Mostly, it's slow, tedious waiting," he said, locating Townsend's address already entered in the navigation system. "Hope you don't mind peeing in the bushes."

She laughed. "I've done worse."

Cutting his eyes to hers, he asked, "What's worse than peeing in the bushes?"

"A whole bunch of things."

The banter helped him think about something other than Darcy marrying her fiancé, his battered friend in the hospital, and,

BIG CITY HEAT   143

most tragically, Nina's family mourning the loss of a wife and mother.

The GPS let them know with a beep it had homed in on their destination and was ready to show them where to go.

He said, "You can share only the PG version with me if you want. It could be a long night."

"Some things are meant to be remembered, not shared."

Having his own file of memories he never disclosed, he understood the concept. "Sorry, didn't mean to pry."

She said, "I'll share a few if you will."

Chapter Twenty-Two

Wednesday, ten p.m.

Atlanta's Midtown. Artsy. Yuppie. Alternative. Expensive. All good for Brack and Tara, because he could think of more than a few circumstances in which an attractive black woman sporting inked-up arms sitting together with an unkempt white man might raise suspicion. This location would not be one of them.

The neighborhood was gentrified in the late seventies and lit up by streetlights that showed trees lining the sidewalks and nice cars parked on the street.

Brack did a slow roll-by on the lookout for the black SUV. It wasn't parked in Townsend's driveway.

One spot was close enough to provide a decent view.

Before he picked up Tara, he'd stopped at a convenience store and purchased stakeout food—peanut M&Ms and bottles of water. Now he took the bag from the backseat and offered her water and candy. She took the water and resisted the sugar. That was okay. After an hour of sitting, all refusals would go out the window.

A hundred and thirty-five minutes later, the pound bag of candy was gone. So was half of the water. They'd each adopted a strict regimen so as to reduce the need to relieve themselves and possibly give their position away, bushes or not.

At a hundred and thirty-six minutes, the SUV drove up to the house and parked in the drive.

A man got out and entered the brownstone.

"Showtime," Brack said.

Tara said, "Are we in a movie?"

"Nah. Reality is so much more interesting."

Saying excuse me, he reached over and popped the glovebox. Mutt's thirty-eight felt cold to the touch.

"This *is* serious, isn't it?"

Sensing the change in mood, he recognized that a new reality had set in for her. "This guy is not to be taken lightly."

"What's our plan?"

He sucked in some air and exhaled a long breath. "Recon the house. See if we can get in there. I'd like to grab Townsend and see what he knows, but he is dangerous. We shouldn't forget that." And, Brack thought, try not to kill him before he talked. Tara didn't need to know the kill part. If things went south, she'd have an out on premeditation.

He stuck the gun down the front waistband of his cargo shorts. "Let's circle the house first."

They got out and he placed the car's key fob on top of the front tire. Pointing to it, he said, "If this doesn't end well, you need to split. Immediately."

In situations like this, direct routes made the most sense. Also best not to give the impression of anything other than visiting a friend.

Townsend's place had a decent front porch. The light was off. In fact, all the lights in the house were off, even though the SUV had arrived ten minutes earlier. They walked past the front of the house and cut down the darkened left side, away from the streetlamps.

All the windows appeared closed. In the shadows, Brack pulled out the thirty-eight and raised his hand to Tara to stop. They were two steps from the backyard, also dark. Aside from the sounds of the city, all was quiet. No dogs or cats. No crickets.

With his free hand, he motioned to Tara to stay put. He cocked the hammer back, extended the revolver out in front of him, and took a step into the backyard.

A gun fired and the bullet ricocheted off the back of the house, missing Brack by inches. He hit the deck and made a slow retreat.

The flash had been in front of him, to the left. It was tough to see in the darkness and he hoped Tara had already run for cover.

He said, "Hey, Townsend, we only want to talk."

Anther blast. The bullet thumped into the siding just above Brack's head. He backed around the corner to where he'd left Tara. She was gone.

Without knowing where Townsend hid, Brack didn't want to start firing. The neighborhood was dense enough that a stray bullet could hit another home, and maybe someone inside that home.

He stood, his back against Townsend's house, and eased his way to the street, his eyes and aim still trained on the rear. At the corner of the house, Brack took his attention away from the direction where Townsend had fired from and scanned the street. The familiar sound of a police siren could be heard in the distance, but getting closer. From experience, he calculated they'd be here in less than three minutes.

That gave him enough time to make one more run at Townsend. He crossed the front of the house and eased along the other side, glad he had the thirty-eight in his hands. Although his weapon of choice was a forty-five, he liked the way Mutt's gun punched holes in whatever it hit. If Townsend remained in a less than agreeable mood, the thirty-eight would do the trick.

Coming to the rear corner of the home from the opposite side, Brack peered around. The lighting was a little better, thanks to some porch lights that were turned on, presumably by the same folks who called the cops.

The backyard was empty. Brack lowered the weapon.

A car horn sounding a lot like the Mazda's blared from the street. Brack took that as his cue and ran toward it.

Tara waved frantically at him from the driver's seat. As soon as he got in, she floored it. He watched blue lights bounce off the homes behind them as they shot through a four-way stop and turned onto a side street.

"I heard gunshots," she said, out of breath. "I got so scared." She put a hand to her face.

He saw they were about to hit a parked car and grabbed the steering wheel.

Tara screamed and got the car back under control.

He said, "We need to pull over."

She slammed on the brakes at the next stop sign, stalling the engine. Then she rested her head against her hands on the steering wheel and cried.

There were no cars behind them at the moment.

He pulled the emergency brake, pushed the button to turn on the hazard lights, and put a hand on her to rub her shoulder while she shook and shuddered. He realized that calling her had been another one of his mistakes. He and Mutt had served in war. They were used to gunfire. Ordinary civilians were not. Darcy might have been an exception because she was anything but ordinary.

Brack said, "I'm sorry."

Her sobs subsided. She held up a hand. "No, I'm sorry."

"First time you ever been shot at?" Brack asked.

She looked at him. "We could have died back there." It was a statement, not a question.

"True," he said. "But we didn't."

Wiping her eyes with a tissue from her pocketbook, she asked, "How do you do it? I mean, it's as if you're already past it all."

"You need to hang around my friend, Brother Thomas. He quotes Psalm twenty-three, verse four whenever it gets tough."

A car sped around them.

She said, "I don't read the Bible."

He said, "'Even though I walk through the valley of the shadow of death, I will fear no evil, for You are with me.'"

"That helps you relax?"

"There's always a good side and a bad side. At least, there's a light gray side and a dark gray side."

"And we're on the right side, aren't we?"

"Yes. That's all we have to know."

"But aren't you afraid of dying?"

He said, "I should have died a long time ago."

"So what is this?" she asked. "You don't care? Thanks a lot. It would have been nice to know I got into a car with someone with a death wish."

"I don't have a death wish," he said. "I just don't worry about it. At least my own death."

"You do worry about other people dying?"

"Of course. Especially those I'm responsible for."

She touched his face with the back of her hand. "You're not responsible for me. I'm a big girl."

"Yeah," he said, "but I got careless."

People think they're okay with danger, but most don't have a clue. Brack had forgotten that fact and now Tara would have nightmares of gunshots for a while, tough act or not.

Someone honked a horn behind them. Brack rolled down his window and flagged them around. They passed by, flipping him the bird.

Watching the car and its rude occupants pass, Tara said, "I guess we should get going. Where to now?"

"I think it's time to take you home."

"Don't be like that," she said. "I'm okay. As long as no one else shoots at us."

"That's the problem," he said. "I can't make any promises. Townsend might have attacked Cassie and killed Nina. This has already been taken up a few notches."

With a sigh, she opened her car door and got out. He did the same.

They crossed the front of the car at the same time, the headlights illuminating them. He stopped. So did she.

Eye to eye, hers a little puffy, she gave him a smile. "You really are crazy, aren't you?"

"Where'd you hear that?"

"Cassie. She said that for the right reason, you and Mutt will stop at nothing."

He had no response.

"Is Regan the right reason?" she asked.

The question surprised Brack. But he already knew the answer.

"No. Mutt is." At that moment, he thought she understood.

She said, "You're here to protect Mutt."

"I'm here to keep him from doing anything stupid. Like going after Vito himself." And I'm here to see Darcy, if only for one last time, he thought.

Stepping back, she said, "So you go after him yourself? Is that really any smarter?"

"At least Mutt's not in the crosshairs." Something occurred to Brack. "Tara, you took on three guys at one time and probably would have beaten them all whether I helped or not."

"So?"

"Any one of them could have had a gun," he said.

She bit the inside of her cheek, her mouth forming a sideways kiss.

He said, "See what I mean? It wasn't your time or mine. All we can do is keep moving forward."

"That was in reaction to the unexpected," she said. "This is deliberate retaliation. I'm not sure if I can do this."

"I don't blame you."

"But you're still going after Vito, aren't you?"

He propped a sandal on the car's front bumper.

"Okay," she said. "I'm in. All the way. But first let's go see Cassie."

"Good."

"Really?" she asked, moving in close. "You aren't worried I might freak out again?"

Her face was inches from his. He could smell her light perfume and feel her breath.

They stood that way for a few seconds.

She said, "You don't rattle easily, do you?"

"No." Not since Afghanistan.

*   *   *

As he piloted them through Midtown Brack used the hands-free option to dial Darcy. This time of night, traffic was lighter, but still no picnic.

She answered with a question. "Find Townsend?"

"Yeah," he said. "He shot at me and Tara."

"You guys got shot at? How's Tara?"

"I'm fine," came the voice to Brack's right. "Just a little rattled."

Darcy said, "So Townsend's our man."

"One of them," he agreed.

His favorite reporter said, "Where are you now?"

"Tara wants to check on Cassie," he said. "We're heading to the hospital." Besides, he thought, it's the safest place he could think of for the time being. Even though visiting hours were over, at the moment Tara probably couldn't handle any more gunfire.

"I can log into my network's database from home," Darcy said. "I'll see what else I can find on Townsend."

They hung up and he parked in the same spot in the hospital lot he'd used before. He led Tara past the receptionist to the waiting room where he'd last seen Mutt.

Mutt wasn't there.

One of the nurses said she thought he'd left about thirty minutes ago but didn't say where he was going. She didn't know if he'd gotten a cab or not. Brack asked to see Cassie.

Against the rules, they were led to the Intensive Care Unit. Cassie's room looked similar to any other hospital room he'd been in before. She lay sleeping. Wires hung off her connected to the monitoring machines beside her that blinked quietly in the background. The nurse said Cassie had been in and out of consciousness since she arrived and the police were on standby to get a statement.

Cassie's face was beaten pretty badly. One eye had swollen shut.

Tara touched Cassie's hand, grasping it lightly, and bent down and kissed her forehead.

Brack stepped out of the room and called Mutt. He answered on the second ring.

"Where are you?" he asked.

Mutt said, "On my way to see Hugh. Nina's husband."

"Want some company?"

"You wanna come?"

He said, "Me and Tara."

"She wit you?"

"Yeah." Brack told him what happened with Townsend. "Darcy's getting us all the intel she has on this cold-blooded murderer."

"Good. Get over to my house. I'll pick you up there."

Brack hung up and went back to the room. Tara had pulled a chair close to the bed. She sat looking at Cassie and holding her hand.

He said, "You're welcome to hang around here if you want. I'll come back for you."

Looking away from Cassie to him, she asked, "Are you leaving?"

"Mutt will meet me at his house. Then we're heading over to visit Nina's husband."

Tara said, "This is so terrible what happened. I can't believe this is real."

"I'm sorry."

He waited to see what she wanted to do. Eventually she got up and moved the chair back to the corner of the room.

With a deep breath, she said, "Okay."

Twenty minutes later they pulled into Mutt's driveway. His white Cadillac was there. So was Brother Thomas's Volvo. That answered the question about whether Mutt had taken a cab when leaving the hospital.

They found Brother Thomas and Mutt seated at the kitchen table, untouched cups of coffee in front of them. Brack introduced

Tara to Brother Thomas. Mutt got two more mugs and filled them with coffee. Brack took his black. Tara added a few splashes of milk to hers.

"This is bad, Opie."

Brack nodded.

Brother Thomas said, "You didn't start this mess, mm-hmm."

But Brack knew they were going to finish it.

As if reading his thoughts, both his friend and his pastor looked at him. "You don't have to finish it either."

Brack didn't play poker with his friends for several reasons, one being that they could already tell what was in his mind.

Tara said, "Vito's got money and connections and power."

"And a whole lotta guns and muscle," Mutt added, no doubt thinking of Cassie's heavy bruising.

"But he isn't on the right side of the line," Brack said. "Sooner or later he's bound to fall."

Brother Thomas said, "I suggest we visit with Nina's husband and go from there."

The apartment where Nina had lived with her family was located close to Lenox Mall. The visitors trudged to the second floor of a three-story unit. Hugh answered the door with a solemn look while he held a little boy in his arms. Another small boy stood by his side, clutching his father's leg.

Mutt introduced everyone.

Brother Thomas said, "You mind if we come in and say a few prayers with you and your sons?"

Hugh nodded and opened the door wider so the visitors could enter.

Within the last year, Brother Thomas and Brack had worked with the Charleston Police Department and informed a murder victim's next of kin. That was a very somber situation, but easy compared to trying to look these boys in the eye to offer condolences. How did one attempt to encourage kids when their mother would never come home again?

The longer Brack stayed in this grief-heavy home, the angrier he got. At the ones who killed Nina, sure. But also at himself. He'd seen the Expedition in the restaurant's parking lot. And thanks to Darcy he'd already gotten the requisite tie-in to Vito. But he didn't react quickly enough. In a way, this tragedy was his fault too.

And he'd have to carry that with him.

Brother Thomas had all of them sit around the living room holding hands while he prayed for Hugh and the boys, Travis and Monte.

By the time the four visitors got out of there, Brack was far from at peace. He wanted blood. No, he really wanted more death. It was the only punishment left. The men who did this would pay for it with their lives. And he would have no regrets about *that*.

They rode back to Mutt's in Brother Thomas's Volvo, Tara and Brack in the backseat.

Seeming to sense Brack's mood, Brother Thomas said, "Before you go off and blow up everything in the city, Brother Brack, we ought to have a little talk."

"What's there to talk about?" Brack asked, not taking his eyes off the late-night scene along of Peachtree Street.

The pastor said, "I think we better have us a plan first, mm-hmm."

"Sure. My plan involves gunshots and blunt force trauma."

Tara asked, "Yours or theirs?"

Brack said, "Et tu, Brutus?"

"She right, Opie," Mutt said. "I don't wanna have to go to your funeral along with Nina's."

"All right, Mutt. Tell me about Regan."

"What you wanna know?"

What came to mind was that she better be worth all this. Otherwise Brack might shoot her himself. "Why did she choose to go with Vito?"

"Cassie thinks she got brainwashed," Mutt said.

Tara asked, "Is that what you think?"

"I think no. She got a drug addiction. And she crazy."

Brack said, "She could die in all this."

Brother Thomas asked, "What do you mean, Brother Brack?"

"Vito understands that all the trouble we are causing and about to cause is because of her. He might not think quite so highly of her anymore. Especially when it begins to hurt his wallet."

"She made her bed," Mutt said.

An interesting observation, because Brack was thinking exactly that but didn't consider it appropriate to say.

Brother Thomas said, "First things first, mm-hmm."

Chapter Twenty-Three

Vito sat at a desk in his home office talking on the phone with a broker from the West Coast.

He said, "I've got the shipment ready. Six crates, twenty in each crate."

"Excellent," came the voice over the phone.

As he ended the call and sat the phone on the desk, Regan entered the room, and Vito smiled at his woman.

She walked behind him and wrapped her arms around his neck, kissing his cheek. "You look happy."

He reached up and took her hands in his. "I am. We've got a buyer for the ivory."

Regan circled around him and sat in his lap. "Wanna celebrate?"

Before he could reply, his phone buzzed. Again. He noted it was Townsend and, to Regan, said, "Hold that thought." He answered the call.

Townsend said, "Pelton was at my house."

Suddenly concerned, Vito said, "You didn't kill him, did you?"

"No. I shot at him but missed on purpose."

"Good. We have to let the plan work out."

Townsend said, "I hope you know what you're doing. Personally, I think we need to kill him now before he gets too close. I had the perfect opportunity tonight to get rid of him for good."

Vito said, "My business, my plan. You run security. It's your job to make sure he doesn't get too close."

Chapter Twenty-Four

Thursday, one a.m.

Brack stood around the table with Brother Thomas and Mutt discussing their options when Darcy walked in Mutt's house.

She kissed Brother Thomas and Mutt on their cheeks and shook Tara's hand. All Brack got was a nod, as if he were the town leper.

Mutt said, "This is bad news, girl."

Darcy said, "I'm so sorry."

"Ain't yo' fault. But we gotta stop 'em."

To Darcy, Brother Thomas said, "I'm afraid I've failed to convince them to let the po-lice handle this, mm-hmm."

Brack said, "You won't get her to agree with you either. She's as gung ho as I am. Maybe even more ruthless."

Darcy arched an eyebrow. "Maybe?"

"You're right," he said. "Definitely more ruthless."

"Now that we have my feelings clear," Darcy said, "here are a few things I learned recently. The first is that Vito is trying to expand his empire. The added heat we've put on him so far is why he's lashing out."

"Who's he taking market share from?" Brack asked.

Mutt said, "Xavier Kualas."

Darcy nodded. "Right. Only he's no featherweight either."

Tara said, "He's the biggest thug in the city."

"Except he wears twenty-thousand-dollar suits and has a chauffeur." Darcy took out her phone and tapped the screen. "This is him."

She showed Brack and Brother Thomas a picture of a clean-cut white man about Brack's age. Kualas looked more like a game-show host than a thug, with a thick head of dark politician's hair parted on the side, a clean-shaven face, and perfect white teeth.

Tara said, "He's skated on every arrest." She looked at her watch. "Look, I've got work in the morning. I need to go home and get some sleep."

Darcy and Brack dropped Tara off at her apartment and stopped for breakfast at the Majestic diner. After he devoured a plate of eggs, bacon, and hash browns, Brack found himself feeling the effects of a long night.

"How's Paige?" she asked.

"Busy with our second location."

"How long do you think she'll stay with you?"

He'd already wondered how long she'd want to continue as his manager after her nuptials. "Unless she decides to have more children or open up her own place, I think she'll stay." And if she decided to buy Brack out, he might sell. After all, Hawaii was waiting.

"How are you doing?" he asked.

Checking her face with a compact mirror from her purse, Darcy answered, "Busy."

"Seems you're adapting well to your new environment."

She snapped the compact shut. "Was there any doubt?"

He smiled. "Still the same old weather girl."

"'Old' being relative to what, exactly?"

"Certainly not me," he said. "So what's next?"

"You look like you need some sleep."

Stretching his arms above his head, he said, "Sleep would be nice."

"It really doesn't get to you, does it?"

"What?"

"Being shot at."

Truth be told, he liked the adrenaline rush. He liked it a lot. Afghanistan had chewed him up and spit him out. When he returned to the States, both damaged and healed, he was a different person. And he knew it. One who rolled the danger dice as often as he could. He found it best not to dwell too much on what that meant.

"Not when I know I'm on the good side," he said.

"It won't matter which side you're on if you get killed."

He took out his wallet and placed thirty dollars on the table. "Probably not in the grand scheme of things. But I believe we've got to make the most of the life we've been given while we have it. I don't want to get to the pearly gates and have to explain the things I should have done but didn't."

She slid out of her seat like a teenager, giving him a glimpse of the girl she'd been in high school. He continually enjoyed finding something new to like about her.

The sky was getting ready for dawn when Brack fell into bed. Six hours of sleep later, he awoke and got some lunch, since it was close to noon. While seated in a Wendy's dining area, he got a phone call and recognized the Atlanta number.

"Hey, Shana from Gecko Row," he said.

"Hey, yourself," she replied.

"I'd ask you to join me for breakfast, but I'm almost finished."

"Too bad for you," she said. "Twelve o'clock is considered lunchtime here in the big city, by the way. Listen, I overheard Levin and a few others talking last night in the bar, and I didn't put it together until this morning that they were probably talking about you."

Levin was the name Sonia had given him when he interviewed her at the women's shelter last Sunday. But Shana had not spoken that name to him before this, so he asked, "Who is Levin to Vito?"

"His number-one guy on the street."

"What made you think they were talking about me?"

"They mentioned they were looking for the guy who accosted Mindy and Kai three nights ago in some restaurant. At first I thought it must be some creep, until I realized the girls were already out with a creep. That foreign businessman. So this morning it hit me that it was probably you they were talking about. Am I right?"

"I did try to talk with the girls in a restaurant, but they screamed so I had to take off."

"Be careful," she said. "You are 'a person of interest,' as they put it. Is it true they blew up your Porsche?"

"Unfortunately."

"These guys like to spend their off time at this dive called the Lion's Den." She gave him the details.

A plan formulated in his head, and, to his surprise, Shana wanted to play along. Apparently she didn't like these guys any more than he did.

An hour later, Brack walked alone into the Lion's Den. TSTL could describe his life sometimes—too stupid to live. Five familiar-looking motorcycles in the lot behind the building told him members of the gang were here.

The bar, constructed of old steel shipping containers stacked and welded together, defined industrial recycling. He liked the concept, which could probably withstand a hurricane. Not that Atlanta got too many category fivers. He thought about how to adopt the style to his next beach bar back home, if there were ever to be a third.

Probably because no one liked being in the vicinity of Vito's henchmen, the bar was empty of customers other than the bikers. And their women. A quick count turned up five men and five women, plus two other females comprising the wait staff.

As usual when Brack walked into something like this, all eyes fell on him. So before anyone got the grand idea to start shooting, he announced, "I've got a message for Vito."

All five bikers pulled out pistols and aimed them at him.

The bartender reached for a phone and punched three numbers. Into the phone she said, "Come quick. There are men with guns."

The biker Brack sensed to be in charge, Levin, he guessed, said, "You're a dead man."

Brack said, "Since the cops are already on their way, today is probably not my day. Or yours. Tell Vito he went too far this time. You idiots killed an innocent mother and put another woman in the ICU."

One of the bikers said, "Innocent? Waren't no one innocent."

Levin said, "Shut up, Johnny."

Behind Brack, five armed police officers stormed in the door, knocking him to the ground. After that, all hell broke loose.

Johnny shot the officer closest to him. The four other bikers immediately up-ended tables to use as shields as they all opened fire. The police ducked for cover and returned fire. And Brack, in the middle of it all, and the only one without a gun, crawled out the door. More police arrived, two of them dragging him off the ground and dumping him behind one of the cruisers.

A loud explosion blew through the front door, followed by smoke. In the chaos, Brack thought he heard motorcycles start up and roar away.

Seconds later, in a cloud of smoke, two officers walked through the door, one of them supporting the other.

An ambulance pulled up behind the police cruisers and was immediately waved back.

Five more officers entered the building, guns drawn and bulletproof vests in place.

Brack overheard one of the cops say, "Dammit! They got away."

Later, he learned that one of the bikers had set off a smoke canister while another threw a grenade, which was what blew out the front door. Those guys were prepared for an ambush.

Two officers got shot and Brack knew he was responsible.

Several more received shrapnel injuries from the grenade. But if the cops hadn't shown up, thereby validating his bluff, he would have been killed. And if he hadn't walked into the Lion's Den to start with, four officers wouldn't be on their way to the hospital.

All in all, not a good day.

Detective Nichols arrived at the scene and took Brack's statement.

He asked, "Why did you think this was a good idea?"

"I wanted Vito to get a message."

"What message was that?" he asked. "That you're dumb enough to let them take you out?"

Brack didn't respond.

"And what would have happened if we hadn't shown up?" Nichols seemed to think about what he'd just said. "You knew we'd show up, didn't you?"

Brack didn't say anything.

Nichols's jaw muscle twitched and he balled his fists.

"You bastard!" Nichols got in Brack's face. "Four good men are in the ICU all because of your little stunt."

Anything Brack said would be the wrong thing, so he kept silent. It hadn't occurred to him that the police would storm the place. Brack thought they would follow protocol, which stressed caution over aggression. Or that the bikers would shoot at cops. The stakes were inching higher.

Chapter Twenty-Five

Thursday, five p.m.

Darcy and a one-man crew showed up outside the Lion's Den.

While the cameraman set up, she asked Brack, "How dumb are you?"

Pretty dumb, he supposed. "They opened fire on the police."

"I know. Word is you are responsible for getting two officers shot."

"Actually," Brack said, "bad tactics got them shot. What set the ball rolling was poor judgment on my part. And unfortunately there are four heading to the hospital, not two."

"Did you really confront them by yourself?"

"Yes."

"What's going on?"

"What do you mean?"

"It's not like you to be that stupid."

He took out a piece of gum, unwrapped it, and popped it in his mouth. "I had inside help."

She chewed her lip, processing this new information. "The one who called the police?"

"Yes."

"How was that an inside job? She would have done that anyway."

"She called them two minutes before I walked inside. The call she made that everyone in the room saw after I walked in was fake." Shana had hooked me up on that one, he thought.

Hands on hips, Darcy said, "They still could have blown your head off."

"True, but the risk had been reduced."

"Not enough."

She was right. When all the bikers simultaneously pulled their guns on him, Brack thought his time was up. That was the closest shave he ever had, but he wasn't about to admit it to Darcy.

Vito's men must now be numero uno on the Atlanta Police Department's apprehension list. For attempted murder of even one cop, the department probably had an unofficial "shoot on sight" mentality. And in this case, Brack didn't mind one bit. With any luck, by the end of the week there would be five fewer bikers on the road. If the police didn't get them, Brack planned to take Mutt's Caddy and run them over.

Darcy asked, "Why are you so careless with your life?"

"That's fresh coming from the gal who traded blackmail material for access to an underground brothel run by Chinese hoods."

She opened her mouth to say something, then stopped.

Brack knew he could be very stubborn when he was in the wrong. Arguing with him at those times was an exercise in futility, and this was one of those times. His phone vibrated. He didn't recognize the number except for the Atlanta area code. He answered.

"Mr. Pelton," a male voice said. "This is Xavier Kualas."

The infamous Xavier Kualas requested a private meeting to discuss—as he put it—current events. Brack figured he had nothing to lose. Darcy believed meeting with the biggest hood in Atlanta was a bad idea, so of course Brack thought it was a great idea.

Their meeting was to take place at seven p.m. on the roof of the tallest building in the city. Kualas had arranged that they not be disturbed, which in itself was disturbing.

At the first floor reception desk, Brack gave the name Kualas to the security guard and was shown where to find the elevators. After a nearly instantaneous ride up, he was still dealing with his loss of hearing when the doors opened and two men greeted him. They could have been ex-Atlanta Falcon defensive linemen. Each stood half a foot taller and a hundred pounds heavier than Brack. For once, he kept his smart mouth shut while they patted him down. One ran some sort of scanner over him, probably checking for a wire.

With the TSA-style preboarding exercise complete, Kualas's security detail led him to a stairwell and motioned for him to head up. The door at the top opened before he reached it, as if someone were monitoring his progress. Another large bodyguard gestured with an open hand toward the center of the roof. The next images that filled Brack's sight were the rooftops of the surrounding buildings, then the sprawling city that stretched as far as he could see.

Xavier Kualas watched him, hands behind his back.

Inhaling the high altitude air mixed with city smog, Brack approached the most powerful man in Atlanta.

Kualas did not look like the thug he was. He wore a conservative navy suit, white shirt, and maroon silk tie. Brack sensed Saville Row more than Versace. Kualas did not offer a hand. "Mr. Pelton. Thank you for coming."

A slight breeze wasn't enough to blow this evil man off the roof. Brack contemplated throwing him off, knowing his guards would make sure he went next.

Kualas turned and gestured for him to follow. They walked slowly away from his bodyguards.

Brack said, "You called this meeting."

"Have you heard the expression, 'The enemy of my enemy is my friend'?"

Recognizing immediately where this conversation was headed, Brack merely said, "Yes."

Glancing at Brack as they walked, Kualas said, "Consider me a friend."

Great, Brack thought. Friended by the biggest pimp in the southeast. "Thanks, but I already have enough."

"But you don't know what I have to offer," he said.

"Sure I do. Pain, suffering, and misery. Not necessarily in that order."

Kualas stopped. "Don't be naïve. I've a larger collection of emissaries than your friend, Darcy Wells, does. And you and I both know that is saying something."

Brack knew he was right. Mutt had told him that Darcy's impact on local Atlanta news could best be described as a brick through a plate-glass window. She had that kind of effect on situations.

Continuing, Kualas said, "I have two hundred men ready to go now and I can have another five hundred with the snap of my fingers."

"If you did your research," Brack said, "then you know I already fought a war."

"Yes."

"These walking refrigerators you have are not soldiers. They're just big targets."

Kualas looked away. "I see."

"No, I don't think you do," Brack said. "I came to town to help with a missing person case. It's gone downhill since."

"From what I know about you, downhill is exactly the situation in which you excel."

"There will be more death before this is over," Brack said. "You may think you have some leverage on me up here surrounded by your overgrown lapdogs, but you and I both know what you really are scared about is collateral damage. Well, my advice to you is to clean up your act and get out of town, because I'm going to blow up Vito and anyone else involved. When I get done, everyone associated with him will wish they hadn't been."

Holding out a hand, Kualas said, "Then I guess I don't have anything to worry about."

Brack met his gaze but didn't shake his hand. "If I see you or any of the men here within a hundred yards of me or my friends, I'll shoot to kill."

A hand rested on his shoulder and Brack felt something hard poke him in the small of his back. One of the goons said, "I think it's time for you to leave."

Kualas said, "It didn't have to go down like this."

Smiling, Brack said, "I wouldn't have it any other way."

In actuality, he'd rather not have a gun jammed into his back and be surrounded by all these meatheads. He'd have preferred a one-on-one with Kualas. But it never worked out that way.

The next ten seconds unfolded in a blur.

The door to the roof blew off its hinges. Twenty armed men in black body armor poured through the opening. In an instant they subdued all of Kualas's men. A helicopter appeared out of the proverbial blue.

Detective Nichols hung out the open door with a bullhorn. "Xavier Kualas, you're surrounded."

The bodyguards raised their hands in surrender.

Kualas reached into his jacket.

"Don't!" Brack shouted.

Four S.W.A.T. team members shot Kualas.

The particular section of the Atlanta police headquarters where Brack happened to be placed smelled of heavy disinfectant and the unwashed odor of broken lives. This time, instead of being made to wait in an interrogation room, he sat alone at a long metal table in a bare-walled conference room. Without his phone or his dog to keep him company, he did what he usually did when detained by the police. He put his head on the table and closed his eyes.

Last year, when he'd been in a similar situation in Charleston, an attractive detective named Rosalita Jackson interrogated him. Detective Nichols, who seemed assigned to Brack specifically, did not possess Rosalita's attributes, but at least he acted like an honorable man.

Brack raised his head when the door opened.

Detective Nichols pulled out a chair across from him and sat.

Yawning, Brack said, "You want to tell me why you had to take out the biggest hood in Atlanta?"

"He took himself out."

"Yeah, right."

"The real question is why you were with him."

It occurred to Brack that Nichols knew more than he let on. This game of the police trying to get him to talk while giving nothing away was beyond old. "I'm sure you already have an idea."

"You're in a lot of trouble, Pelton," Nichols said.

"Yeah, well, go figure."

"For starters, interfering with a police investigation, conspiring with a known criminal, and trespassing."

Sitting back, Brack said, "My lawyer will eat you alive."

"Kualas has been under surveillance for possible terrorist activities. We can hold you without a lawyer and file it under national security."

Even though Nichols and his entourage did save him from being thrown off the building, Brack nevertheless felt the urge to pop Nichols in the mouth. He let it pass.

"Of course," Nichols said, his face suddenly all chipper, "there's a way out of this."

Of course there was. "And what would that be?"

Nichols hooked an arm over the back of his chair, as if totally relaxed.

When it became apparent he wasn't answering the question, Brack prompted, "You want me to work with you."

"Not exactly."

"Not exactly," Brack repeated.

"We'd like you to work *for* us. Unofficially, of course."

Brack looked up, not exactly for divine guidance. More to think about the offer without having to see Nichols's face. Water had stained several tiles of the dropped ceiling. "Why would I want to do that?"

"Because we can help you."

"What makes you think I need help?"

Nichols inhaled through his nose and blew out a long breath. "The last time Kualas had someone on the roof, they ended up on the sidewalk. And not by taking the down elevator."

"That was then. This is now. I haven't taken orders since I left the Marines and I don't plan on starting again any time soon."

"Still," he said, "you don't have a whole lot of options."

There it was. Jail or slavery. Nichols was right, Brack didn't have much of a choice. Both options were equally restricting. Brack chose the option that allowed him to at least walk around outside.

Chapter Twenty-Six

Thursday, two minutes to midnight

The cork popped off, and champagne erupted from the bottle like lava from a volcano, the expensive libation spilling on the equally expensive carpet of the penthouse. Vito grinned and poured the celebratory liquid into the three waiting flutes. With that taken care of, he poured a fourth for himself, set the bottle back in the ice, and lifted his own glass.

Levin, Townsend, and Regan raised theirs.

Vito said, "To Kualas. May he burn in hell."

In unison, his three companions said, "Hear, hear!"

They clinked glasses and sipped the bubbly.

"There is no stopping us now," Vito said. "The world is our oyster." What he said to himself was, "The world is *my* oyster and Regan is my princess. You other two are along for the ride only as long as you help me get more."

Regan kissed him. "It's all ours now, baby."

Vito smiled at her. It certainly was. He looked at Levin and Townsend. "Gentlemen, it's time to get to work expanding our new empire."

Chapter Twenty-Seven

An hour later, Brack stood on the balcony of Tara's second-floor apartment staring at the cars below, his deal with Nichols still on his mind. For various reasons, he'd asked Darcy to meet him here.

Tara came out and handed him the glass of water he'd asked for. "You're saying the police coerced you into working for them?"

"Something like that."

"I thought you said Nichols threatened you with some form of National Security violation."

"He did. I wanted to tell him to go pound sand. Personally, I think they like me on the street. I'm helping them clean up a few of their messes."

The doorbell rang and Tara went to answer it. Through the open screen door, he heard Darcy's voice. The two women walked out onto the patio.

Brack said, "I miss the ocean."

Darcy said, "Me too. But right now, we have bigger issues."

Facing her, he said, "Yeah, like Kualas almost throwing me off the roof."

"I called Detective Nichols to tip him off, and guess what? He already knew about it."

He had to let that register. Several things came directly to mind. Like how conveniently Kualas met his maker. And how it could have gone really bad for him if the cops hadn't shown up. "You think Vito had a hand in it?"

"Of course," Darcy said. "He is the one who would benefit the most if Kualas died."

Tara suggested that they bring this kind of talk inside. Brack and Darcy followed her in and she shut the sliding-glass door.

Darcy said, "You charge headfirst into brick walls. Meetings with Kualas seldom end well. In fact, five murders in the last six months have him as a common denominator."

Brack folded his arms across his chest.

Darcy continued, "I'm not going to apologize for doing what I could to save your life. Thanks to me, we know that you were probably set up on both sides by Vito. Now, you can stand here and pout or we can pool our resources and go after Vito."

After another six-hour stretch in his hotel bed, Brack sat at the kitchen table in Mutt's house across from Brother Thomas and drank a glass of sweet tea. He missed his dog. It was the second day Shelby was "vacationing" with Trish in the north Georgia mountains without him. Realizing it was a good idea for them to be away from the city, Brack didn't object—aloud. He didn't want Vito to have any more leverage on him than he already had.

With Kualas out of the picture, Vito could now control all of Atlanta. Logic would dictate he'd begin by consolidating and eliminating any of Kualas's loyal henchmen. Brack didn't have long to wait for the fallout.

Friday morning's breaking news reported not only the death of Kualas by the police, but also several immediate murders of members of his organization by persons unknown. Vito had lost no time in eliminating most of his wannabe competition.

Detective Nichols, Darcy, and Brack had done together what Vito would never have been able to do alone. Enabled him to grow more powerful.

Brother Thomas said, "What you gonna do now?"

Every few seconds Brack flicked his uncle's Vietnam Zippo open and closed. Since he'd become a reformed smoker after puking his guts out into a trash can thanks to Tara, he'd considered taking up Mutt's vapor habit. But he'd already replaced his vice reacquired from his time in Afghanistan, cigarettes, with his more recent addiction of choice, cigars. He didn't need another one at the moment.

He said, "I'm kind of stumped here. Vito just doubled the size of his organization."

"Remember, Brother Brack, Vito is not yo' focus. Neither is vengeance, mm-hmm."

"You're right. I really need to be spending my time and energies trying to get Regan out of the situation she seems perfectly content to be in."

"Just because she think it's the right thing for her don't mean it is."

All that girl wanted was more sex, more drugs, more money, more perceived power, and more abuse, in whatever order it was dished out to her. And she'd found the perfect place to get her cocktail of self-annihilation.

"So what you're saying is all I need do is figure out how to bust into Vito's stronghold and remove one of his women."

"No," Brother Thomas said. "What I'm sayin' is we need to catch her outside unawares and drag her miserable behind back to reality."

"I know what you want, Brother Thomas. I want it too. But—and I can't believe I'm the one saying this—we cannot go in blasting."

From the doorway, Darcy said, "I can't believe you're the one saying that either."

The men looked up.

She said, "What we need is to go after his money. I might have a way to do that."

In an empty parking lot off Peachtree Street, Detective Nichols sat on the hood of his cruiser when Darcy's Honda pulled up to it.

The detective walked up to Brack's open window. "What's this all about, Pelton? And why'd you bring the press?"

Brack said, "Thanks to me, you have only one dirtbag to deal with instead of two."

"Actually, I still have half a city full of dirtbags. Though you did help me get the biggest."

"We're here," Darcy said, "to help you get the other half."

"Tell me, how will 'we' do that?"

Brack said, "We need what you have on Vito."

"Why would I give you that?"

"You wanted me to sign on with you. Consider this my way of making good."

"I can't simply hand over evidence to you."

"I realize what you want, Nichols, is a nice public arrest and guilty verdict. That is not our goal, but we'll help where we can."

"I'm still not hearing anything that says I should violate protocol."

Darcy said, "What if I told you I have an informant in Vito's camp?"

"Big deal. We've got twenty."

"Obviously," Brack said, "they are quite the help."

Nichols smirked. "More than you know."

This wasn't going the way Brack wanted. His uncle had taught him about the rules of negotiation. Based on that instruction, he knew the next person who spoke would be conceding victory. He kept quiet. So did Darcy.

"Okay," Detective Nichols said. "I'll give you what I have. Sadly, it isn't much."

Before Brack could speak, Darcy said, "We're supposed to believe that you don't have much information on Vito. After all these years? I've got a fair amount and I've been in Atlanta less than a year."

Nichols opened his hands in a surrendering gesture. "I don't expect you to, but due to his immunity and the fact that he doesn't personally get his hands dirty, that is the truth."

"What about Townsend or Levin?" Brack asked him.

"Those two are a different story."

*   *   *

When their ten a.m. meeting with Nichols ended, Darcy left to review the information he provided. Needing a break, Brack took a daytrip to visit his dog in the mountains where Trish had taken him. The hour-long drive gave him a chance to reflect on the present situation. Overall, it was pretty dreary. Despite the demise of Kualas, he was no closer to Regan, or to the further entrenched Vito. Cassie was still in critical condition in the hospital. Nina was dead. And his beloved Porsche was a pile of ash.

Shelby greeted him by running out the door of Trish's mountain cabin and almost knocking him down. Was he really glad to see Brack or grateful that he'd been allowed to spend so much time with his best girlfriend?

Either way, the sight of his dog did Brack's heart good. He'd missed Shelby. Badly.

Trish said, "You don't look so good."

Probably because I'm still getting over almost falling from a hundred-story skyscraper, he thought.

He said, "Not getting much sleep."

"Well," she said, "there's a hammock on the back porch. Why don't you take a nap with Shelby while I prepare lunch?"

Who would argue with that? Within minutes, Shelby lay on his back at Brack's side and both were in dreamland.

An hour later Trish woke them. She'd prepared a nice lunch of pimento cheese and tuna salad sandwich wedges, and spinach leaves drizzled with balsamic vinegar. For dessert, peach cobbler. Brack washed it all down with a gallon of sweet tea.

She asked, "How are you really doing?"

Scratching behind Shelby's ears, he said, "Just peachy."

"Yeah, right. Chauncey says you have a horrible game face. He wants you to give him a call. Phone reception is best on the back porch."

Trish's husband was Brack's lawyer. He and Brack had a bit of a strained relationship last year when Chauncey withdrew as

Brack's counsel because he also represented a family trying to take over his Pirate's Cove bar.

To be fair, Chauncey withdrew from representing the family as well—a good thing because the whole mess ended up in a huge scandal for the family.

Brack stepped out onto the back porch of the cabin. From this setting high in the north Georgia mountains, the view of Kennesaw Mountain was amazing. And Brack had two bars of coverage available.

Chauncey's receptionist answered on the second ring and put him through.

Chauncey spoke in his smooth Charlestonian way. "Hey they-ah, Brack."

"Hey yourself," he said. "I'm up in the mountains in a cabin with your wife and my dog."

"Sounds like I should be wor-ried." A soft chuckle characterized the attorney's voice.

"Depends on what you have to tell me," Brack said. "You already know Trish has a crush on Shelby. One false step by either of us and I see her packing up and taking him with her."

"You don't have to ra-mind me about that," he said.

"She said you wanted me to give you a call."

"Yes." His tone changed from light-hearted to all business. "I understand you have some trouble over they-ah."

"What would give you that idea?"

"Way-ell, for one, you called my wife to come and watch your dog. You yourself told me she's li-able to run away and start a new life with him. The fact that you're takin' that risk means things are not currently in your fay-vah."

Brack smiled. "I guess I tipped my hand a little, didn't I? Yes, things are not going exactly as I'd planned." Cassie's getting attacked had not been a risk ever imagined.

"Kelvin Vito is an in-te-esting character," Chauncey said. "His business interests run the ga-ye-mut from real estate to drugs and prostitution and exotic animal poaching."

"Thanks to Darcy I did learn most of that," Brack said.

"Our famous news repor-tah is still he'ping you out, huh?" He already knew the background on Darcy and Brack.

"She's still willing to go slumming with me."

"Good, Brack. That's real good. You're going to need he'p with this one."

Brack thought about walking into a deathtrap less than twenty-four hours ago and had to agree with him. "I can think of a few reasons why you're right. Why do you think so?"

"Vito is a very powerful man. And I understand his main adversary is now off the books. But there's something you praw-bably don't know. He's got a handler."

"Handler?"

"He repor-arts to someone else."

"No kidding? Well, don't drag this out like some TV show. Who?"

"His grandfath-ah, Marcus. He lives in Mexico."

Brack thought about that. "I'd like you to send everything you have on this Marcus to Darcy." What he heard next sounded like a tap on a keyboard.

"Done."

"Thanks, Chauncey."

"Don't thank me," he said. "If something happens to you, my wife will take your dog. And she just might give me the boot in the pro-cess."

"You and I both know it. Better do all you can to keep me alive then." He hung up.

It took Darcy all of sixty seconds from the time Brack heard Chauncey send the file for her to call him.

Brack asked, "What's the weather forecast for today?"

"Very funny," she said. "I just got the file from Chauncey. Why'd you have him send it to me?"

"I'm out of town right now."

"Out of town? With whom? Wait, don't tell me. It's none of my business."

Did he hear a slight hint of jealousy in her tone? Hadn't ever heard that before. He let her think the worst. "How about if I meet you in an hour?" he asked.

"How about if I think about it?"

"Suit yourself," he said. "I'll be on my way back to the city in a few minutes. You can call me on the way, or whenever you want. I'd like to see what Chauncey sent you."

"You're with Trish, aren't you?" A pause. "You jerk." She hung up.

Another successful attempt to win her over. Zero for four? Six?

Chapter Twenty-Eight

Friday, six p.m.

That evening, Brother Thomas and Reverend Cleophus met Brack at Mutt's house. Mutt was still with Cassie at the hospital.

Brack said, "The situation is worse than we thought."

"How so?" Brother Thomas asked.

"Did you know Vito has to answer to someone else?"

"How is that worse?" Cleophus asked.

After a moment of contemplation, Brother Thomas explained, "Because Vito can't do anything without considering how he'll look to the boss."

Cleophus said, "Well, we all gotta answer to somebody."

"Yeah," Brack said, "but Vito would be much easier to deal with if he were the head of the snake. Instead of just cutting him out, we have to worry about his boss coming to town and taking over where Vito leaves off."

"There won't be no vacuum effect," Brother Thomas said.

"I'm not sure I understand what you two are really saying." Cleophus scratched his chin. "But I'll go along since both of you are saying the same thing."

The last time Brother Thomas and Brack agreed on something, they almost set a course for their own incarceration. Brack had to keep in mind that he didn't need to once again drag his good friend into the gutter with him.

That good friend then asked, "How is Trish doing?"

"Great. She's got this luxury cabin at the top of a mountain and complete access to my dog, who by the way, has the run of the place. And his diet is shot."

"So what's our plan?" Cleophus asked.

Brack wanted to say, "Kill Vito and drag Regan back to Cassie." Didn't, though.

As if sensing Brack's reluctance to answer, Brother Thomas said, "We gotta see exactly who Vito reports to."

A rap on the counter had them turn around, where Brack hoped that information was about to be shared.

Darcy smiled. "You guys need to be more careful. The door wasn't locked. I thought the whole reason you're staying at the hotel is to protect Mutt."

Brother Thomas said, "You can't be sneaking up on us, girl."

"Sorry if I scared you, Brother," she said, kissing him on the cheek.

Flustered, he said, "Well, okay then."

Brack said, "Rogue reporters are always lurking about."

"Save it." She held up her printouts. "Who wants to read about Marcus Valenzueala?"

Cleophus said, "I seen you on the news. You're real good, Miss." He introduced himself.

Darcy shook his hand. "Nice to meet you, Reverend. And thank you."

Brack said, "Are you going to share the file or just taunt us?"

She looked at Brack but handed the file to Brother Thomas.

As if suddenly thirsty, Brack stood, got four glasses out of Mutt's kitchen cupboard, and filled them with ice and sweet tea. Back in Charleston, Mutt's home was always clean but had slightly fewer accommodations than his current digs. Sweet tea being one of them.

As the glasses were handed around, Darcy reviewed the contents of the police file aloud. This Marcus was an interesting fellow. Seventy years old, he ran a very large empire that, in addition to Mexico, stretched across the southeast United States, from Texas to Florida to Virginia. The file showed his specialty to be methamphetamine, but he also ran girls and guns, whatever and wherever the demand was.

Cleophus said, "Meth seems low-rent for Vito."

"I agree," Darcy said. "I think he tolerates it in order to keep in good standing with his grandfather, Marcus."

"That might be how we get to him," Brack said.

Brother Thomas asked, "How does this Marcus get around the competition?"

Darcy said, "He tries to eliminate it where he can. Otherwise seems they all have loose agreements that are always in flux."

"With Kualas out of the picture," Brack said, "apparently thanks to me and Nichols, Vito now has the run of the city."

A little before nine p.m. a knock at the front door interrupted their conversation. Brack went to see who it was. Tara and her brother stood on the stoop holding two white shopping bags.

She held up hers. "We brought Chinese."

Her brother said, "Enough for an army."

"Good," Brack said, "because an army is what's here."

He led them to the kitchen and got plates out of a cupboard while they set out the food. The good Reverends eyed the food like vultures homing in on a fresh kill.

All exchanged the latest news and shared the great takeout until they were stuffed. Then, after they'd cleaned up and cracked wise over their fortune cookies, they sat around Mutt's living room discussing their next moves. Generally Brack preferred stirring the pot and seeing what popped up. But Vito did not rattle easy. Certainly not as easily as his goons.

Wanting input from Mutt, they took two cars to the hospital to visit with him and Cassie, who'd been moved out of the ICU.

Mutt was sitting in Cassie's room when the group walked in. He looked at the six of them and chuckled. "Dang if y'all don't look like you belong on one a' them bad reality shows."

Tara gave him a hug. "Very funny, Clarence."

At the sound of his given name, the smile left Mutt's face. Brack knew he hated his name.

"I ain't never seen you without a quick comeback," Brother Thomas said. "I'll have to remember that, mm-hmm."

Darcy asked Mutt how Cassie was.

"She's a strong woman. Have to be to put up wit me. She's doin' better than yesterday."

"Good," Brack said. "How are you doing?"

"I'm sicka hospital food, that's how I am."

Darnel held up a bag with what remained to feed the army. "This should make you happy."

Mutt opened the bag, saw the Chinese food containers, and gave a big grin.

Darcy said. "Eat something. We'll sit with Cassie for a while."

Darcy left to film a segment. The church men wanted to stay and pray over Cassie. Mutt and Brack rode with Tara and Darnel into the city in her SUV. And Brack reflected on life.

Whenever the hygrometer pegged with near hundred percent humidity in Charleston, nights became so hot and sticky that the Pirate's Cove sold out of longnecks and whisky sours. The live band playing on stage got the sunburnt crowd up and dancing, all inhibition left in the backwash of their shotglasses. A charge of energy radiated around the mass of people with a feeling Brack could only describe as pure electricity.

Tonight, Friday night, Atlanta, the self-proclaimed Capital of the South, felt like that. It might have been seeing Darcy and knowing things would never again be the same between them. Or Tara and Darnel wanting to give Mutt a break from hospital vigil by taking him for a night on the town. Brack was sure the former had no permanent cure, but he hoped his new friends understood what they'd signed up for in suggesting the latter. Mutt, Brack knew, was so wound up from sequestering himself in that small room with the blinking monitors that he'd be like the Tasmanian Devil as soon they reached whatever destination they had in mind.

A city of almost half-a-million people, Atlanta provided an infinite choice of entertainment. With Tara in the car, Brack wouldn't have to worry that Mutt would demand they head to the closest gentlemen's club. They settled on an older bar known for having the best Motown and R&B cover band in town.

Get Back, the name of the establishment, was already hopping when Brack, et al, joined the frenzy a shade past ten. The night crowd represented the full gamut of the color chart but seemed predominantly African-American. With Vito's crew white and Hispanic, Brack thought that here, at least, they'd have a good chance of avoiding any nasty confrontations.

Mutt led the charge to the bar. He ordered three tequila shots with beer chasers for the non-teetotalers among them, Tara, her brother, and himself. For Brack, he ordered a Coke. They toasted Vito's imminent demise, and Brack's three companions then licked salt, downed shots, and sucked on lime.

There were times when Brack missed feeding the beast. The slow burn down the throat. The dulled senses. The temporary fade of memories.

But tonight was not one of those times. Every day he felt the loss of his late wife, Jo. And soon he'd have to deal all over again with losing Darcy. But right now his friend Mutt was hurting and needed a diversion. Tonight was for him.

While Brack talked with Tara, Darnel and Mutt chatted up two fifty-year-old women who didn't seem to be visiting Get Back for only the music. They had squeezed size-twelve bodies into size-ten outfits and inhaled clove vapor while tickling the stems of their wineglasses. The band lived up to its reputation, hopping from Ray Charles to the Commodores to Stevie Wonder without a hiccup. It didn't take long before the group jumped up from their seats to hit the dance floor. Mutt led one of the cougars. Darnel caught the other. And Tara and Brack once again paired nicely, though he worked to keep up with her. She anticipated every move he threw at her, spinning into and out of his arms as if they'd been practicing for years, instead of only a single night before—the night his car blew up.

During a slow number, Brack caught sight of Mutt dirty dancing with his quick picker-upper. Darnel had already disappeared from the dance floor with his. Brack also noticed a few sneers directed his way from some of the men in the place. He figured they disliked seeing a white man with a black woman— especially a woman as eye-catching as Tara. Not that it bothered Brack. If push came to shove, he and Tara could take on most of them without much effort.

At the break he and his dance partner found two seats at the bar. Brack laid down a five and asked for two waters.

The bartender pocketed the bill and filled the two glasses.

When the bartender moved on to serve someone else, Brack said, "You realize we may have to drag Mutt away from that woman out there, don't you?"

"I thought about it," she said. "But he and Cassie are not doing that well right now anyway."

Not the impression Brack had gotten when Cassie originally called him, all upset about her sister missing and worried about Mutt's doings. Or when Cassie was beaten and Mutt practically lived at the hospital. Brack didn't reply.

She continued, "I'm more worried about Darnel. His date is twice his age."

He nodded. "It was good of you two showing up with food and joining us at the hospital."

"This whole situation is crazy," she said.

At that moment, Brack felt something jab into his back. He guessed it was a pistol, a familiar sensation that always led to pain and suffering in one form or another.

A voice said, "Why don't we step outside, Pelton." It wasn't a question.

Glancing at Tara, Brack saw her wide-eyed stare. A man stood behind her too, his hand on her shoulder. Brack guessed his other hand similarly had a gun stuck in her back.

Brack said, "I'm happy right where I am. So is she."

"I'm not gonna ask again," the voice said, rising in volume.

From behind, Brack heard Mutt say, "Good," then the sound of glass smashing on his captor's head.

As soon as the gun left his back, Brack threw an elbow and caught the man in the nose. In the same instant, the man behind Tara hesitated, as if stunned by his partner being taken out. Tara spun around, twisted the gun from the goon's hand, and slammed the butt of it into the side of his face. He joined his buddy on the floor.

Things happened even faster after that. Brack grabbed Tara's free hand and they followed Mutt toward the emergency exit at the back of the night club.

But three men formed a blockade between them and the exit door. Their mistake, because Brack grabbed the gun still in Tara's hand, a nine millimeter, and pointed it at the men.

As soon as the three thugs reached for their own pistols, Brack pulled the trigger six times, nailing each of them twice. The Marines had taught him not to waste shots.

The men went down and Brack, Tara, and Mutt stepped over them, bounding out the back door expecting its alarm to go off. It didn't. Tara quickly tossed Brack her keys. Five feet from her 4Runner, he pressed the unlock button. The three of them each opened a different door and discovered Darnel in a compromised position with his elder date. He must have had his own key to the truck.

The woman with him screamed.

Mutt yelled, "Shove over!" and climbed in the backseat over them.

Tara and Brack jumped in the front seats. Brack started the engine and got them out of there in a hurry.

The woman screamed again.

Tara turned around and Brack thought she would slap the screamer. Instead, in her soft Mr. Grumpy voice, she said, "Calm down. We're not kidnapping you."

In the rearview mirror, Brack saw the woman trying to cover herself with her dress. Fat chance of cramming herself back into her size ten from her current position despite all the deep breaths she took.

Tara continued her explanation. "Someone started shooting up the club so we thought it best to leave."

Brack guessed that wanting to avoid further spooking the poor embarrassed woman, Tara chose to omit the detail that he'd been the one shooting up the club.

"What about Wanda?" the woman said.

Mutt said, "Don't you worry 'bout yo' friend. She made it out okay."

The certainty in his voice told Brack more than he really wanted to know.

To make sure they weren't followed, Brack took a few erroneous turns. Then Mutt said, "Let me know when you think we in the clear, Opie."

"We're okay," Brack said. "No one's tailing us."

"In that case," Mutt said, "follow this for a few blocks. I'll tell you where to turn."

Brack followed his directions and they ended up parked at a meter outside a run-down hotel not far from the Get Back club where they'd been. Tara, Mutt, and Brack got out of the SUV to give Darnel and his date time to get dressed.

Tara leaned against her 4Runner and put her head in her hands. "This is so crazy."

Now would have been a great time for a cigar, except for Brack's memory of the trash can.

To Mutt he said, "Thanks for showing up when you did."

Mutt sucked on vapor and exhaled. "I was actually comin' over to let you know I was leavin'."

A detail came to mind that Brack had skimmed over before, but with Tara standing nearby, he didn't speak.

Darnel exited the vehicle and Tara said to him, "I didn't know you still had a key to my 4Runner."

He gave a smirk and shrugged. "Sorry about that, sis."

Mutt said, "Good thing he did or he'd still be back in the club."

"Yeah," Tara said. "A real good thing." Her voice lacked conviction.

Thirty more seconds passed without another word spoken and Brack wondered if Darnel's date was ever coming out of the backseat.

When the door finally opened, the woman shimmied out. She said, "Darnel, sweetie? Can you zip my back?"

Brack had to give her an A for effort. It couldn't have been easy getting into that outfit again, especially in the backseat of someone else's vehicle.

Darnel managed to raise her zipper, moving in close and whispering something in her ear.

She giggled.

He then turned to the others. "Um, we're gonna check out the inside of this here establishment. Don't worry about us. We'll take a cab later."

Brack said, "Mutt, maybe you should make sure this place is safe for them."

Mutt gave him a sideways smirk and said, "Okay, Opie. I think I'll do that. You two can take off. The po-lice are probably lookin' for three people fittin' our descriptions. Best to split up anyways."

Tara shook her head no when Brack offered to return her keys.

A mile down the road, he said, "You'll have to direct me where to go."

Tara looked straight ahead. "Men can be such pigs."

"Huh?"

"Don't play dumb with me. Mutt's date was already at that hotel. It's why he directed you there."

"We don't know that."

"You certainly thought it. Even gave him a really lame cover story."

"It was his choice."

"You could've talked him out of it."

"Maybe."

"Well, *maybe* was worth trying for, don'cha think? I mean, his woman is in the hospital and he's out looking to get his rocks off?"

"Personally," Brack said, "those two ladies gave me the willies.

I would have steered clear of anything beyond the dance floor with either of them."

He couldn't answer for Mutt's intentions.

Chapter Twenty-Nine

Friday, eleven p.m.

Tara kept quiet for the rest of the drive back to Mutt's house. When Brack pulled into the drive and got out, she said she needed to get home, bade him goodnight, and drove off.

Gunplay wound Brack up like a coiled spring. With sleep out of the question for a while, he pulled out his phone to call Darcy, only to find three messages from her that he'd missed. She already knew about the shooting. He hit the call back button.

She answered on the first ring. "I'm on my way to Get Back. Whatever did you guys get yourselves into?"

"I'm guessing it was Levin and his goons. They took us by surprise."

"One of them is dead, and the rest are seriously injured. Levin wasn't among them."

"They pulled guns on us," Brack said.

"Detective Nichols has an A.P.B. out on you."

There were times he felt like the dumbest man on earth. A lot of those times occurred in the vicinity of Darcy Wells. He'd first gotten to know her the two years prior to her abandoning Charleston and moving here, so if he were placing bets, he'd put all he had on his next move.

He said, "I'm heading to my hotel. Why don't you meet me there?"

"Give me ten minutes."

The call ended.

If that had been a real bet, Brack would have doubled his money. He knew Darcy would always go for the exclusive, which she'd get from him on the ride back to the bar—before he made his statement to the police.

And he'd get to spend a little more time with her before he went to jail. A one-sided win-win if there ever was one.

After giving Darcy the details, leaving out only Mutt's alleged clandestine interlude, Brack surrendered the pistol he'd used and turned himself in to Nichols. He was read his rights, got a pleasant ride into the city in a new cruiser, but skipped the usual fingerprinting and paperwork. Instead, he was again escorted directly to an interrogation room. Staring at his reflection in the phony mirror, he realized how much older he looked since the last time he'd been in the same position. Was it only a year ago? He wondered, not for the first time, why he kept putting himself in situations that landed him in this kind of place.

Detective Nichols walked in wearing his sport-coat ensemble and carrying two cups of coffee. Someone closed the door behind him, probably the same person now monitoring them from behind the so-called mirror.

Nichols sat one of the cups on the table in front of Brack.

"Thanks."

"No problem." From the inside pocket of his jacket, Nichols pulled out a folded sheet of paper. "Care to hear about the unfortunate guy you capped?"

"I capped three of them," Brack said. "Which one are you talking about?"

Nichols eyed him. "You are aware of your rights, aren't you?"

"Yes, I've been Mirandized."

"Good," he said. "I'm talking about the dead one. The other two are in critical condition."

"Let's hear about the good citizen then." Brack eased back in his chair and took a sip of some fairly decent coffee.

"He was no good citizen. But he was connected."

By connected, Nichols meant protected.

By Vito.

Or had been until Brack put two slugs in him.

"Aren't they all?" he asked.

"Not like this," Nichols said. "At least not in this city."

"We were running away from two guys who'd each put a gun in my back and my date's. In addition, three more guys were blocking the exit. I showed them the nine millimeter I'd picked up from one of the two guys who'd confronted me and my date before we subdued them. All three drew down. I shot them. Case closed."

"What angle are you working here, Pelton?"

"No angle," Brack said. "I respect you. You're a decent man. I'm playing this straight up."

"We could be talking jail time."

"I doubt it. That night club probably has surveillance cameras. If not for its own security, then from Atlanta Vice."

Nichols scratched his chin. "Why do you say that?"

"I'm being straight with you. Don't jerk me around. If you wanted to arrest me, I'd already be in cuffs and in a holding cell." Brack knew how this game was played.

"Good guess. The DEA was there. They caught the whole thing on video too. Like you said."

"The question I don't have an answer for is how Levin found us. We didn't have a game plan when we left the house. None of us knew Get Back was our destination until we were on our way."

Nichols tapped the table. "So they were tracking you."

Brack looked at him and felt his stomach tighten. "And the only way to do that is through cell phones, credit cards, or some car tracking device like Lo-Jack."

Nichols nodded.

"So which is it?"

"I'm not sure," he said.

"I need my phone to make a call."

"Are you requesting your one phone call?"

"I need to warn Tara. She'd be in the same video I'm in. It was her car we were in last night."

Nichols stood. "I'll take care of it. Anything else?"

"Yeah," Brack said. "Since we weren't alone last night, why didn't your buddies help?"

"The story I heard was that by the time everything went down, you three were out the door. Frankly, the DEA guys are ticked off they had to clean up your mess." The detective said it with almost a smile.

"And you aren't too upset about that, are you?"

"No." Nichols walked out of the room and shut the door, leaving his coffee untouched.

Brack finished his own cup and got to work on Nichols's.

At eight a.m. when Nichols released Brack, Darcy was waiting for him in what could best be described as a busy lobby. Of all his friends, she'd spent the most time chauffeuring him from police stations.

Brack went up to where she stood waiting. "Thanks."

She smiled. "Like I told you, you make good copy. Right now, all the other networks are eating my dust." Then she really surprised him. She kissed his cheek.

Brack tried not to think what that meant as they walked out to her Honda. Instead, he asked, "Could we stop by the hospital to see Cassie? I mean, after I get something to eat."

Five minutes later they crept out of a McDonald's drive thru and into Atlanta's morning traffic. A few minutes after that, enough time for Brack to wolf down a bacon, egg, and cheese biscuit and chug a large orange juice, they parked in the hospital lot.

Cassie was awake, sitting up, and eating breakfast. Brack gave her a soft hug.

She said, "Hi, handsome. You smell like you been in jail."

"That's because he was," Darcy said.

"Is Mutt there too?"

"No," Brack said. "We had a late night. I'm guessing he's home sleeping." At least, he hoped so.

Darcy asked Cassie, "How are you feeling? You look much better."

"Thanks, sweetie," she said. "I do feel better."

"Can you tell us what happened?"

Cassie drank the rest of her orange juice and wiped her mouth with a napkin. "I was in the kitchen getting the prep ready when these two men walked in. They tried to grab me and I hit one of them across the face with a cast-iron skillet."

Brack laughed.

"I tried to hit the other one, but he was too quick. He punched me so hard I dropped the pan. Next thing I know I'm waking up in here."

Darcy asked, "Only you and Nina were working at the time?"

Her eyes filled with tears. "I heard she didn't make it."

Brack said, "I'm sorry."

Cassie sobbed, then fought to get herself under control.

He asked, "Can you describe the men who did this?"

Cassie nodded.

Darcy said, "I'm sorry to have to ask, but can you look at a photo of someone and tell me if he was one of the attackers?"

"Yes."

Darcy opened her phone and pulled up a picture of Townsend, the Aryan mercenary who shot at Brack and Tara when they'd staked out his house in Midtown.

After one look, Cassie averted her eyes. "The police already showed me his picture. He was the main one."

"That's good, Cassie," Darcy said. "The police will probably bring in a sketch artist for the rest of them. Are there any other details you can think of? Anything that comes to mind. Sometimes the smallest thing becomes the key."

Cassie thought for a moment. Then she said, "Well, I guess I'm wondering why they killed Nina and left me alive."

Brack had wondered that as well. One of the bikers at the Lion's Den said Nina wasn't innocent right before they opened up on the police.

Darcy persisted gently, "Anything else seem odd to you?"

"They somehow knew I was the only one in the kitchen."

"How so?"

"I don't know," Cassie said. "Just like they knew I was back there."

"Okay," Brack said. "That's real good."

Darcy patted her on the shoulder. "You get better. We'll find out who did this."

"It's connected to Regan, isn't it?" she asked.

Brack said, "I think so. We've been stirring the pot."

"Don't get yourself killed now, handsome."

"Wouldn't dream of it," he said.

"You neither, Miss Darcy."

"I'll be fine, but the boy wonder over there thinks he's invincible."

"It's worked for me so far," he said.

Chapter Thirty

Saturday, ten a.m.

Riding in Darcy's Accord along Peachtree and listening to Katy Perry croon about Friday nights, Brack thought again about Mutt. What a mess of a situation.

Darcy said, "Where *is* Mutt?"

"I hope he isn't still at the hotel we left him at last night."

"Hotel?"

He realized he'd let one of their several black cats out of the proverbial bag. "Ye-es," he said, with more than a hint of hesitation. "Our getaway ended at the South Side Hotel, where we left Darnel and his date. Mutt stayed behind."

"Was Mutt alone?" she asked.

"On the dance floor, no. But in the car and in front of the hotel, yes."

She said, "I always find that when someone gets real specific with the details, an implication is in the air."

"I just told you everything I know as fact."

"Okay," she said. "How'd you end up at that particular hotel?"

"I drove us there." The next question she asked would not be good.

"I don't think you're familiar enough with the city to head there without help. Was it a random choice?"

Rubbing the headache out of his temples, Brack said, "No."

"Tara knew about it?"

"I'm not sure."

"But she wasn't the one who guided you there, was she?"

"No."

"Her brother, perhaps? Please tell me it was him."

"I cannot tell a lie," Brack said. "I chopped down the cherry tree."

"So Mutt guided you there. Any reason why Mutt would want to go there and not somewhere else, like an all-night coffee shop or something?"

All the words that came to mind would be filtered through a lie before they left Brack's mouth so he kept it shut.

"Uh-huh," she said. "Okay. Let's pray for the best, plan for the worst."

"Levin must have tracked us to the club from Mutt's house or from the hospital. I used a credit card for the cover charge and several rounds of drinks. It's either that or my phone or there's a tracker on Tara's SUV."

She said, "I've got a guy who can check for bugs and things. Let's rule the car out first, for her safety. He can also check your phone, but that takes a little more time."

"Nichols said he'd take care of it."

After a smirk, Darcy said, "My guy is better than anyone they've got. Trust me."

After two phone calls, one to Darcy's tech guy and one to Tara, he and Darcy headed to the Preservation parking lot to pick up the 4Runner. Tara handed over the keys, giving Brack an awkward smile. Darcy took a call and stepped away.

Brack said, "How're you doing?"

"Well," she said, "I can say I haven't had this much excitement since college."

"Full-contact fighting and gunshots, huh. Which college did you go to?"

She laughed. "You know what I meant. And thanks for doing this."

"They found us somehow," he said. "Either it's this"—he tapped the hood of her SUV—"or it's my credit card. I have a feeling it's me, but we need to rule out your car. I'll bring it back to you. It'll take a few hours."

Darcy came back to them and gave Tara a hug. "I'd never had anyone shoot at me until I met him either. I learned it goes with the territory."

Brack wanted to say that wasn't a fair assessment, except he couldn't dispute the accuracy of her statement. Intent was always hard to prove, though he never intended anyone to get shot. Especially Darcy. But that was two years ago.

Darcy drove her Honda through an industrial section of town and Brack followed behind in the 4Runner, sampling Tara's music, which was mostly jazz. They pulled up to an abandoned warehouse. The big roll-up door opened automatically, and a short round man stepped out and waved them to drive in.

They parked, got out of the vehicles, and the man pressed a button to lower the door.

"Jim," Darcy said, "this is Brack Pelton."

Jim wore overalls and his bald head shone under the fluorescent lighting. He smiled and held out a hand. "The guy making the headlines."

Brack shook his hand.

"In the flesh," Darcy said.

Motioning to Tara's SUV, Jim asked, "Key in it?"

"No." Brack fished out the ring and handed it to him.

"Take your time with it, Jim," Darcy said. "We need to be sure it's clean."

"No problem," he said. "Network paying?"

Brack said, handing him his phone. "I am. You take cash, right?"

Jim said, "Always, and twice on Sundays."

They left Jim to his devices and drove into the city.

"Where're you taking me now?" Brack asked.

"I thought you might like a tour."

Not sure what to make of that, nor did he care, he reclined the seatback and stretched out. The next thing he knew, Darcy was nudging him awake.

"We're here, sleeping beauty."

He opened his eyes. "Where are we?" It looked like a parking garage.

"You'll see. Come on." She got out.

He rubbed his eyes and followed.

It turned out they were at Turner Field and Darcy had tickets to a baseball game. The Braves were playing the Pittsburgh Pirates. He hadn't been to a baseball game in a long time.

Brack bought them each ball caps because the sun was fierce and the sky was clear, with no clouds in sight for relief. After raiding the closest vendor of nachos, hot dogs, and peanuts, they found their seats—right behind home plate.

Darcy had a beer and he stuck with bottled water. They ate until they were stuffed.

Around the seventh inning, Brack finally got around to saying, "Thanks."

"For what?" Her eyes were green, which told him she was happy. With her hair pulled up under the cap to keep her neck cool, she was everything he wanted but couldn't have.

"For this. Today."

"You say that now," she said. "But you don't know how much Jim is going to charge you."

"True," he said. "I've got a couple thousand in cash. If it's more than that, we better stop at an ATM. But I don't care how much he charges. If he wasn't worth it, you wouldn't be using him."

"You are correct." She sipped her beer.

At that moment, something sparkled, catching his attention. Her engagement ring. Already sober, he was ready to move on.

"What's next?" he asked.

"The eighth inning."

"I mean after that."

"Why rush things? It's a nice day. We don't have to be anywhere else. Can't you relax and enjoy the moment?"

Not as long as you're marrying that peckerwood, he thought.

What he said was, "I'm sorry. Paige and I've been so busy with the new place that I haven't had time to breathe."

"So stop talking shop. Now is your chance."

He signaled a soft-drink vendor making his rounds with a tray full of Cokes. He bought two, handing one to Darcy after she'd finished her beer.

The Braves handily won the game and they walked to the car with the celebratory crowd. Brack and Darcy, however, were in no hurry.

Jim found nothing wrong with Tara's 4Runner but a leaking valve cover gasket, which he fixed. Given the skill set required to check the SUV for any tracking devices, fix the leak, and look for any traces on the phone, the bill seemed reasonable to Brack, although it did clean him out of cash. On the way back to drop off Tara's 4Runner, he stopped at a bank and made the max ATM withdrawal. Since the 4Runner and his phone were clean, the only other source he could think of was his credit card, so he decided against using it anymore.

Returning to the Preserve, Darcy and Brack helped Tara and a coworker feed Mr. Grumpy and the other elephants. One of the huge females took a fancy to Darcy and gave her a trunk hug.

Tara said, "Her name's Princess."

Darcy turned to Brack. "Don't say it."

"What am I gonna say?"

"Some comment. Us being namesakes or twins or something."

Tara laughed.

Brack handed Grumpy a bundle of hay. "You said it, I didn't."

"Yeah, but you were thinking it, or something worse."

"How long have you two known each other?" Tara asked.

He said, "About two years."

Darcy said, "It feels longer."

Tara changed the subject. "The guy who looked over my 4Runner—he found nothing wrong with it? I mean, no tracking device?"

"Just a leaking valve cover gasket, which he replaced. We think

Vito's been tracking me by my credit card. I'll be using cash from now on."

"Okay," Tara said. "Thank you both. What's our next step?"

Surprised by her willingness to continue to hang with them, given the likelihood of violence to follow him like a rabid dog ready to bite, he swallowed hard and said, "Did you have something in mind?"

"Yes," she said. "I've been thinking we need to just go in there and kidnap Regan."

It was a crazy idea, but he'd been thinking along the same lines. He asked, "How would we do that?"

"Hijack her limo."

Darcy said, "That's not a bad idea. Limited guards. They're vulnerable."

"Except that Mutt and I are the trigger pullers. And the targets."

Tara said, "I was thinking more like a distraction. You and the other guys keep their attention long enough for Darcy and me to grab Regan."

"What if she doesn't want to come?" he asked.

"Then I'll knock her upside the head."

Darcy put her arm around Tara. "My kind of woman."

Princess nudged Brack out of the way of the two women and blew a loud trumpet blast from her trunk, as if to say "we girls have to stick together."

But all Brack could think at that moment was, this is a suicide mission. Hope Mutt is up for another one.

Chapter Thirty-One

Saturday, six p.m.

Sitting with Darcy in a trendy coffee shop that evening, its big windows overlooking a busy street, Brack stared at all the unanswered questions he'd written on a sheet of paper. He tapped the side of his cup, which now held cold coffee.

"Regan's not surrounded by bright people," Darcy said.

"That only adds to the difficulty," he said. "It means they are apt to do anything. Not follow a script." He stared at the coffee shop's steady influx of customers. Most wanted their coffee doctored in a way Maxwell House had never intended.

Downing the last of her latte, Darcy stood and threw away her empty cup.

Brack tapped on his cup some more.

At the table next to him a baby dressed in pink sat on her father's lap, gurgled, and reached out to him.

He waved.

She waved back.

Darcy interrupted, "What a cute baby."

Brack asked her if she and the peckerwood were planning to procreate, except he used Welcott's given name.

His favorite reporter made a "goo-goo" sound, completely enamored of the infant, ignoring his question.

Brack ignored her ignoring him and said, "We need to have Regan tailed. Why don't you work on that?"

Darcy held out a finger and the baby grabbed it.

"I've been here only a year, Brack. It takes a while to get things organized."

Brack drank cold coffee, wondering if she were talking about her work or her personal life. "No, it doesn't. Not for you." He set the cup down.

Sitting back in her chair, now refocused on the problem at hand, she said, "You're right." She pulled out her phone and touched the screen. "Regan's still at home. Been there for the last twelve hours."

"Anything else you're not telling me?"

"Not as far as you know."

Brother Thomas called at that moment and asked what they were up to, because, as he put it, "If they weren't doing anything, there was always something needing done." Which in his parlance meant volunteer work.

Brack and Darcy left the coffee shop and headed south on Peachtree, the evening traffic already a slight nuisance. Forty-five minutes to travel a distance that in Charleston would take all of five minutes, they parked at Three Crosses Church. Brother Thomas and another man were busy unloading a delivery truck.

Without asking, Darcy and Brack grabbed boxes from the back of the truck and carted them inside the church. These turned out to contain cans of vegetables. Like the Church of Redemption of Brother Thomas, this church of Reverend Cleophus also moonlighted as a soup kitchen. Here, in the capital of the South, the patrons were similar to those in Charleston—the difference being how many. The number of people lined up waiting for a meal staggered him. And it would take another two hours before serving them could even begin.

Within the hour, Tara and her younger brother joined them. Brother Thomas never met anyone he wouldn't eventually hit up to help out. The evening went by fast, and after the clean-up, Brack, Darcy, Tara, and Darnel were ready to drop. As they sat around a table sipping sweet tea, Reverend Cleophus came in, a somber look on his face.

Brack asked if everything was okay.

The preacher took a seat, his hands shaking in front of him. "I got some bad news."

Brack had experienced a lot of tragedy in his life, his wife's death at the top of the list. They hadn't had any children yet and so he'd been left to deal with the pain alone.

To Reverend Cleophus's statement, Brack said, "Okay."

"Remember I told you to look for Mindy and Kai," the Reverend said.

Immediately Brack knew he did not like where this was going. "Yes."

The preacher put his head in his hands.

Brother Thomas put a hand on his friend's shoulder.

"The police found two girls matching their description in a dumpster."

Brack felt Darcy's and Tara's eyes on him. He did not look at them. Instead, he got up from the table and walked outside the church. When he was alone, he called Nichols.

When the detective answered, Brack asked, "Can you check on a couple of dead bodies for me?"

"Maybe," came the reply.

"Two eighteen-year-olds. First names Mindy and Kai."

Nichols asked, "What's your connection with them?"

"I met their mothers."

"Under what circumstance?"

Brack took a deep breath and tried to calm down. "I'm guessing by answering my question with your questions means you do know about them and they are indeed dead."

"Yes."

He closed his eyes. He did not want to deal with being responsible for two more deaths, innocent or not.

Nichols continued, "They were cut up pretty bad. Some john paid a lot of money for that trick."

Brack opened his eyes.

"What are you talking about?"

"For the right amount of money," Nichols said, "anything is possible."

"What if I told you I tried to talk to them?"

Nichols didn't respond right away. When he did, he asked, "You think because you spoke with them, they were killed."

"Yes."

"Did they give you any information?"

Brack shook his head in frustration. He realized Nichols could not see his nonverbal answer over the phone. "That's what's so sick about this. When I approached them, they screamed and alerted their handlers. I got nothing from them except to be chased by two armed thugs."

"Jesus."

Brack hung up and called Mutt, who'd been with Cassie at the hospital, and told him they needed more weapons. A lot more. Now he wanted to unleash the hounds of hell on Vito.

Mutt said he knew just the place.

Brack, dressed in the clothes Darcy picked out for him, parallel parked at a meter a block away from Mutt's source for guns. Before stepping out of the Mazda, he scanned the area. Cars and trucks from all walks of life filled the street. The sidewalk was cracked and worn but fairly litter-free. Mutt and Brack got out of the car and crossed the intersection. The target building loomed across from them, a brick two-story with hazy windows. The thump of bass within resonated across the street. The beat was not gangsta rap. It wasn't blues or even the strip club Kid Rock "Cowboy" ballad. It was reggae.

A fixture with a single bulb illuminated two black men perched on stools outside of the establishment's entrance. A rastacap bearing the colors of Africa covered each man's mountains of dreadlocks.

Brack and Mutt approached the doormen.

The closest one said, "Dis a pri-vate club, mon."

Mutt folded his arms across his chest. "Well, dis a private matter."

"Beat it, mon," the other said. "Before we have to get up off our stools."

Behind them, the door to the "private" club was nothing more than a metal screen, its rusty frame held in place by corroded hinges. An idea formed in Brack's vengeance-focused brain around the temptation to shove these two dread heads right through the makeshift door.

Brack's savvy companion must have sensed his thoughts. He said, "Easy, Opie."

Brack spotted the cause of his concern. Both rastas were packing more than yards of unwashed hair. The shape of the butt of a gun could be seen through each of their t-shirts.

"How about this?" Brack asked. "You let us through without a hassle and we'll buy you a beer inside."

The Rasta on Brack's right looked at his partner and both laughed.

Mutt shook his head.

In one motion, Brack raised his foot and kicked, catching the laughing instigator in the gut. He flew backwards off the stool and through the screen door.

Before the other could react, Mutt grabbed the guy's gun and trained it on him. Brack jumped on the one he'd used as a door opener and grabbed his piece.

The pungent aroma of marijuana wafted through the now-open entry. Brack held the rusty screen door open for Mutt who escorted the other doorman in with a nudge of the pistol. A thick layer of smoke danced around the rafters, dimming the illumination. A quick scan of the room revealed at least ten men, all with long dreads visible or partially showing under their rasta-caps.

All had pistols.

Pointed at them.

One man sat higher than the others on a sort of throne, sporting shoulder-length dreadlocks and holding a fat three-inch-long spliff between the fingers of one hand. His other hand was raised as if commanding his soldiers to hold back.

Every eye in the room focused on Brack and Mutt, all the men seemingly ready to attack them upon command.

The man on high—figuratively and literally—took a hit off his smoke, exhaled, and said, "I saw you comin' long before you got here."

Folding his arms across his chest, Brack asked, "How's that?"

The Rasta king tilted his head back and inhaled air through his nostrils deeply. To his men he said, "Help Julian up." To Brack and Mutt he said, "You carry the stench of death. Chaos and destruction follow you. And you brought it to my kingdom."

Two Rastas came forward and helped up the man Brack had kicked through the door.

Brack said, "I heard Vito was muscling in on your kingdom."

With a tight grin, the Rasta king said, "You heard wrong. Vito is a serpent crawling on de ground."

"Well, my preacher told me the story of one snake that caused a whole lot of damage."

"Why you here?" the king asked.

"Someone else told me the enemy of my enemy was my friend. And I'm the man who wants to stand over your problem snake with a shovel and chop its head off. If you saw us coming, you know who we are."

Drawing deeply on his smoke again, the king held his breath a few seconds, then let out a steady stream. "You do not answer my question."

Mutt, who'd been quiet the whole time, said, "Reason we here is we need some a them shovels."

"I see." The Rasta king's eyes appeared to focus on something to his left, as if in deep thought, then came back to his two customers. "Yes. I believe we con help you gentlemen with your endeavah."

With a wave of his free hand he summoned one of his men. They spoke in whispers. Then the man scurried off.

Mutt and Brack stood quietly, arms at their sides holding the guns they'd taken off the door guards, ready for anything.

Four men entered the room, each pair of them carrying a rectangular wooden crate a little smaller than a coffin. They set the crates down in front of Brack and Mutt and removed the lids. Inside was a gangster's paradise: AKs, Tech Nines, Berettas, pump-action shotguns, Glocks, H&Ks. And many more.

Brack's eyes opened wide and he selected a Colt forty-five to replace the one that Vito's men had blown up with his car. "How much?"

The king on his throne smiled, took another drag, and exhaled again. "If you are successful, you will have paid your debt. If not, well..."

His implication was clear. Either they cut the head off Vito or they come back here and deal with all these armed Rastas. One serpent was easier than a dozen Rastafarians. Brack and Mutt took the deal, along with a forty-five, a telescopic baton, and a nine millimeter.

Chapter Thirty-Two

Sunday, ten a.m.

Through her never-ending network of sources, Darcy found a hole in Vito's armor big enough for Brack to punch a fist through. Vito had weekly appointments in a luxury hotel suite with a certain masseuse. Brack, Mutt, and Darcy wondered if Regan knew about it. The best part was that Vito kept it on the down low by using only one security guard—Jack Townsend—to accompany him. Everyone knew the head of Vito's security was the best, so nobody messed with him.

Vito believed himself safe.

That was up until Sunday morning at ten when Brack and Mutt knocked on the masseuse's door dressed like bellmen. Brass buttons glinted against the itchy black material. Their attire came from a local uniform store and fit well enough for the occasion. The short-billed caps they wore when seen through a peephole would make it tough for even their own mothers to recognize them.

This was one of those times when Brack didn't want to think too hard about what was about to happen next. They wanted Vito, preferably alive. They needed him breathing at least long enough to tell them where they could find Regan. But with everything that had happened, nothing was a given any more.

Townsend opened the door and Brack hit him square across the jaw. The Aryan stumbled backward. Mutt and Brack entered. Brack pulled out the telescopic baton and with a flick of his wrist extended the weapon.

Mutt moved around him and went to the back of the suite.

Townsend stepped back, eyes on Brack, and rubbed his face.

He gave his head two quick shakes.

Brack wanted blood today. Now. For beating and torturing Cassie. For killing Nina, and Mindy, and Kai.

From somewhere in the apartment, a woman screamed.

Townsend said, "You're a dead man."

Brack swung the baton.

Townsend side-stepped the blow and punched Brack in his exposed gut.

Brack felt the pain but gritted through the jolt. He knew he could not take his attention off his opponent, who bounced around like a lightweight champion.

Townsend came in low.

Brack swung the baton again.

Townsend ducked it a second time and gave Brack a one-two blow to his gut.

It was harder to grit through the pain a second time. One more blow and Brack knew he would be in trouble.

Townsend bounced back and then forward. Brack swung the baton again. It cracked across Townsend's face. Townsend spun with the blow and Brack took the opportunity to smash his left knee. The giant collapsed. There was no mercy from Brack for this man. The pain and suffering he'd caused many others was immeasurable. Brack decided that Townsend would die here today.

From where he lay on the floor, Townsend saw Brack raise the baton again. He tried to roll away from the blow but was too late. Brack slammed the weapon across an exposed wrist and heard bone snap. The once-great warrior curled into a fetal position, so Brack kicked him in the middle of his back.

From behind Brack, Mutt said, "Opie, we gotta go."

"I'm not finished."

Mutt grabbed the back of his shirt and pulled him away. "Give 'im a rain check. Vito left the building. We gotta go now."

"How'd he get away?"

"He shoved the girl at me," Mutt said. "There musta been another exit."

"Okay."

Mutt let go and Brack kicked Townsend in the face twice before Mutt grabbed him again and shoved him out the door.

They ran from the masseuse's suite. The fact that it was located on the fiftieth floor meant they had to take the elevator. But less than sixty seconds after pressing the call button, the doors swished open and they got on. Mutt hit "L" and they were off. Brack could only pray they wouldn't stop at too many floors on the way.

Mutt pulled out his Beretta and checked to make sure a round was chambered. "We been in some crazy situations before, but nothin' like this."

"You know we might not make it," Brack said.

Mutt tucked the pistol in the front waistband of his trousers. "You say that before. Let's work on havin' a positive attitude."

"Okay, I'm positive we *might* not make it this time. You didn't let me finish off Sasquatch upstairs. He's still a threat."

"You broke his jaw, his nose, his knee, and his wrist. I think we're safe from him for now."

Brack wanted a cigar. Instead, he took out a piece of Bubblicious, grape flavor, and popped it in his mouth.

Mutt toked on vapor.

The doors opened on the twenty-fifth floor. A well-dressed older white man and woman started to get on, took one look at Brack and Mutt—even though their attire du jour was of bellmen—and stepped back. Mutt waved as the doors closed.

"Guess we scared them," Brack said.

"Guess so."

The next stop was the ground floor. As soon as the doors slid open, they bolted from the elevator, raced through the lobby, and ran out the front door, their bellman caps still in place. Darnel, Tara's brother, waited for them in his Mercedes sedan. They jumped in the idling car and Mutt shouted, "Hit it!"

Darnel sped away and Mutt and Brack changed back to their street clothes. At the first stoplight Darnel turned to Mutt. "You guys all right?"

"Opie took down Townsend, but Vito got away."

The light turned green and Darnel took off again. "Where to now?"

"Opie, you got any ideas?"

"Yes." Brack pulled out his iPhone and called Darcy.

She answered with, "The police were called to the Towers. I'm guessing you're not dead and you need something."

"We lost Vito," he said. "Any idea where he could be?"

"Where are you now?"

"Traveling down Peachtree."

A pause, then, "Meet me at the Varsity," and she ended the call.

Brack told Darnel.

Mutt said, "Good. I'm hungry."

Ten minutes later they pulled into the parking lot of Atlanta's original, the Varsity. Mutt jumped out and went to the counter. Before Darnel or Brack could object, he ordered six burgers, a mound of fries, and four large Varsity orange drinks.

Within ten minutes, they were busy stuffing their faces.

Darcy approached their table. "I see you guys didn't bother waiting."

Mutt swallowed half a cow, smiled, and said, "You know how disrespectful Opie can be."

Back-doored by his own comrade, Brack said, "You look great."

And she did. Blonde hair pinned off her neck, light blue V-neck t-shirt, cream-colored walking shorts, and sandals. Minimal, if any, makeup.

"Thanks."

Brack slid over and she sat next to him. A burger, fries, and the fourth drink sat in a tray that he pushed in front of her.

"What have you found out?" she asked.

"I found out Opie here can still do some damage."

She said, "I heard it was Townsend. That guy deserved a lot worse."

Brack looked at Mutt. "That's what I said."

Darcy took a sip of her drink. "Since you're being so professional and all, what else did you gumshoes learn?"

Brack didn't reply.

Mutt didn't reply.

Finally, Darnel said, "We were kind of hoping you could tell us where to go next."

Darcy looked at him, then Mutt, then Brack. "I don't know how you guys handle tying your shoes every morning."

"I usually wear sandals," Brack said.

She smirked. "Not in this town." Pulling out her phone, she got up from the table and made a call.

Darnel asked, "Is she always this friendly?"

Mutt guffawed.

Brack cleared his throat. "Um, wait 'til we have to ask her for bail money. Then she's a real peach."

Darnell said, "Sounds like you three have a lot of history."

Brack's sidekick answered. "You could say that. See, that foxy lady over there love a good story. Anything to get her pretty face on the television. Me and Mr. Opie here, we make news. She helps us along, but when the bullets start flyin' and the bad guys start dyin', it's us droppin' the hammer."

Brack said, "You've been working on that last line for a while, haven't you?"

"That obvious?"

Darcy came back to the table.

"Is what obvious?"

"Uh, how many times we gotta ask for your help," Mutt said.

"Let's see," she said. "I moved six hours away from Mr. Romeo and here I am right back where I left off. But I don't mind. Vito just walked into the City Club."

Brack stood. "What are we waiting for?"

"Easy there, Opie. We gotta problem."

"We had a problem," Brack said. "Now thanks to our favorite weather girl, we're down one."

"I appreciate the compliment," Darcy said, "but what Mutt is trying to say is that we can't simply walk into the City Club."

Darnel said, "It's the most exclusive club in Atlanta."

"How much will it take?" Brack asked.

Darcy put her phone in her purse. "I know you want to show off how much money you have, Mr. Ex-Porsche, but we are talking the nine-figure crowd. That means a one and eight zeroes in the bank just to shake hands."

"Okay," Brack said, "so how do we get to him?"

"I'm thinking," she said.

Mutt said, "You two are worse now than when you was back in Charleston."

Instead of replying, and because he craved a cigar, Brack pulled out his pack of gum and stuck a piece in his mouth.

Darcy watched Brack chew. "I have got to ask. What's with the Bubblicious?"

"Opie here realized that maybe all that smoking ain't too good for him."

"Huh?" She looked totally amazed.

Brack's favorite sidekick pulled out his vapor stick and took a few puffs. "Tara give him one of her personal trainer sessions. From what I hear, someone puked his guts out at the end."

She laughed. "Really?"

"Can we get back to the task at hand?" Brack asked.

Darnel said, "Well, to Brack's credit he matched my sister set for set for two hours. Most men can't hang with her for more than thirty minutes before they drop out. One of the other trainers there told me it was the last bit on the stair machine that did him in."

"But," Darcy said, "*that* got you to stop smoking?"

"I'm not going to say that. All I'll say is that every time I think I want a cigar, I remember my head in that trash can."

Darcy sat back. "I have to take that gal to lunch."

"Whatever," Brack said. "So how do we get to Vito now?"

Darcy looked at her watch. "It's afternoon and I have today's deadline to meet. Let's pick this up tomorrow."

*   *   *

While Brack licked his wounds in his hotel room, his cell phone buzzed. He recognized the number and answered. "Hello, Shana from Gecko Row."

She said, "I heard Mindy and Kai are dead."

No "hello" or "how's it going." None of her normal flirting. None of his either.

Brack inhaled and exhaled. "Yes."

A long pause.

He said, "Shana? Are you still there?"

She said, "This started out fun, you know. I liked you and I liked that you were giving Vito and his thugs a hard time."

"Yes."

"I didn't think anyone I knew would actually die."

He said, "You knew the girls?"

"Only to look at them. But still, no matter what they were doing, hooking or stripping or whatever, they didn't deserve to die."

Certainly not just because I wanted to talk to them, Brack thought. He simply said, "I agree."

She said, "Am I in danger?"

The six-million-dollar question. Brack thought about all the ways he could answer the question. In the end, the truth was the only answer that would protect her. He said, "If Vito finds out you were talking to me, then yes."

He heard a gasp.

"Shana?" he said again.

"I'm still here," she said.

"The best thing for you to do is get out of town," he said. "At least until this blows over. Do you have any place you can go?"

"My mother lives in Florida," she said. "I've been thinking about moving down there and starting over anyway."

Brack said, "Pack light. Leave as soon as you can. Do you have money?"

"Yes," she said. "I have enough to get there, anyway."

"Good."

Another pause.

"Shana," he said, "I want to thank you for everything you did for me. You didn't have to do any of it, but you did. I'm not with the police, but I believe I'm on the right side of this one. No matter what happens, you were trying to do the right thing. Remember that."

He heard her sniffle through the phone. "I know. I can't believe I ever got into the situation where I had to work for a man like Vito."

"You can change that right now," he said. "And if you ever get to Charleston, look me up."

"You know, Mr. Pelton, I might just do that."

Chapter Thirty-Three

Sunday, eight a.m.

A buzzing cell phone woke Brack from a deep sleep. He sat up in bed, looking around trying to figure out where he was. The white room came into focus and he remembered—still crashing at the pet-friendly hotel.

He answered the call and Darcy said, "We need to hit the road. I'm on my way with Mutt. You've got ten minutes."

"What happened to 'good morning'?"

His only answer was silence because Darcy had hung up. With time for a quick shave and shower, he dressed in his old shorts and upgraded to a decent polo, swallowed a couple of vitamins, and gargled with Listerine before heading out.

Mutt waited for him in the lobby, talking with Darcy. When Brack joined them, Mutt said, "You better pack somethin' beside that pocket knife for this one."

Brack went back to his room, stuck the forty-five down the waistband of his shorts, and grabbed three full clips before returning.

When he returned, he noticed Darcy held a coffee and a McDonald's bag. "Good morning." She handed Brack the coffee and bag. "You can eat in the car."

"Hooray!" Brack took the offered meal. "Breakfast and guns. This ought to be good."

"It isn't," Darcy said. "But we'll make the most of it."

He and Mutt followed her outside to her undercover car, Brack chewing a mouthful of Egg McMuffin. "Make the most of what?"

She turned to them. "The airport isn't just one of the busiest places for travelers. It's also the hub for human trafficking in the U.S."

"No kidding."

Her eyes, which changed color depending on her mood, were now a gray-green. Ignoring him again, she said, "Johns fly in, are chauffeured to some location to rendezvous with a sex slave, then fly out."

"Please tell me Regan isn't mixed up with this somehow."

"Not sure," she said. "But Vito is."

Brack finished off the sandwich and took a gulp of coffee, thinking this meant a whole lot of people were involved.

"Ready to get in?" She gestured to the Honda.

"You've got a line on one of the johns, don't you?"

A smile crept across her pretty face. "And I'm going to love burning him with this."

Brack downed the rest of the coffee and tossed the empty cup and balled-up sandwich wrapper in a trash can at the curb. He opened the passenger door and sat. "This is a little bigger than that Chinese brothel sting back in Charleston, you know?"

Darcy had broken that story and Brack had killed a few of the hoods running the joint.

"I know."

"Good," he said. "We just need about a thousand more of us."

Darcy said, "Don't be so dramatic. All we're going to do today is get pictures and have a little discussion with the john."

Brack asked, "You got a tracker on him or something? I mean, the Atlanta airport isn't a small place."

Mutt said, "I got a line on the one pickin' up the john."

"How'd you get that exactly?"

"Exactly by him bein' one of my own customers," Mutt said. "Fool got drunk and started gabbin' to me last night. Lucky the place was otherwise empty. I figured you was asleep, Opie, so I called Wonder Woman over here early this mornin'."

"The john's flying in this morning?" Brack asked.

Darcy said, "We have an hour to get set up."

And that was what they did. Perched in her Honda, they staked out the chauffeur's apartment. The Lincoln Town Car he drove was a polished black chariot of sin parked in front of his unit. He'd mentioned to Mutt an arrival time for the john. They calculated that he'd leave about an hour before the flight touched down. Their calculation was within five minutes.

The chauffeur, a small, wiry African-American man with a mustache going gray, exited his apartment shortly after they arrived. Wearing a dark suit and tie, a white shirt, and polished shoes, he got into the Lincoln, backed it from its spot, and pulled out of his apartment complex.

Darcy let a few cars get between him and them before giving chase. Brack wondered why Mutt thought they needed the heaters, given the small stature of the driver, though he found it best to err on the side of too many guns rather than too few. He'd had sufficient experience with the latter to desire never having to relive that again.

A sweet aroma filled the car and Brack looked back to find Mutt vaping. He asked, "There's no other flavor besides vanilla?"

Mutt said, "I like it."

Brack thought Cassie had done her darnedest to domesticate Mutt. A haircut, tooth bridge, and fancy clothes had cleaned up the exterior along with the switch from cigarettes to vapor. Not a whole lot could be done about the rest though. Like Brack. They were both tomcats ready to scrap. And Brack loved him for it.

Darcy said, "We're on the job here, gentlemen. Why don't we try to focus?"

Brack said, "This is how we roll."

From the backseat, Mutt cackled and said, "How!"

They followed the Lincoln through traffic all the way to Hartsfield Airport, and then to "Arrivals." Mutt's bar patron pulled to the curb and waited. They drove past the Town Car and two more taxis, then grabbed an open spot. Brack got out and walked back toward the limo with his cell phone out, snapping pics as discreetly as he could. A dark-skinned man in a sharp houndstooth sport coat approached the Lincoln. The man looked around, spotted Brack, and stared. Brack passed him, kept walking, and entered the airport, the man's image now immortalized in digital.

Once inside the terminal, Brack reversed course, upped his pace to a brisk walk past three baggage-claim conveyors to the next exit, pushed the doors open, and hopped in Darcy's car, which had moved ahead when he'd gotten out.

As soon as he was seated she took off. Good thing his feet had cleared the doorsill because her acceleration slammed his door shut with no effort on Brack's part.

"He spotted you, didn't he?" she asked.

"Yep. But I got his picture."

"This isn't good, Brack," she said. "You've been compromised."

"We don't know that," Brack said, although he suspected he might regret his words.

Mutt said, "Right now, we gotta stay with that Lincoln. I don't know where they're goin'."

Darcy kept the target car in sight. Because of its heavily tinted back window, they couldn't see inside the car. The driver headed for the center of town, but thirty minutes into the trip he made an unexpected turn down a one-way side street. They followed. The Lincoln stopped in the middle of it. Too late they saw this street was more like an alley. Worse, parked cars on each side meant they couldn't go around.

Darcy slowed and looked in her rearview mirror. "We've got a problem."

Brack looked back and saw a Chevrolet Tahoe approaching and yelled, "Throw it in reverse and ram him."

"What?"

Mutt pulled out his pistol. "Do it! And with your head down."

Brack pulled his forty-five, opened the window, and fired two shots in the air.

The Tahoe stopped, the two front doors opened, but no one emerged. Yet.

Darcy put the Honda in reverse and accelerated toward the SUV.

The two men in the Tahoe fired at them.

The Accord's rear window shattered in a spider-web pattern.

Mutt and Brack twisted in their seats to return fire and unloaded their weapons into the Tahoe.

Two seconds later Darcy rammed it.

The force jarred Brack and he bounced off his seat and slammed against the dash.

He slid a full clip into the forty-five, opened his door, and jumped out rolling, attempting to draw the gunfire away from Mutt and Darcy. His back let him know it was not in any kind of shape for this maneuver.

He rolled to one of the parked cars, ducked behind its trunk, and raised up briefly to fire into the Tahoe. His shot caught one of the men and the force of the bullet nearly took his face off. The man went down.

The other one in the smashed SUV reversed out of the alley.

Brack looked at the Accord. Darcy and Mutt appeared to be okay. The Lincoln was gone. In its place was another vehicle, an F-150, coming up fast the wrong way. Brack aimed and shot at the truck's tires, blowing one out. It veered right and crashed into several parked cars.

Mutt must have understood what was happening because he opened the rear door, leaned out, and fired shots into the pickup.

The front-seat passenger got out of the F-150 with bad news. Real bad news. Like a freaking submachine gun.

Brack emptied his clip at the truck. Mutt ducked back inside the Accord.

With a click, the forty-five told Brack it was empty. One more clip left. In less than two seconds he ejected the empty and jammed in the fresh.

Without taking his eyes off the man with the submachine gun, Brack heard Darcy continue reversing the Honda out of the street, now clear of the Tahoe she'd rammed. It had disappeared.

The man with the submachine gun hadn't. Brack took several shots at him, attempting to provide cover so Darcy and Mutt could escape. But Brack was too late.

Chapter Thirty-Four

Darcy pushed the accelerator to the floor, her head and shoulder facing the rear as she steered. The Honda shot backwards. The car's little engine screamed, its transmission whining for mercy. The only thought in Darcy's mind was Brack. The lug was on foot in the alley. But he knew how to take care of himself in these situations. That was for sure.

With that machine gun trained on them, she and Mutt were sitting ducks if she didn't get them out of there. Almost reaching the end of the alley, she slowed when the Tahoe returned and blocked her in, maneuvering so its length sat roughly across the entry to prevent escape.

"Ram him again," Mutt yelled. "Don't let up."

The driver got out and peppered the back of the Honda with bullets.

Mutt returned fire through the already busted back window.

Darcy didn't like any of this. She closed the distance to the Tahoe, and at the last moment, cut the wheel left and caught the front fender of the truck and rear quarter panel of a parked car. The impact jarred them in their seats. And to her surprise, the impact moved the SUV. But not enough.

Mutt fired his gun at its driver, yelling to her, "Get out and run!"

Darcy pulled her thirty-two. "You first."

"Dammit, girl! Git!"

She crawled over the console and opened the passenger door.

"Mutt," she said, "as soon as I get out, you follow. I'll cover. We both need to get out of here."

At that moment a muzzle pressed against her head.

A man said, "I wouldn't do that if I were you."

She watched Mutt turn to see what was happening and to swing his pistol around.

Someone shot him twice in the chest.

Darcy screamed and tried to turn to face her attacker.

That's when she was clubbed on the head and the lights went out.

Chapter Thirty-Five

Sunday, ten a.m.

Brack kept suppressive fire on the man with the submachine gun. With only seven bullets in a full mag, he had four left. Then it was on to plan B. In his case, run like the wind.

Boom. Pause. *Boom.* Pause. *Boom.* Pause. *Boom.* Click.

Empty.

Run.

Brack turned and caught a fist in the mouth. The next thing he knew he was in the air. Then a very hard crash into something solid. His already injured back erupted in pain. He crumpled to the ground, unable to move anything.

"So," a voice said above him, "you're the one causing all this ruckus."

His brain scrambled to make sense of his situation. He couldn't get up, couldn't formulate words, couldn't shoot. He was a dead man. So he did the only thing he could, physically. He spat in the direction of the voice.

"Aw, man!"

Then Brack heard another voice say, "Townsend sends his regards." Next, a shoe kicked him. Hard.

He blacked out.

Chapter Thirty-Six

Darcy came to at the jostle of the floor beneath her. She blinked a few times and realized her situation. She lay in the back of a large SUV, her hands bound behind her back, her feet tied together.

The interior of the vehicle smelled like vanilla. Either the owner liked the scent or they'd taken Mutt's vaporizer.

Brack lay facing her. She stared at him, thinking not about how to escape, but about their history together. The last time they were this close, she'd been shot and he was saving her life by stanching her blood loss. But even before that, when they'd first met, there'd been a connection between them—despite his having been so hard to get close to. It began as a lingering attraction, but she soon found herself needing to be near him. And she didn't like that one bit, which is why she'd pushed him away. When he found comfort in the arms of another woman, she had bolted to Atlanta.

All of it one big mistake after another.

And now Mutt was dead and they were next.

At that moment, the SUV hit a pothole and Brack stirred.

Chapter Thirty-Seven

Brack opened his eyes and found himself looking at a bound and gagged Darcy. Her eyes were slate gray, a piece of duct tape stuck across her mouth. He realized he had tape across his own as well. His hands were bound behind his back. And his ankles were tied together. His back hurt.

Not good.

The floor bounced again. He winced. They lay in the very back of a moving SUV. Probably the Tahoe.

Really not good.

The interior smelled like Mutt's vanilla vapor.

Brack tested the binds on his hands. Tight, but with some movement. Which was all he needed. Afghanistan taught him a lot. Like shoot first or die hesitating. Trust his instincts. And zip ties are less flexible than twine and far superior for binding legs and arms. He worked the knot at his wrists, tied by inexperience and twine, and wriggled free in thirty seconds.

Darcy watched him gain freedom of his hands and turned to give him access to her bound hands. But like the airplane stewards say during their safety instructions to passengers, first make sure you can breathe before helping someone else. So Brack knew he had to be a hundred percent unbound, ready to fight, before he could help Darcy.

The moment he freed his ankles, a man riding in the backseat turned. He saw Brack at the same time Brack saw him. In the man's mouth was Mutt's vaporizer. Before he could speak, Brack sprung, grabbed the man's already turned head and twisted it further, breaking his neck.

The driver skidded to a stop.

Brack dove over the dead man in the backseat and shoved both the driver and the front passenger forward. Neither wore seatbelts. The driver's head slammed into the steering wheel. His partner had more distance to travel so his forward motion smashed him into the windshield.

Before the driver roused himself, Brack punched him twice in the face, then turned to the passenger. The man was dazed. Seeing his own forty-five stuck in the man's waistband, Brack pulled it out and cracked the man across the skull. He did the same to the driver.

Horns blew and Brack realized the SUV was stopped in the middle of busy Peachtree Street, holding up traffic.

Brack reached across the seat to the passenger door handle, opened the door, and shoved the man out onto the street. Then he opened the other door and did the same for the driver, got behind the wheel, and accelerated away.

When he reached Lenox Mall, Brack pulled in, parked in one of the garages, and freed Darcy. He also found Mutt's vaporizer and put it in his pocket.

Without a word, they got out of the SUV, walked through the mall, and escaped out a side door.

A Marta station sign loomed across the outdoor parking lot. The three idiots in the SUV hadn't taken Brack's wallet, so he paid for two tickets and he and Darcy walked to the platform to wait for the next train.

Not until they made it to a bench did Darcy collapse, cry, and heave.

Brack stooped next to her. "Breathe...Breathe...Breathe..."

The small crowd on the platform stared but kept their distance.

She heaved a few more times. "Mutt—"

The train came.

Brack helped her up. "Tell me when we get moving."

They boarded the train and found two seats away from the other passengers, several of whom kept an eye on the pair.

When the doors closed, Darcy took a deep breath and spoke. "They shot Mutt."

"Did they kill him?"

She put her head in her hands. "I think so. They shot at him twice before they knocked me out and dragged me from the car."

Although the idiots hadn't taken his wallet, his iPhone was fair game. Not that they could have done anything with it unless they broke his passcode. Darcy didn't have either her purse or her phone.

Brack said, "We need to call Brother Thomas."

They rode the gold line to Five Points Station, the heart of Atlanta, and exited the Marta system. Brack bought them two Cokes, breaking a twenty to get change, and found something of a relic: a phone booth.

Darcy called her news office and spoke to someone named Dana. Apparently the word was already out about their little O.K. Corral gunfight. Their captors had left her car, and Mutt, at the scene.

"Mutt's alive?" she yelled into the payphone. "Where is he?"

A tightness in Brack's chest lightened. His friend lived.

Darcy told Dana, "We're going to the hospital. Tell Ben when I get an Emmy for this, he's going to double my salary or I quit." She hung up. "The police are looking for us."

"I'm not ready to talk to them yet." Brack called Brother Thomas and told him where Mutt was.

Darcy and Brack rode the Marta train to the East Point stop and walked to the hospital.

Mutt was in the ICU. One of the two shots to his chest punctured a lung, which had the doctors worried.

Brack pulled the vaporizer out of his pocket as if to show Mutt he'd recovered it.

Shortly after he and Darcy arrived, Brother Thomas rushed into the waiting area. "You all got some explaining to do."

The last thing Brack wanted to hear was how Brother Thomas thought they'd screwed up. They were doing what they were supposed to: trying to find Regan.

He said, "No, we don't."

Brother Thomas stopped in his tracks and looked at Brack.

Darcy also looked at him.

"Before you start," Brack said to his friend and pastor, "I want to say that I wish it were me lying in that bed there instead of Mutt. I wish we hadn't gotten into a gunfight that ended the lives of at least two bad men. I wish I hadn't put Darcy's life in danger. Again. I wish a lot of things. We did the best we could. Mutt got hit. And that's that."

Brack walked from the room, went down the hall, and rode the elevator to the ground floor. Outside, he figured out how to operate Mutt's vaporizer and got ready to vape for the first time. And realized how upset he really was at seeing his friend in the hospital. He meant everything he'd said to Brother Thomas. He needed only to get it out.

Resting his hand against a post in a covered area designated for smoking, he took a few puffs off the vaporizer. The jolt he got told him Mutt had really dialed up the nicotine. His fingertips and toes tingled from the vapor.

Two women sitting on a bench at the opposite end smoked real cigarettes.

Brack felt an arm on his shoulder and turned. It was Darcy. She didn't say anything. He put the vaporizer in his pocket and faced her. She kept her eyes on his and tears streaked down her face. He wiped them with his hands. She moved in close and rested her head on his shoulder. He held her in his arms for the first time in two years, since when she'd been shot, and let her cry some more.

After enough time for a slow dance, she said, "Thanks for getting us out of that alive."

"We were set up real good today."

"Yes, we were."

"What do you want to do about it?"

She pushed herself gently away. Still looking at him, she said, "I want some payback for what they did to Mutt."

"Me too," came a voice from behind them. Brother Thomas added, "I'm sorry, Brother Brack."

Still looking at Darcy, Brack said, "Me too."

"Let me finish," he said.

Brack turned to meet his gaze. "Okay."

"I wasn't trying to accuse you of anything except not callin' me."

"Then you might have gotten shot too."

"True," he said. "But maybe I could have said a few prayers for us all, mm-hmm."

"Still can."

"Already have," he said. "What we gonna do now?"

Darcy said, "Let me make a few calls. Though I no longer have my speed dial."

Within the hour, Detective Nichols came and took their statements. He said three men had died in the alley. All were Vito's men. They'd found the Tahoe parked at the mall with the dead guy in the backseat, his neck snapped. And the police had lifted Brack's and Darcy's prints from the interior, plus several others, and were trying to match those. The dazed driver and his passenger, whom Brack had kicked out onto Peachtree Street, alive, were nowhere to be found.

After visiting hours were over, Brack spent the rest of the night sitting in a chair in the waiting room. Brother Thomas sat in a chair facing him. Neither of them spoke. There was nothing to say. Brother Thomas knew that Brack, as well as Darcy, who'd gone home to clean up and get another phone, would go after those who'd shot Mutt. But he said he didn't want them to. The pastor and Brack and Darcy were at an impasse.

Chapter Thirty-Eight

Monday, seven a.m.

For the second day in a row, Brack's morning sleep was interrupted. Except this time it was by Cassie.

He'd slouched in his chair in the hospital waiting area and used the magazine table as a footrest, the closest to horizontal he could manage. On waking, his foot knocked a stack of magazines onto the floor.

"Brack," she said. "Mutt's awake. He asked for you."

Rubbing his eyes, Brack said, "What are you doing out of bed?"

She showed him the cane she'd been practicing with for the last couple of days and had used to help her walk to Mutt's room. "Don't you worry about me. Go on and see him."

Brack stood, stretched, felt his back complain, and twisted his head from side to side. Then he walked into the room where Mutt lay. Tubes following surgery still stuck out of everywhere. But he was off the respirator and conscious.

He watched Brack approach.

"Opie." He coughed. "I heard you got a few of 'em."

He held out his hand and Brack took it in both of his.

"We both did," Brack said, "but I missed a few too."

"How you think they got onto us?"

"The john spotted me taking his picture at the airport. Or the talkative chauffeur was a plant. Either way, it was downhill from there."

"What's the next plan?"

"For you to get better."

Mutt coughed again and winced with pain. "I'm sorry I'm gonna have to sit the rest of this one out."

"Don't worry," Brack said. "I'll make sure you get regular news updates."

His eyes met Brack's. "Don't you go and get yourself killed now. Hear?"

Brack nodded but didn't reply.

"Regan ain't worth all this trouble."

He was thinking the same thing.

Brack took a cab back to his room to get his things and moved into Mutt's house because he was tired of the hotel. After a shower and some breakfast, he sat on the patio, Mutt's portable phone by his side, and called Darcy's office to get her the message where he was since he didn't have a number for her new phone yet.

As he cleaned his gun, Darcy drove up in a brand-new Range Rover and parked in the driveway.

"Old Hondas not cutting it for you any more?" Brack asked.

"Very funny. This is Justin's." She sat down in a chair next to him on the patio.

Being reminded of the peckerwood was not what Brack wanted at the moment. He concentrated on wiping the oil residue off his forty-five.

Mutt's landline rang. Brack, with no cell phone of his own, knew to pick up. It was Brother Thomas asking, "You seen Cassie?"

In that instant, Brack knew the situation had plummeted from bad to worse. "No." At least he thought he answered. He felt dazed.

Darcy focused on his face and he shook his head.

Brother Thomas continued, "She checked herself out of the hospital against her doctor's orders and hasn't been seen since."

Brack said, "What comes to mind is that she's going after her sister."

"That's what I was thinkin'," he said. "We got to find her before she do something stupid. Whatever that is."

Brack thought he had a monopoly on stupid. But anger and fear and overconfidence apparently had similar effects on the judgment of others at times. Like right now. Cassie's decision to confront her sister, if that's what she planned to do, was straight-out suicidal.

Darcy said, "This is a trap."

"Of course it is," Brack said. "Vito probably assigned someone to keep tabs on Cassie since she landed in the hospital, if not before. But what choice do we have?"

"We can call in the police."

"Good idea," Brack said. "We're going to need them."

Brack sensed that Darcy might not believe he was sincere, so he pulled out his wallet, found Detective Nichols's card, and dialed the number on the landline.

Nichols answered and Brack explained that Cassie was missing and why he feared trouble.

The detective said, "Don't do anything stupid."

A recurring theme. Sometimes Brack listened to reason. And he tried real hard to make this one of those times.

Chapter Thirty-Nine

Cassie knew she didn't have a lot of time before people started looking for her. She had managed to dress and check herself out of the hospital without much of a fuss. A cab ride back to her house to get her car and now, noon, she was on her way.

As she drove she mentally kicked herself, not for the first time, for calling Brack at all two weeks ago. He was a sweet boy, and damn if he warn't fine. All it took to get him here was a few white lies. She knew if Brack thought Mutt was in danger he'd come runnin'. It was true. Mutt was in danger. But she let on like she didn't know about his juke joint.

She shoulda handled this with Regan herself.

Cassie had an address from, of all things, the society papers. She'd seen a picture of Vito hosting a cocktail party at a lavish West Paces Ferry home and figured her sister was probably there.

Brack and the others didn't need be involved any more than they already was, she thought. All she'd wanted was her sister back. Mutt, bein' who he was, Cassie figured would be dead within a week if he went looking for her alone. It took her less time than that to find out about his bar and get her friend Tara to work there and keep tabs on him.

With Nina dead and Mutt in the hospital, Tara, Brack, or Darcy could be next. Enough was enough. She would go get Regan herself, snatch that tramp up bald-headed if that was what it took.

Cassie pulled into the spacious drive, stopped at the gate with a keypad, and pressed the intercom button.

A voice said, "May I help you?"

Cassie yelled, "I'm here for Regan."

Chapter Forty

Another fundraiser was taking place. Even in an off-election year, this city was filled with them. Darcy, of course, would be there with her fiancé. Brack needed backup, but Mutt was in the hospital. The cost was a cool five grand for two tickets, whether Brack used both or not. So he visited the bank once more and showed up with Tara to his second black-tie function in less than a week.

He'd had to replace his favorite, and only, tux with a new one since it didn't survive the explosion unscathed. To pay for it, he'd decided to use his credit card. He hoped that would confuse Vito when he discovered the charge.

This event was held at a swanky downtown hotel. One of Darcy's many sources said Vito and his entourage had checked into a suite. The source also said that with them was a short plump woman. Her description matched Cassie's.

The valet didn't say much when Brack showed up in his turbo Mazda. But every male in the vicinity checked out Tara in her strapless gown.

Even that, unfortunately, failed to get them front-row parking.

Tara and Brack found the right ballroom, walked in, and handed the tickets to a pretty twenty-something in a sequined dress. Brack's goal was to find Vito and confirm whether he had Cassie. The killer's so-called diplomatic immunity kept him from being arrested, but it didn't prevent them from harassing him. Or beating him to death, whichever came first.

Tara, nervous, excused herself and went to the ladies' room.

Someone Brack didn't expect to see was Detective Nichols. He stood at the bar in a tux and Brack joined him.

"Here goes my evening," Nichols said.

Brack said, "Glad you could make it. I didn't know you were a socialite."

Nichols's smile told him to go pound salt. "I'm working."

"Me too."

"No, you're not."

"First you want my help and now you don't. Make up your mind."

"The Governor's here," Nichols said. "If something bad goes down, I will probably lose my job."

"Don't worry," Brack said, popping a piece of Bubblicious in his mouth. "I'll make sure to take it outside."

"Vito's not at the event," he said.

Apparently Nichols didn't have Darcy's intel about Vito's sighting. Brack thought about telling him this time but elected not to. If the detective was already acting paranoid, that wouldn't help.

"I'll take my chances," Brack said.

"Part of the reason I'm here." Nichols now smiled. "A special team is raiding three of Vito's stockyards right now."

"Stockyards?" Brack asked.

Nichols said, "What he calls the apartment buildings where he keeps the young girls. As soon as we have them in custody, it's only a matter of time before one of them sells out their boss."

"You weren't going to share this with me?"

"It was strictly need to know."

Brack walked away from the big city heat.

The new phone he'd picked up earlier in the afternoon vibrated inside the pocket of his new tux jacket. He pulled it out and saw a text message from Darcy. It read, "Room 7500."

Tara returned. He showed her the message and texted back what Nichols said. Then he told Tara about the raids.

She said, "What's our plan?"

"Find the elevators, head to the seventy-fifth floor, and unleash the hounds of hell."

"Oh, is that all?"

"He's got Cassie," Brack said. "If you want out, I'll understand."

"She's like a sister to me," Tara said. "I'm in all the way."

If Cassie had been standing with them, he'd have suggested that she disown Regan and adopt Tara as her real sister.

Instead, he looked for the elevators.

To get to the seventy-fifth floor, the elevator required a specially coded room key.

"What do you say we get a room?" Brack asked Tara.

She laughed and touched his collar. "As handsome as you are in your tux, I don't think tonight is your lucky night."

"Too bad for me," he said. "But we still need to get to the upper floors."

She gave him a peck on the cheek. "Lead the way."

Hotel guest services had two suites available, both on the eightieth floor. Because his credit card was being tracked by Vito, he didn't want to tip his hand. Tara charged the room on her card.

In the elevator, their key card opened the electronic lock that allowed them to travel above the fiftieth floor.

Brack pressed eighty.

Tara said, "I thought we wanted seventy-five?"

"Let's check out the layout before we venture into harm's way."

And that's exactly what they did. Assuming the seventy-fifth floor was arranged identically to the eightieth, Vito's room would lie in the hotel's northeastern corner. After checking out how their own suite was laid out, they rode the elevator down five floors and got out.

Lucky for them, the floors were identical in layout. Their plan was for Tara to walk down the corridor toward Vito's room. If there was a guard, he'd most likely be looking for Brack, not her.

Brack waited around the closest corner, counting seconds while Tara did reconnaissance. If she didn't return in two minutes, he was charging the door.

Forty seconds into his count, he heard a man's voice start to say, "What—"

A thump followed. None of it sounded good.

Brack drew his forty-five and charged around the corner. Tara stood over an unconscious man lying on the floor. The door to the suite opened five inches and a hand extending from it held a pistol. Still moving forward, Brack lowered his gun, brushed past Tara, and crashed into the door. Whoever stood behind it was knocked back into the room. Brack wasted no time smashing his forty-five into the head of the man trying to regain his footing and hang onto the gun. The man failed both tries and fell.

Darcy's earlier information said Vito had a short plump woman and two guards with him. That should have been it as far as guards went, Brack thought.

Except two more rushed him, weapons drawn. A mistake on their part.

Brack shot both of them and lowered his gun. The three men inside were sprawled on the floor, all bleeding. The man Tara cold-cocked outside still lay there.

From the walkthrough Tara and Brack had done of "their" room on the eightieth floor, he knew the bedroom was located past the lounge area to the left. A young woman—not Cassie—stepped out of the bedroom, Vito right behind her, a gun to her head.

Tara gasped.

Brack aimed his forty-five. "The police are raiding your stockyards as we speak, Vito. I don't know who this woman is. But if you kill her, we'll kill you. There's no win here for you. It's over."

At that moment Tara turned, saw a guard sneaking up behind them, and caught him with an elbow to the throat. He was the unconscious one from outside the door who'd obviously come to. Now he writhed on the ground, his face blue, clutching his throat.

The action occupied Tara and momentarily distracted Brack. Vito quickly shoved the woman to him and ran out of the suite.

The woman collided into Brack and they fell to the floor. Brack got to his feet and gave chase, leaving Tara to deal with the woman.

Chapter Forty-One

Monday, nine p.m.

The elevator corridor was empty of people. He pressed the down button and phoned Darcy.

She answered, "The cops just finished raiding three of Vito's brothels. Where are you?"

"Waiting on an elevator. Tonight, here, was another setup. Cassie wasn't in his suite, but four more of Vito's goons are now out of commission. He's on his way down. Probably on the run now. Where are you?"

"In the lobby with Justin. Wait—Vito is just getting off an elevator. He is heading out the door."

"Watch where he goes." He ended the call.

The bell dinged, he checked inside the elevator before he stepped into it, then pressed the lobby. It stopped once and a couple got on. With no further interruptions, they were in the lobby in less than a minute. Brack brushed past the man and woman. She said something snarky to him, but he ignored her and ran to the main entrance.

Outside, Darcy waited with Justin for a valet to bring their car.

"He just pulled away," Darcy said, and pointed. "He's in his black Mercedes G."

Justin's new Range Rover pulled to the curb.

Darcy watched Brack, used to his antics.

He shouted to Justin, "I need to borrow your wheels," handed the valet a ten, got in, and sped off.

If Brack hadn't been in such a hurry, he might have pondered

Darcy's shaking her head, as if saying "tsk, tsk, tsk" to a naughty boy.

In the first five seconds as he looked around for the black Benz, Brack guessed she'd warn Justin that he'd likely not see his SUV in one piece again. Too bad, because it was a very nice ride.

The Supercharged V-8 roared down the avenue as Brack gave the heavy vehicle more speed than seemed logical.

By the first intersection, his mind focused completely on Vito's worthlessness. He'd put Mutt and Cassie in the hospital, ruined countless lives, and was a death-causing parasite. He deserved to be taken out, no matter what Brother Thomas thought.

Brack's phone buzzed again and he hit the speaker button.

"Where do you think you're going with our car?" Darcy asked.

Ignoring her question, he said, "If he's on the run, where do you think he would be going?"

In the background he heard Justin yelling at her to demand that he bring back his Range Rover.

She said, "Vito owns a small private plane."

Brack said, "Lead me to it."

The background noise suggested she was arguing with Justin. She came back on the line. "Let me see what I can find out. Just don't hurt Justin's car. It's the love of his life."

It could have been the way the speaker amplified her voice, but Brack detected a hint of resentment, or maybe it was resignation.

The next voice Brack heard was Justin's. He said, "Hey you— Pelton—you better bring my—"

Brack hit end call.

A large pothole jarred him back to the task at hand. So much for taking care of the peckerwood's wheels. That crater was a doozy.

Right about now Darcy would be trying to talk Justin out of calling the police, because he dreaded the condition of the "love of his life" after Brack was done with it. If Brack managed to catch Vito before he left for the Caribbean—or wherever—and ended up totaling Justin's prized possession in the process, he'd buy him a new one. He was already out a $125K Porsche anyway.

Why he was calculating the cost of vehicles when he should be focused on stopping Vito was not clear to him. Maybe because he couldn't bear to think that his recklessness had already put two of his friends in the hospital. He wouldn't stop until he'd delivered payback, expensive German sports cars and peckerwood Range Rovers be damned.

Brack pulled over and consulted his new iPhone for the addresses of airports Vito could be headed to. The big one, Hartsfield-Jackson Atlanta, probably wasn't it for a private plane. There were three others, Dekalb Peachtree, Fulton County, and Gwinnett County. He ruled out Gwinnett County as it was too far away, but he wasn't sure about the other two. A wrong choice would put him on the opposite side of the city from the right choice, with no time left on the clock. As if reading his mind, Darcy called back.

She said, "I just learned that his plane is at Fulton County."

She gave him the address and he entered it in the Range Rover's GPS. It lay west of downtown.

"Hurry, because he is really running. His plane is scheduled to leave within the hour." She ended the call.

Bless all her contacts.

A glance at the gas gauge reassured Brack that the peckerwood had recently filled it. A straight drag race between the supercharged Range Rover and Vito's G63 AMG turbocharged Mercedes would end in a dead heat. Brack could only hope that Vito was in less of a hurry to leave than he was in trying to prevent it.

Twenty minutes later and five miles from the target airport, what should he see ahead of him but one of those German tank SUVs. Brack pushed the accelerator harder and the Rover rocketed forward. When he pulled even with the suspicious SUV, he saw the color and décor to be spot on. Black paint, dark windows, and black wheels.

The four-lane road was mostly clear of traffic. With now only about four miles left, Brack had to act fast. A light ahead turned yellow, then red. He ran it. Vito did not. Planting his foot to the floor, Brack accelerated to a hundred miles an hour, then a mile down the road at an intersection he slammed on the brakes and made a U-turn, heading east back toward Vito.

If now were an updated peacetime World War II, he was driving one of the best trucks Britain made and Vito was driving Germany's pinnacle in pedestrian SUVs. Brack wondered, not idly, how each would fare in a head-on collision with the other.

He drove toward Vito on the wrong side of the road and turned on the HID brights. The landscape in front of him exploded with light. The headlights of Vito's oncoming Benz cut through the glare. Brack rotated the steering wheel from side to side, taking up the whole lane.

At sixty miles an hour, one mile would take exactly a minute. With both objects traveling toward each other at that velocity, impact would occur in thirty seconds. Brack accelerated to run out the clock.

They approached each other and the front of Vito's truck loomed. Brack's lights revealed Vito was his own driver, jerking the wheel to Brack's left to avoid impact. Brack mirrored his movements with his own. He saw Vito's eyes grow wide realizing the inevitable.

Five seconds before impact, the Range Rover shut down. Brack lost all control of the steering wheel. It locked. The engine cut off and its lack of aerodynamics kicked in, slowing the brick-shaped SUV down dramatically. In the same five seconds Vito's Mercedes slammed into the curb and bounced up onto the sidewalk. Sparks flew and it crashed into a telephone pole. The Range Rover crawled to a stop, its front wheels gently kissing the same curb, missing the Benz by what had to be the thinnest margin in history.

Aside from the slight chance of a vehicle malfunction, the only cause for the Range Rover's complete shutdown could be some kind of theft prevention system. For a second, Brack imagined punching Justin Welcott the third in the mouth. Regardless, he had to check on Vito.

His door refused to unlock, so Brack crawled over the seats and tried the other doors. Same thing. He decided the rear glass would be the easiest to break so he gave it two solid kicks. It shattered and fell onto the road. He crawled through the opening, grateful for safety glass and its lack of sharp edges.

Vito's two-hundred-thousand-dollar rig was a steaming mess. His own evasive steering caused him to hit the telephone pole head on, pushing the front grill into the radiator, and the radiator into the engine. He was still inside. Thanks to the logic programmed into the Merc's onboard computer, in the event of an accident the doors unlocked. Brack grabbed the handle and hefted the door open. Vito looked dazed and confused, his tanned face red and blotchy from the airbag's explosion. But otherwise uninjured.

However, Vito's condition was about to take a turn for the worse. Brack grabbed his shirt and cocked a fist in time to hear sirens and see a squadron of blue lights fast approaching from the east. That forced an immediate decision. He punched Vito in the face as hard as he could. Three times. He raced back to the Range Rover, crawled back in, and stuck his gun under the front seat. By the time the approaching headlights illuminated his actions, Brack was pulling a now unconscious Vito from the Mercedes and laying him gently on the asphalt.

In his ear, Brack whispered, "You got off easy just now. I'm not done with you."

The police cars pulled to a stop. Two officers helped him up and asked if he was okay. Brack said he was, except for a pulled back. They next asked if he was Brack Pelton. Again he said he was. Then they detained him.

Turns out that Justin had activated the Range Rover's customized internal security system via a cell phone call to the vehicle. Doing that had shut everything down before the love of his life became a hunk of scrap steel and aluminum to be recycled. That reflex action Brack attributed to Justin's selfish denial of public responsibility, not brains. He didn't seem smart enough to warrant any sort of compliment for foresight.

What Brack wouldn't admit even to himself was that Justin's action had probably saved him from a head-on collision and a trip to the hospital—if he survived the inevitable crash. But he would never acknowledge that truth for the rest of his days.

Brack stood by the police cruiser in the glare of its rotating blue lights, his hands zip-tied in front of him, and watched Darcy and Justin arrive on the scene by cab. At first he thought the anti-carjacking system on the Range Rover must have told them where he was. Then he remembered that Darcy knew just about everything that went on anywhere, anytime anyway.

Justin strode toward Brack with his left fist clenched to throw a punch. Brack made a split-second decision to let him get it out of his system and Justin tagged him on the right jaw. That punch probably hurt his own hand more than Brack's face. Justin balled his fist for another hit, but Darcy grabbed his hand.

"Stop it!" she yelled.

The way Darcy looked at Brack he could tell she feared he might hurt her fiancé. Brack gave her a slight head shake, letting her know he wasn't going to. Instead, he raised his bound hands to his jaw, making a display of his helplessness.

Detective Nichols spun Justin around and pushed him against the cruiser.

Brack said, "I'm not going to press charges."

Nichols looked at Brack.

A new thought occurred to Brack. "At least, I won't if you let me make a phone call right now. Otherwise, well, I might just have to file against your department too."

Nichols smirked, understanding how it would look if a civilian punched someone in custody and they let it happen. He cut the binding on Brack's wrists.

As Brack walked away, he heard Detective Nichols say, "Don't leave the scene, Pelton."

"No problem, boss."

He pulled out his new cell phone.

Brother Thomas answered on the second ring.

Before he could say a word, Brack told him, "I got Vito, but I don't think this is done yet. Cassie wasn't with him."

"Where is Regan?" he asked.

"I don't know." Brack realized he hadn't even considered that she might have been in the SUV with Vito. Vengeance had blinded him to the possibility that he could have killed her in the crash. Idiot. Instead, he said, "We have to find Cassie. I bet she went after her sister. But first, I need a lawyer."

How one wild girl could start a series of dominoes falling to bring together all these tragedies was beyond comprehension. Regrettably, this happened around Brack a lot.

Chapter Forty-Two

Monday, quarter to midnight

The police did not release Brack. Thanks to Justin Welcott the third—and over Darcy's protest—Brack was charged with grand theft auto. He sensed trouble brewing in paradise, but didn't mind seeing another man's pride take him down. Especially that man. Brack's own pride had done enough damage over the years.

He was placed in a holding cell with mostly minority folks coming down from whatever chemicals had gotten them into trouble and landed them in there. The Latinos stood together on one side and the African-Americans held the other side. There were only three whites, including Brack. He still wore his new tux. Keeping to himself, he stood in a corner and thought about where, once he was released, he might find Regan. Brother Thomas was currently very busy trying to find him a lawyer for the hearing.

Predictably, it didn't take long before Brack's loner strategy for self-preservation was tested. Two Latino thugs, tats up and down their arms and necks, approached.

"Ese," one said, "what you in for?" His nose displayed a red sore where, Brack assumed, some form of jewelry had resided before the police made him remove it before locking him up.

"I stole a Range Rover," Brack said, already tired and not in the mood for this. "How about you guys?"

The holding cell became quiet. Everyone focused their attention on the new floor show.

The second thug, who wore red sneakers, said, "We took a sweet white boy like you into the bushes and made him our bitch."

Brack nodded. "You must have been hard up."

Chuckles came from the African-American section.

"You think that funny, ese?" asked Red Sneakers.

"Hey man," Brack said, "I don't judge. You like white guys. I get it."

The two squinted at him, as if trying to decide what to do next. All this time Brack had been looking them in the eyes, which he'd heard was a mistake. His failure to cower at their implied threats was likely to get him killed.

Another Latino from the group in the corner called out, "Hey, Raoul, he call you a homo. You gonna take that?"

Before either of the two facing Brack could respond, one of the black men said, "He call it like he see it."

All eyes in the Latinos' corner turned from Brack to the group of African-Americans.

Red Sneakers said, "You stay out of this, *mayate*."

Brack's Spanish was more than a little rusty, but he knew that was not the smartest insult to be used in a place like this.

The African-Americans grew in stature. Brack hadn't realized it before, but the shortest man matched his own six-foot height and the rest stretched upwards of six-five, six-six. They formed a wall.

The Latino contingent, all of them under six feet, lined up in opposition.

Brack's two fellow whites did their best to slink away from the middle. It was about to become a war zone, and the three of them would be collateral damage if Brack didn't do some—

Too late.

One of the Latinos pulled out a shiv that a decent search should have confiscated and stabbed the closest black man. Then all hell broke loose.

Brack jumped into the fray, deciding at the last minute to team up with the African-Americans whether they liked it or not. He grabbed the first Latino he found who also possessed a heretofore hidden shiv and broke his arm. Then Brack punched another and elbowed a third in the face.

The Latino with red sneakers swung his own shiv at one of the African-Americans who'd had his back turned. Brack caught the hand with the shiv and wrenched the wrist backwards until it popped. Brack caught a fist in the face and all of a sudden had two shivs swinging at him from two different directions. An African-American turned around in time to realize Brack saved him from getting stuck. The black man slammed the heads of the two Latinos together and they collapsed.

Brack turned to face another attacker only to find there weren't any. All the Latinos lay on the floor, along with three black men. The rest stood breathing hard but victorious.

"You fight pretty good for a cracker," said the man Brack saved.

"Thanks."

"What make you think we ain't gonna finish you off too?"

"You're not into white guys?"

The man gave Brack a hard glare. Several others also faced him, ready to finish him off, he supposed. The man Brack took to be their leader then faced the ceiling and laughed. A second or two later, the others began to laugh.

"You real funny."

As if knowing the threat was over, two guards appeared who should have heard all the ruckus from the start but failed to intervene. They stood at the cell door and one of them said, "All right, what happened?"

Brack held up his hands. "There weren't enough white guys for them to play house with. So they started fighting over us."

All the cellmates still standing laughed even harder.

The guards looked at everyone laughing, then at the men bleeding and busted up on the floor, and called for reinforcements.

The situation couldn't have worked out better for Brack. The guards split up the Latinos who hadn't been stabbed or had a broken bone and moved them to their own cell. The bleeding and unconscious, including Brack's two fellow crackers, got an express trip to the infirmary. And Brack got put in isolation.

With his newfound solitude, Brack stretched out on a fairly clean bunk and passed out, secure that he wouldn't be carried into the bushes by any strapping tattooed young men.

Thanks to Brother Thomas's connections, when Brack entered the attorney-client meeting room at nine the next morning, his new lawyer awaited. For the first time this week he'd gotten a great night's sleep, but he looked like he'd been in a jail fight. His face was bruised and scratched, and his new tux was now torn.

The attorney representing Brack was a tall slender African-American woman about fifty who filled out a serious business suit. She reminded him a lot of Pam Grier in the film *Jackie Brown*. Draped across one of the chairs was a garment bag. She gave Brack a disapproving onceover but held out a hand. "Mr. Pelton, I'm Jacqueline Boyd. Brother Thomas sent me to represent you."

Okay, Jackie *Boyd*. "Great, but you can call me Brack."

"Mr. Pelton," she said, "I need to know how you want to plead. With the few facts I have been able to ascertain, I'd recommend not guilty. Promise to pay for the car's rear window and any inconvenience and leave it at that. The judges have too many cases to waste time on something that could be construed as a misunderstanding."

"You really think you can construe it that way?"

"Are you patronizing me?"

"A little," he said. "What I'm guessing you don't know, and which will probably make it hard for you to construe much of anything, is my past record."

She pulled a thick file from her very nice, very expensive briefcase. "You mean this?" Dropping it on the table, the rubber-banded overstuffed folder made a loud thump when it hit the wood surface. "Interesting reading. I usually develop a profile from the contents."

"Let me guess," he said. "You just found the man of your dreams."

A stiff grin lightened her face a fraction. "Actually, I already found him. He's my husband."

"Too bad for the rest of us," Brack said. "So skip the psycho-babble and give me a rundown of the profile you have of yours truly."

"Impulsive, heroic, manic, masochistic, loyal, arrogant, lost, direct, immature, dangerous, and self-destructive."

"You forgot hedonistic and chaotic."

"I was trying to be nice."

Brack chuckled. "Gee, thanks."

"Word is there was a bad fight in your cell last night."

"I had a cell to myself," he said, waiting to see just how good her info was.

"Yeah," she said, "you did. *After* the fight ended and they had to cart fourteen men out, several with stab wounds and broken bones."

"No thanks to the officers supposedly guarding the holding cell. Anyway, I'm here in one piece, aren't I?"

"Barely." She handed him the garment bag. "Put this on before court. When you go in front of the judge we can't have you looking like you had too many drinks at a party and went joy-riding in someone else's car."

"I'll try to keep that in mind."

"Do that." She gathered the file folder that constituted his record.

Brack noticed the name written on it was not his own.

His attorney watched and gave a sly grin. "We're scheduled for ten a.m."

It occurred to Brack that her mostly spot-on profile of him had come not from the file in her hands but from their brief meeting just now. Plus maybe from Brother Thomas. Brack considered it "mostly spot-on" because he thought she threw in the masochistic part only to rattle him. It almost worked. Or maybe he *was* masochistic.

*   *   *

Jacqueline Boyd worked the judge so well that Brack thought even Darcy could take lessons. When his attorney described his incarceration as a big misunderstanding, batting her eyes and pursing her lips, the judge watched her with a loopy grin on his face. The Assistant D.A., a wet-behind-the-ears wannabe all of twenty-five, didn't have a chance. His thick glasses and bad complexion did not work in his favor. Too bad, because he'd done a lot of homework digging up Brack's past. Prepared he was. Unfortunately, he could not overcome the judge's appreciation of the defense attorney's many skills.

Brack walked out a free man, thanks to Jackie Boyd and the judge's generous dismissal of the charges against him. As long as she defended cases in front of him prosecuted by a pimply kid, the District Attorney's office had no chance—a scandal in the making.

Vito, on the other hand, had not fared so well. After a police-guarded hospital stay, he was detained for a whole slew of activities. His diplomatic status would save him from jail in the States, but Brack had a feeling he would be deported within the week.

"Can I at least buy you a cup of coffee?" Brack asked his attorney.

"Even with the new suit, you look like you just got out of jail, and I don't socialize with clients."

"I'd say your representation of me ended as soon as the judge banged the gavel. Call it a thank-you gesture. Or stay on the clock and call it a business meeting."

She slipped her phone out of her briefcase. "You have an answer for everything, don't you?"

"That's your job," he said. "I'm only trying to be friendly."

The grin returned. The one that mesmerized the judge. It was working on Brack too. "Okay. There's a Starbucks around the corner. My treat. Or ultimately yours after I bill you."

With the heat of the day just coming on, they found shade on a bench under a tree. Turned out she really was happily married. And had been an A.D.A. until the dark side of defense lured her with large stacks of cash, which Brack would be adding to.

"Brother Thomas said I stood to make a lot of money off you," she said. "How long can I count on your being in town and in trouble?"

"As long as it takes."

"I'm guessing that not knowing your business would be in my best interest."

"Correct," he said. "Sounds like you want to stay on retainer."

"You're the perfect client," she said. "You can afford my fees and you have a propensity for staying in trouble."

Brack raised his cup. "Cheers to that."

"Mr. Pelton," she said, tapping his cup with hers, "this could be the start of a beautiful friendship."

Chapter Forty-Three

Tuesday afternoon

Brack had previously discovered that life was easier when he had a good lawyer to get him out of jams. Today looked like he'd retained the Wonder Woman of barristers.

He tooled down Peachtree in the turbo hatchback, thinking he was luckier than he deserved to be. Except that Mutt was still recovering in the hospital and no one had yet found Regan or Cassie. So he still had to remain in town. Oh, and Darcy was still marrying the peckerwood.

His pocket vibrated as he slowed for a light. Darcy was calling.

"Speak of the devil," he said.

"Whatever," she said. "Sounds like you survived your night in jail."

"Best sleep I had in months. That's after they moved me into solitary confinement."

"For everyone else's safety, no doubt," she said. "Listen, I'm sorry."

Brack didn't know how to respond to that.

She continued. "Justin has issues about his things."

"Well, to be honest, I was playing a bad game of chicken with his Range Rover when he shut it down. The situation could have ended much worse." He didn't add how close he'd been to ending it all in an intentional head-on collision.

After a pause, she said, "I wish you'd have totaled it."

Brack's turn to pause, surprised.

"Then I would have had to pay for it. Probably better for my bank balance that it washed out the way it did. I already have to replace my Porsche, you know."

"I know."

"Of course you know," he said. "You were kind enough to film a clip and put the carcass—as you put it—on Atlanta's number-one news channel."

"How could I pass up such an opportunity?"

"So what's next?"

She said, "Vito's in custody. Townsend's out of the picture for the time being. We still need to find Cassie. And when we do, I'll bet we find Regan."

Brack said, "We never did find out what was in those warehouses—both the ones by the airport with the old guard, and those the kid tipped Mutt to that the bikers visited at night."

"Maybe you should check it out," she said. "I'm going back through Vito's assets to see if I can find any place Regan could be that Cassie might have known about. Let's regroup later."

"What does the fiancé say of our alliance?"

"This is business. I don't care what he has to say about that."

While Darcy researched Vito's properties to find where Cassie might be, Brack picked up Tara, and the two of them headed to the warehouse where Mutt and he got into their little disagreement and Mutt kicked him out of the car. On the way, they stopped and purchased a set of bolt cutters, a sledge hammer, and a stout pry bar. They had most of the day left before the bikers returned in the dark and he planned on a heck of a lot of breaking and entering.

Trolling the run-down streets of the old warehouse district once again, Brack had to think hard to remember exactly which warehouse. After three failed attempts, they found the one Mutt and he had been shown by young Jacob. Brack recognized the dock by its recent refurbishing.

He and Tara looked around, mostly for motorcycles. No other vehicles were in sight. They got out of the Mazda and carried the tools to the doors. After examining the lock on the side door next to the roll ups, Brack pulled out two thin screwdrivers from their bag.

A voice behind them said, "Whatcha doin?"

To say Brack was startled was an understatement. When he recognized the voice he turned. "Jacob?"

The lanky boy who'd previously guided Mutt and Brack to this location stood behind Brack and Tara. Jacob had managed to successfully sneak up on them both, an extremely unnerving experience.

Tara said, "We want to see what's inside this place."

"Oh," the boy said.

Brack said, "I'm afraid I forgot to bring some baseball cards with me. We'll come back with some."

"That's okay," he said.

Thanks to some training Darcy had given Brack when she'd lived in Charleston, Brack picked the lock. The door swung open to reveal a dark cavernous space. A keypad glowed next to the door, flashing red. No alarm sounded, so Brack guessed the alert signal went somewhere other than a security agency. Although that meant the police were unlikely to show up, he wondered who might. Then he thought if anyone did, it would be Levin and his pathetic road hogs. With their boss in jail, Brack figured they'd be itching for even greater revenge that their barroom bust. He decided they needed to work quickly.

Inside next to the keypad Tara found the light switches. When she flipped them on, the three of them saw a fairly large space, probably a hundred feet wide by three-hundred feet deep. Six large wooden crates stacked in the center were nailed shut. Using the pry bar on one of them, Brack worked the lid, one side at a time. Tara used the handle of the sledge to help pry it up. After about five minutes of sweaty work, the lid came free. They lifted it off and sat it on top of another crate, then looked inside.

Brack stood in shock.

Tara screamed.

Jacob looked at both of them. "What is it?"

In a hoarse voice, Brack said, "Elephant tusks."

Each had been completely removed from the head of a slaughtered elephant so the only thing shipped was the ivory.

Vito really needed to burn in hell. This was federal. International.

Brack called Nichols and told him what they found. And he suggested Nichols get here fast in case the bikers were already on their way. Before any motorcycles showed up, Nichols arrived with ten uniformed officers. Five minutes behind him, Darcy brought her film crew and set up camp. Brack knew that if the contents of all the crates were similar, this was big news.

What would become the largest find of illegal ivory outside of the Atlanta airport made the headline news. And Darcy got the scoop. Further, for what Brack and Tara thought would create good public awareness of the global crime—along with great fundraising possibilities for the local Piedmont Preserve—Darcy interviewed Tara on the spot. The crates of tusks stood behind them, an ominous backdrop. Nichols neglected to press any charges for breaking and entering. As far as he knew, Brack and Tara had found the door open.

With its newfound publicity, not to mention the public outrage that would reverberate around the globe for the next several months, the Piedmont Preserve needed Tara there. So directly after her filmed debut was finished, she took a cab back to her apartment, got her vehicle, then headed to work.

Well into the next day and more than two weeks from when Brack had arrived in town, Darcy and one of her administrative assistants at the network pored over a list of assets they'd compiled from Vito's businesses. It was Darcy who found a listing for a home on Lake Lanier, about sixty miles northeast of the city.

When she met Brack at Mutt's house later that night, she handed him the forty-five, which he'd left under the seat of Justin's Range Rover.

Nichols called ten minutes after midnight.

"There's nobody at Vito's penthouse," Nichols said. "Same with the one in West Paces Ferry."

"What?" Brack said.

"Nobody. I got a judge to sign the warrants based on the disappearance of Cassie and the ivory we found. I have a dozen officers at each place. That's two jurisdictions involved. And now I'm going to be on the short list for ball washer at the next Brave's game."

"Neither Cassie nor Regan were there?"

"Didn't you hear me?" Nichols asked. "Nobody. Nada. Zilch. Both places are deserted."

"Darcy just found out there's another house on Lake Lanier."

Nichols said, "There's no way I can ask for another search warrant in yet another jurisdiction. Not after being zero for two, plus twenty-four officers on overtime."

"You know what this means?" Brack asked.

"Yes. It means before I get fired I'll have to clean up another one of your messes."

"Don't be so negative. You've already caught the man himself. Beat it out of him." Brack wanted to slam the receiver, but that was before expensive iPhones.

Darcy said, "He can't get a warrant?"

"No."

She grabbed her handbag. "I guess it's you and me."

"You better call what's-his-name."

She stopped in mid-motion. "Excuse me?"

"Call Justin. Tell him where we'll be."

"I don't work for you," she said.

Brack said, "Get your uptight feminist panties out of the bunch they're in and call your fiancé." He walked past her toward the Mazda. Without turning to look at her, he continued, "I don't like the guy one bit, but he deserves to know where you'll be."

Chapter Forty-Four

Cassie sat in a chair overlooking Lake Lanier and watched her sister. Two men who'd escorted them from the mansion in West Paces Ferry to here stayed in the room with them, both with guns in holsters under their arms.

Regan paced back and forth. "What would ever make you think I'd wanna come back wit you?"

On a table in front of Regan lay a small mirror with two lines of white powder and a small straw on it.

Cassie said, "Because you're my sister."

Regan stopped. "I *was* your sister. Now look at me. Thanks to your friends I run this whole thing." She leaned over the mirror and did a line of the powder.

Cassie asked, "What do you mean?"

Regan raised her head. "Who you think got Vito to check into that fancy hotel suite with someone who looked like you? You know, someone short an' fat." She approached Cassie and put a hand on her shoulder. "An' your friends come a runnin'. We wanted that dumb Marine to get what was comin' to him. I had four men there with guns waiting for him." She tilted her head back and sniffed the air as if to capture any escaping cocaine.

"You set up my friends?" Cassie realized for the first time that Regan was truly crazy. She'd tried to ignore all the signs before. But now crazy was looking straight at her.

Regan said, "My finest plan yet. I figured either way I won. This way though—ha! He put me in charge with nothin' to stop me now."

"Why'd you have Nina killed?" Cassie asked.

Her sister smiled. "You should have done a better job of pickin' people you could trust."

"She worked for you too?" Cassie felt nauseous.

"Let's just say Nina had a little problem with oxycodone and needed someone to help her with it."

Before Cassie could respond, something beeped.

Cassie saw one of the men check his phone, then show the message to his partner.

"What?" Regan asked.

At that moment, a young woman entered the room. Cassie recognized the sniveling little snit as Regan's assistant. She'd been the one who let Cassie in Vito's mansion and then locked her in a room for Regan.

The snit whispered something in Regan's ear.

Cassie saw that whatever she said really upset Regan because her light-skinned face reddened.

To the men, Regan said, "You know what is going on?"

One of them nodded yes.

Regan yelled, "Then get over there and stop them! We already lost three stockyards. I ain't gonna lose them tusks too."

The man who'd nodded at her watched his phone. "It's too late. I'm watching Pelton make a phone call on replay. The police will be there before we will. It's over."

Regan screamed, "We need that shipment!"

Cassie said, "Don't look like you can handle it, you ask me."

Regan looked at her sister. "What you say?"

"I said you're out of your league." Cassie folded her arms across her chest. "Thanks to you, Nina's little children have no mother. Mutt's in the hospital. Good people are risking their lives for me. And for you. You always been beautiful, but you sure are dumb. And you ain't worth a pot to spit in. I'm ashamed you ever was my sister."

"If that the case," Regan said, "then I ain't gonna worry about what I do next."

Cassie realized, too late, that Regan really was crazy. Before she could react, Regan's hands were at her throat. Cassie tried to fight her sister off, but she was in a rage. Cassie couldn't breathe, the pressure on her windpipe was painful. She gasped for breath, but no air could get in. Her head pulsed. Then she blacked out.

Chapter Forty-Five

Wednesday, dusk

The sixty-mile trek to Lake Lanier gave Brack and Darcy time to plan. Assuming most of Vito's employees would have skipped town after he got busted, Brack thought they had a chance of getting to Regan and Cassie.

The three-story residence stood on a five-acre plot with plenty of lake frontage. A black fence made of steel bars protected the immediate grounds. From what Brack could see through the fence, the house itself was surrounded by a tall row of holly bushes. He and Darcy stopped at the gate and he pressed a button on an intercom. Silence.

"Maybe no one is home," she said.

"They're here." Brack could feel it.

He got out of the Mazda and looked around. The sun was low in the sky, but wouldn't set for another hour or so. The house had no lights on that he could see. The gate was chained, so he used his new bolt cutters to remove the lock, and the chain dropped to the ground. After swinging the gate open, he got back in the car and drove to the house. Since the property was in the name of Vito's company, and Vito was currently detained by the Atlanta Police, anyone here—Brack, Darcy, even Regan—was trespassing.

Fifty feet short of the house, he stopped the car.

Darcy asked, "What's wrong?"

"We're sitting ducks in this car. We need to separate and spread out. Are you sure you're up for this?"

She pulled a thirty-two-caliber pistol from her purse. "Yes. You want the front or the back?"

For some really stupid reason, a question came to mind. Not one he should be asking given the circumstances currently facing them, but another one. So he asked it. "What is PC industries?" The business she'd registered her car under.

She smiled. "PC stands for Pirate's Cove."

The Pirate's Cove. His bar in Charleston. If she'd been using the name for the past year, Brack didn't know what that meant. No time now to pursue the issue. He shook it off. "I have a feeling Regan has Cassie tied up in there. I'm not sure what her game plan is, but this ends today. I'll take the front. Cover me until I can get inside. After you hear me fire my gun, head to the back."

She nodded and stood off to the side, using a tree for cover.

He walked to the front door with the pry bar in one hand and his pistol in the other. At the last minute, he decided to announce his presence and used the pry bar to ring the bell.

Again, silence. Brack slipped his gun into his waistband and tried the door handle. Locked. He slid the pry bar into the door jamb, put some pressure on it, slid his hands to the end of the bar, and pulled with all his strength.

At first nothing happened. Then he heard a splinter. The door popped open and Brack fell inside the house. Two men with guns were waiting for him. Darcy fired four shots at them. They scattered—which gave Brack a chance to recover. He dropped the pry bar, grabbed his pistol, sighted one of them, and hit him with a chest shot at ten feet. The second gunman tried to aim at Brack. Brack got another shot off before the goon could. That goon fell too.

Sighting in the entryway from his position on the floor, Brack saw no one else at the moment. Only two large sets of stairs, one on each side of the room. He got to his feet and, aiming his pistol in front to shoot anything that moved that wasn't Cassie, made his way through the first floor rooms to the back door. But instead of opening the back door and risking getting shot by Darcy, Brack unlocked it, then retraced his steps to the main staircase in the entryway.

The house was dead silent. And dark. The marble stairs uttered not a creak as he climbed them, pausing at the first landing where the stairs split. He kept the forty-five trained in front of him, aiming wherever he looked. The second-floor corridor was empty. He turned a corner. A flash of light lit up the darkness, followed by the explosion of a gun firing, followed by pain. He'd been hit.

Chapter Forty-Six

At the back of the house, Darcy tried the door. Unlocked. She guessed that Brack may have unlocked it for her and was now somewhere in the house. She moved from room to room until she found two downed men and a marble staircase that led to the upper floors. Another gunshot went off, this one sounding different from Brack's cannon. A feeling of dread came over her. Creeping up the stairs, her pistol held in front of her, she made it to the second floor. As she turned a corner and entered the first room, she saw a young woman, arms cradled in front of her chest, crying.

Darcy kept her guard up. She aimed her pistol at the woman and said, "Who are you?"

The young woman swayed back and forth. "They're all gone."

"Who's gone?"

"Regan. Cassie. They're gone."

"How long ago did they leave?"

Looking down, she said, "I don't know."

"Who are you?" Darcy asked.

"I work for Regan. I'm her assistant."

The rear window was open, long curtains swaying in the breeze. Darcy sidled up to the opening to see if they might have climbed down some escape to the ground. No sign of anyone.

She heard a sound behind her and turned. The assistant and another woman Darcy swore was Regan rushed toward her. Before Darcy could react, the two of them pushed her out the window.

*   *   *

Darcy hit the bushes hard, their prickly leaves puncturing her skin in a million places. The stout shrubbery and its thick branches acted like a giant spring, compressing with the force of impact, then catapulting her up and onto the ground. She landed with a thud on her belly.

When she came to her senses the first thing she felt was really pissed off. The holly bushes had broken her fall, but she hurt all over from crashing into them.

The second thought that came to mind was to roll under the prickly things as much as possible to avoid being targeted from above.

Gingerly she got to her knees and assessed her condition. Aside from a pretty good-sized cut on her left arm and plenty of smaller pricks and cuts, plus a stiffness forming in her lower back and shoulder, she was better than she could have been. After all, she could have hit the hard ground.

Her pistol was nowhere to be seen.

Rising to her feet, she brushed twigs and dead leaves from her clothes and hair and used a napkin she had in her pocket to apply pressure to the cut on her arm. She knew what she needed to do next. She needed to finish with those two women.

As she crept around to the front of the house, unarmed, she realized she was acting exactly like Brack, wherever he was. He would be doing the very same thing—a frontal assault. Kick the door down. Shoot all the bad guys. Carry the damsel in distress over his shoulder like a barbarian. That's what he was—a barbarian in god-awful cargo shorts.

She shook her head clear of Brack. He was a riddle wrapped in Samsonite luggage. Meaning baggage. The absolute wrong guy for her, she reminded herself for the millionth time since she'd met him. And he was inside this house. Maybe dead already.

The front door stood ajar. The two guards Brack had taken out still lay on the floor where she'd shot at them the first time. Darcy searched them for weapons and hit the jackpot. Each carried a nine-millimeter pistol. She slid one down the back of her walking shorts, found three extra clips, and put one in each of her pockets. Picking up the remaining pistol, she made sure the safety was off.

A figure appeared in the hall from behind the stairs.

Darcy raised the pistol, recognized Regan's assistant with a gun in her hand, and shot her. The assistant's pistol clanged to the floor and she collapsed to her knees, clutching her chest. Blood pooled through the front of her dress.

For a second, the shock in the woman's wide-open eyes startled Darcy. Then the woman fell forward and lay still. Darcy stepped over the body, training the pistol in front of her the way she'd seen Brack do.

The large entryway of the home was interrupted only by the stairwell she'd previously climbed. Darcy took the stairs again, pivoting her sightline from side to side. On the first landing where the stairs split, she took the right side. One of the benefits of marble stairs that she registered was no creaking. The home, she had to admit, was gorgeous. But very cold, and not only in the temperature sense.

Reaching the second floor, from the top of the stairs, she saw light at the far end of the hall. It was coming from the only room with an open doorway.

Darcy took a step toward the room.

A voice behind her said, "You is the dumbest white girl I ever met."

It had to be Regan.

In that moment, Darcy knew her life was over. Knew she'd made a terrible mistake. Unlike Brack, she did not have nine lives. Maybe two. Three at the most. But they'd already been used up. Now she was dead.

Darcy said, "Where's Cassie?"

A laugh. "My *sister* thought she could change me. Got me to move here and play like we was good friends. I hated that bitch. She come here talkin' about how I needed to stop this foolishness and come home. I figured it wasn't gonna stop 'cause her gettin' beat up didn't stop her neither. So I killed her."

"You must be crazy," Darcy said.

"Yeah? Well, I'm not the one who got pushed out a window and came back for more."

She had a point.

The loud click of a cocking revolver hammer echoed across the marble.

This was it.

The explosion was both exciting and mortal. And loud. Darcy flinched. But she still stood. Uninjured. Regan must have missed. But she wouldn't miss a second time.

Darcy dropped to the ground for a last attempt to save herself. She heard Regan give a bloodcurling scream, then something clanged to the ground followed by a dull thump.

Darcy turned to face her executioner and saw Regan on the floor.

Brack stood over Regan's body, his forty-five in his hands. He slid the revolver away from her with his foot, a useless precaution. The way Regan had fallen, her eyes—still open—looked blankly toward Darcy.

Darcy felt no empathy. Regan had eagerly chosen her lifestyle. And she'd chosen to die trying to keep it. She must not have thought she'd actually depart this life. Darcy guessed the girl, and Vito for that matter, had underestimated Brack. A mistake even Darcy made from time to time. A lot of people did. And a lot of people had lost their lives because of it.

Just like Regan.

Chapter Forty-Seven

Brack turned to look at Darcy standing ten feet away staring at Regan's dead body. This was the first time in a long time that he'd killed a woman. As with the others, he hadn't been given an alternative. Because Regan had already chosen death for others, that's what he'd given her.

Darcy said, "She was going to kill me."

"I know."

"I heard a gun," she said. "Thought maybe they shot you."

Brack pointed to his leg. "She grazed me." At that moment, he noticed her arm. "You're bleeding."

She looked down. "Yeah. So are you."

He set his gun on a nearby console table, took out a handkerchief, and wrapped it around her arm. "I found Cassie," he said. "She's dead too."

Chapter Forty-Eight

Wednesday, eight p.m.

Tara went to get her SUV parked in the back lot of her apartment complex. The pavement was faded gray except where Brack's Porsche had exploded. There it was charcoal black. She sensed several men coming up behind her.

One of them said, "Where do you think you're going?"

Tara turned to face Levin. He had four other goons with him.

She said, "I was about to head to your house to shove your face in the toilet, but since you're here, it will save me the trip."

Levin said, "You got a smart mouth for a channdo. You won't be so smart when we finish with you."

Two of the goons approached her. She dropped one with a roundhouse kick. The other fell with a toe to the groin. Then the other three moved in together. One caught her in the face with a set of brass knuckles and she saw stars. Another blow from behind and she was on the ground. Half conscious, she saw them surround her and felt the repeated blows as they kicked at her body. After the first three or four blows, it felt to her as if the beating was happening to someone else.

When she realized they'd stopped, she couldn't see anything.

Levin was close when he said, "It was a big mistake breaking into that warehouse. We lost a lot of money. Gotta make it back somehow. I want you to know that when we leave here, we're going to that zoo you work at. I hope you said goodbye to all your pets, because we've got a buyer who wants all the ivory we can get him. And since we're now short six crates, we need more."

She spit in the direction of his voice and heard him curse. Then she felt the blows on her back and head. Then...nothing.

The loud revving of their motorcycles woke her.

She couldn't move her right arm, but managed to wiggle the fingers of her left hand. She used it to feel around for her purse and found her phone.

Using Siri, she dialed a number.

While Brack stood over Regan's dead body, his phone vibrated. He checked the number and answered, "Tara? Where are you?"

A hoarse voice said, "Get to Grumpy." A cough. "Levin is on his way to kill them all."

"What? Are you all right?"

"Get to the Preserve. Now!"

This wasn't good. "Where are you?" he asked again.

"I'll...be okay. Just...get to Grumpy." The line went dead.

Darcy said, "What's going on?"

"Something's happened to Tara. I have to get to the Preserve. Call Nichols. I'll be back."

The Mazda started, and he raced to the Preserve. En route, he called Tara's brother. Told him what he knew. Darnel said he'd try to find her.

A bad feeling settled in Brack's gut. Levin and his goons had gotten to her. And now they were going after the only thing she really loved—besides her brother. Brack merged onto the interstate and made a promise: they would not succeed. No matter what.

It took twenty minutes of a hundred-mile-an-hour-plus speed to reach the exit to the Preserve. He barely slowed in time for the ninety-degree turn. At the entrance, three things were immediately evident. The security guard was not at his post. Five very expensive motorcycles were already parked. And Brack had left his gun on the table beside Regan's dead body.

He got out and ran to the bikes, hoping to find a gun, or anything, he could use. Inside one of the saddle bags, Brack found a length of chain. Grabbed it. Also a six-inch blade that he holstered under his belt. As Brack ran through the entrance, he heard Grumpy's distinctive trumpet call.

The bikers had already found Tara's baby.

Brack doubled his speed, the chain clinking in his hands.

Another call from Grumpy. Brack rounded the corner to Grumpy's shelter and saw him fifty feet ahead. Levin and four others had cornered the behemoth against the steel fence. Grumpy was trying to use his tusks and front feet to keep them at a distance, but Brack could tell the elephant was scared.

Levin aimed a rifle. Two others had hatchets.

With his right hand, Brack swung the chain over his head. Its length fed out six feet as he approached. It caught Levin around the throat and wrapped twice around his neck. Brack pulled the chain tight with both hands. Levin jerked back and Brack heard the snap of bone. Before the dead body hit the ground, Brack let go of the chain, slid the knife from his belt, and threw it at the closest goon with a hatchet. The business end of the knife struck home in his gut. The three bikers remaining on their feet, one with a hatchet, recovered from their shock. Brack grabbed Levin's rifle lying beside his body and smashed it into the nose of the goon with the hatchet. A fourth biker caught Brack in the face with a hard brass-knuckled punch. Brack saw stars and barely felt his knees hit the dirt.

Even in his dazed condition, something was off. Brack imagined he felt...an earthquake? His eyes regained focus in time to see Mr. Grumpy crash into the brass-knuckles guy. The man did a face-plant against the fence. Without delay, Grumpy scooped up the last biker with his tusks and tossed him into the air.

Brack watched the man sail ten feet above Grumpy, screaming, then drop like a rock directly on top of the spiked fence. Brack knew he would never forget the sickening sound of flesh and bone impaling on steel.

Grumpy let out another trumpet call, came up beside Brack, and swayed his head and body a hundred and eighty degrees, as if ready for another attack.

In the calmest voice he could muster, Brack said, "It's okay, Grumpy. We got them."

The animal belted another cry.

"Good boy." Brack eased to his feet, his balance still off from the brass-knuckled blow.

Grumpy stopped his head movement, did a slow turn, and approached him.

Brack put out his hand. Grumpy lowered his head and nuzzled his trunk against Brack's palm. "That's right, boy."

Darcy's news crew got to the scene even before the police. And well before she did. Grumpy chased a cameraman onto the roof of one of the buildings. Brack felt bad for both, but no way could he do anything. A ten-thousand-pound pachyderm can do pretty much whatever he damn well pleases.

Tara's coworker, Jeanne, arrived next and showed extreme care in getting all the elephants to calm down, bribing Grumpy with watermelon.

When the police arrived, one look at the carnage Grumpy and Brack had inflicted produced calls for several ambulances. Levin and two others were headed straight for the morgue: chalk up two for Brack, one for Grumpy. Not bad for a night's work.

Sadly, the bikers had bound and gagged the security guard. The stress was too much for the elderly man, and he had a heart attack and died. That alone would send the two goons still living to jail for a very long time.

While Brack waited to hear from Tara or her brother or Darcy, he helped Jeanne feed Mr. Grumpy. The elephant had already inhaled the melon and now seemed content munching on apples. As Brack ran his hand along Grumpy's lower shoulder it occurred to him that he'd saved Grumpy's life and Grumpy had saved his. As if sensing Brack's worry over Tara, Grumpy turned his head and gently rubbed Brack's chest with the end of his trunk.

"We'll find her," Brack said. "We'll find her."

Grumpy let out a soft grunt.

One of the police officers got Brack's attention by clearing his throat. He'd been smart enough not to make any loud noises to startle Grumpy. Instead, he stood by the door and motioned Brack over.

The officer said, "We've got word on your friend, Tara. She was assaulted and is at Emory Hospital."

"Will she make it?" Brack asked.

"They roughed her up pretty good. She's in the ICU."

Brack returned to Grumpy, patted him one last time, and told Tara's coworker where he was going.

She sighed and said, "This is all so terrible."

It was, Brack thought, not good. Too many of his friends were hurt, hospitalized, or dead. But they'd run out of bad guys at the moment, so that was positive.

Chapter Forty-Nine

Thursday morning

With Nichols's help, Brack was able to find out how Cassie died. According to the M.E., Regan had apparently strangled her own sister. Brack visited Mutt at the hospital to say goodbye to his friend and inform him of the M.E.'s conclusion. Mutt, already visibly saddened and upset about Cassie's death, turned away and asked to be alone.

"Of course," Brack said as he opened the door to leave Mutt's room. He added, "I love you, my friend. You ever need anything, you know where to reach me."

The doctors said Mutt would eventually make a full recovery from his physical injuries. Brack wasn't sure about the emotional ones.

Tara was at a different hospital and Brack needed to drive across town to visit her. Because she was in such good physical condition at the time of her attack, she would also make a full recovery. With tears in her eyes, she thanked him for saving Grumpy and the other elephants. Brack described Grumpy's heroics. She said she couldn't wait to return to her day job at the Preserve in a week or so. She wouldn't be going back to work at Mutt's bar. He kissed her goodbye and made sure to exact a promise from her to look him up if she ever came to Charleston.

The drive from the hospital gave Brack time to collect his thoughts about the previous weeks. Vito made his flight, but not in the manner in which he most likely preferred. After everything that went down, the police contacted the feds, who contacted Vito's native country—Mexico. When it became apparent that Vito had engaged in crimes of murder, extortion, prostitution, and drugs against citizens of his own country along with the endangered species violation of ivory smuggling, the United States happily changed his status to persona non grata. Vito probably now wished he'd been able to stay in the U.S.

Vito's handler, his grandfather Marcus, was another story. The United States would not grant him entrance. That was why his grandson had carte blanche on how things were run. Without another suitable heir to put in place, all their business holdings were divided up by the remaining underworld figures in the same way a fresh kill was split up by a group of lions in the wild. The strongest got the lion's share.

The Rastas did not come around looking for any money for supplying him with their guns. Brack figured they were thankful Vito was headed for a life or death sentence. For all he knew, they now ran the city's underworld.

The two goons not killed by Grumpy and Brack ended up in jail for breaking into the Preserve and causing the death of the security guard.

Because Jackie Boyd came to the rescue and fought for both Brack and Darcy, no charges were filed against them, despite their having left quite a few bodies on the ground, in the one-way alley, and at Vito's lake house. With Vito and Kualas out of operation, the natural order in the city had shifted.

Brack's last stop before picking up Shelby and heading home was Reverend Cleophus's church. Though the Mazdaspeed3 was a fast car, it wasn't him. He also realized the Porsche hadn't been him either. Brack donated the Mazda to the Reverend, who could have his brother sell it again. The Reverend gave Brack a ride back to Mutt's house, thanking him for the donation. Brack asked about Mindy and Kai's parents. With a sad face, the Reverend said that each woman was grieving over her loss and considering leaving her husband.

The only other disturbing news was that Townsend had

disappeared. He checked himself out of the hospital and vanished. Brack had a feeling he might be meeting up with the monster again, but not any time soon.

Later that day, Brack and Shelby waited in Mutt's driveway for Brother Thomas and Trish to pick them up and take them back to Charleston. They said they had some errands to run and would be by shortly. Brack thought again about how crazy and tragic their Atlanta experience had been. So much death and, in the end, all for nothing. Cassie and Regan were both dead. While he couldn't prevent Cassie's death, he'd caused Regan's and would have done it again if he had to.

At that moment, a brand-new Mustang rumbled into Mutt's drive, interrupting his thoughts. The shiny black paint, chrome wheels, and 5.0 badges put Brack in a trance. As the performance machine pulled to a stop and the engine turned off, its dark-tinted windows kept him from seeing the driver.

Shelby gave a quick but happy bark as Darcy got out of the car.

The sun was just coming up over the Atlanta skyline. Bright rays glistened off her blonde curls. With all three of them a couple of years older than when they first met, she was still a few years away from thirty, and even with bandages all over her face and arms from the holly bushes she'd fallen into, as beautiful as ever. Especially with that crease between her eyebrows when she was focused, like now.

Brack's dog ran to her.

She knelt and kissed his head. "Hello, sweetheart. I missed you too."

Brack said, "Nice ride."

She stood and tossed him the keyfob to the car.

Brack looked at it and then at her.

She said, "Consider this an early wedding present."

"I thought I was supposed to get *you* something."

She didn't answer him.

While trying to puzzle out her meaning, he noticed she was no longer wearing her engagement ring.

Her reply was to wrap her injured arms around his shoulders and kiss him on the lips. She said, "You will."

DAVID BURNSWORTH

David Burnsworth became fascinated with the Deep South at a young age. After a degree in Mechanical Engineering from the University of Tennessee and fifteen years in the corporate world, he made the decision to write a novel. *Big City Heat* is his third mystery. Having lived in Charleston on Sullivan's Island for five years, the setting was a foregone conclusion. He and his wife call South Carolina home.

Books by David Burnsworth

The Brack Pelton Mystery Series

SOUTHERN HEAT (#1)
BURNING HEAT (#2)
BIG CITY HEAT (#3)

The Blu Carraway Mystery Series

BLU HEAT (Prequel Novella)
IN IT FOR THE MONEY (#1)

Available at booksellers nationwide and online

Visit www.henerypress.com for details

Henery Press Mystery Books

And finally, before you go...
Here are a few other mysteries
you might enjoy:

CIRCLE OF INFLUENCE

Annette Dashofy

A Zoe Chambers Mystery (#1)

Zoe Chambers, paramedic and deputy coroner in rural Pennsylvania's tight-knit Vance Township, has been privy to a number of local secrets over the years, some of them her own. But secrets become explosive when a dead body is found in the Township Board President's abandoned car.

As a January blizzard rages, Zoe and Police Chief Pete Adams launch a desperate search for the killer, even if it means uncovering secrets that could not only destroy Zoe and Pete, but also those closest to them.

Available at booksellers nationwide and online

Visit www.henerypress.com for details

LOWCOUNTRY BOIL

Susan M. Boyer

A Liz Talbot Mystery (#1)

Private Investigator Liz Talbot is a modern Southern belle: she blesses hearts and takes names. She carries her Sig 9 in her Kate Spade handbag, and her golden retriever, Rhett, rides shotgun in her hybrid Escape. When her grandmother is murdered, Liz high-tails it back to her South Carolina island home to find the killer.

She's fit to be tied when her police-chief brother shuts her out of the investigation, so she opens her own. Then her long-dead best friend pops in and things really get complicated. When more folks start turning up dead in this small seaside town, Liz must use more than just her wits and charm to keep her family safe, chase down clues from the hereafter, and catch a psychopath before he catches her.

Available at booksellers nationwide and online

Visit www.henerypress.com for details

BOARD STIFF

Kendel Lynn

An Elliott Lisbon Mystery (#1)

As director of the Ballantyne Foundation on Sea Pine Island, SC, Elliott Lisbon scratches her detective itch by performing discreet inquiries for Foundation donors. Usually nothing more serious than retrieving a pilfered Pomeranian. Until Jane Hatting, Ballantyne board chair, is accused of murder. The Ballantyne's reputation tanks, Jane's headed to a jail cell, and Elliott's sexy ex is the new lieutenant in town.

Armed with moxie and her Mini Coop, Elliott uncovers a trail of blackmail schemes, gambling debts, illicit affairs, and investment scams. But the deeper she digs to clear Jane's name, the guiltier Jane looks. The closer she gets to the truth, the more treacherous her investigation becomes. With victims piling up faster than shells at a clambake, Elliott realizes she's next on the killer's list.

Available at booksellers nationwide and online

Visit www.henerypress.com for details